"What's wrong?"

"The tornado. It hit the botanical gardens. I need to see it for myself." Lindsay glanced at the door to the basement, where Evan and Chloe were.

Mason checked his phone, and his chief hadn't called him in. "I'll watch the kids."

"I shouldn't be too long."

He laughed, knowing full well she'd lose track of time once she was actually there. Her passion for her work at the gardens was undeniable. "Take as long as you need."

"Thanks." She grabbed her car keys and rushed for the front door.

He cleared his throat, and she glanced over her shoulder. "Is something wrong?"

"I love pink hippopotamus lounge pants, but you might want to change."

Her cheeks flamed and she rolled her eyes. "Where would I be without my best friend? On the road to making a fool of myself, that's where."

Where would Mason be without *his* best friend was the real question...and one he didn't want answered.

Dear Reader,

I chaperoned my twins' field trip to the local botanical gardens and was awestruck at the exhibits, ranging from structured gardens to colorful topiaries. Out of that trip came Lindsay Hudson, a horticulturist who is clawing her way back to life after mourning the death of her paramedic husband in a line-of-duty crash.

Dedicated to his job, Mason Ruddick is a free spirit who relishes jumping on his motorcycle at a moment's notice. The last thing he ever expected was to fall for his best friend's widow, who also happens to be his next-door neighbor. While fighting those feelings, he makes room for some unexpected houseguests in the form of his grandfather and a lovable dog.

This book touches on a subject close to home for me—childhood asthma. My older daughter was diagnosed with asthma, and I'm forever grateful to the pediatric pulmonologists who helped her face this disease with a sense of calmness and encouraged her to live in awareness but not fear.

Please visit my website at tanyaagler.com, where you can sign up for my newsletter, or follow me on social media.

Happy reading,

Tanya

HEARTWARMING

The Paramedic's Forever Family

Tanya Agler

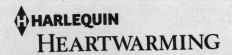

HARLEQUIN
HEARTWARMING

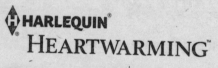

HARLEQUIN®
HEARTWARMING™

ISBN-13: 978-1-335-42667-3

The Paramedic's Forever Family

Copyright © 2022 by Tanya Agler

Recycling programs for this product may not exist in your area.

For questions and comments about the quality of this book, please contact us at CustomerService@Harlequin.com.

Harlequin Enterprises ULC
22 Adelaide St. West, 41st Floor
Toronto, Ontario M5H 4E3, Canada
www.Harlequin.com

Printed in U.S.A.

Tanya Agler remembers the first set of Harlequin books her grandmother gifted her, and she's been in love with romance novels ever since. An award-winning author, Tanya makes her home in Georgia with her wonderful husband, their four children and a lovable basset, who really rules the roost. When she's not writing, Tanya loves classic movies and a good cup of tea. Visit her at tanyaagler.com or email her at tanyaagler@gmail.com.

Books by Tanya Agler

Harlequin Heartwarming

A Ranger for the Twins
The Sheriff's Second Chance
The Soldier's Unexpected Family
The Single Dad's Holiday Match

Visit the Author Profile page
at Harlequin.com for more titles.

For Carrie, my bright, artistic daughter, who sees the beauty of life all around her. Her messages to me on her whiteboard bring me joy and smiles, as do her hugs that greet me in the morning. Her happiness and quiet strength inspire me every day. This one's for you, Cupcake!

CHAPTER ONE

ONE MORE MINUTE on hold and Lindsay Hudson would scream so loud the spring wildflowers in bloom outside her office window would wilt. Since she'd pressed the Speaker button so she wouldn't miss out on a live customer representative, she had answered her morning emails, restructured the volunteer orientation and counted the number of jellybeans on her desk. There were five fewer than there'd been when she agreed to hold eighteen minutes and forty-eight seconds ago. She popped a cherry jellybean into her mouth. Make that six.

A knock almost prompted her to end the call, but she had to speak to someone at the Premier Bronze Engravers today. The door opened, and her best friend popped his head in. "Want to have lunch with me?"

"This is Angela. Is this a prank call?" A voice finally crackled over the speaker. Lindsay groaned at her friend Mason's timing.

Mason must have taken her grunt as a sign to enter. Lindsay held up a finger and grabbed her phone, taking it off Speaker. "No! I've been on hold for nineteen minutes. Don't hang up. I need to speak to someone about the proof for the memorial plaque that was sent to the Hollydale Botanical Garden."

"One moment, please." The familiar sounds of Muzak played once more. As much as Lindsay loved Beyoncé, she much preferred belting out the singer's tunes in her trusty truck than listening to the instrumental version of her top hit.

"Lunch with me would remove those pesky thoughts of tossing your phone out the window." Mason's rich laugh filled her tiny office.

She wrinkled her nose, guilty, as her next-door neighbor knew her too well.

"That new deli downtown has two-for-one pimento cheese sandwiches today."

Considering how often he teased her about being a lifelong North Carolinian who shuddered at the mere smell of pimento cheese, he knew she despised the spread. "You want me along so you can have both for yourself?"

"That's what best friends are for." He shrugged and the light from the afternoon sun bounced off his thick ginger hair, making it almost glow. "I'll buy you a Reuben."

As hard as it was to resist that invitation,

her workload prevented her from accepting his offer. "Could you bring it back here for me?"

Angela came on over the line. "If this is a bad time for you, I'd be more than happy to talk to another customer."

"Not at all." Where did her boss find this place? "Are you the person to speak to about the proof for the botanical garden?"

"I handled this requisition myself. A simple email would have sufficed to okay the order. If that's all?"

The representative's smugness took Lindsay by surprise. "No, that's not all. You've misspelled several of the names."

"That must have been a mistake on your part. That will result in a delay of two to four weeks for the new proof and the finished product. Send me the correct spellings, and I'll email you the updated version in which it was received in the queue." Angela's well-modulated, even voice gave no sign she was the guilty party.

Lindsay shuffled papers until she came upon her original document. "If the mistake is on your end, I expect we can still receive the plaque at the scheduled time. Its unveiling for the memorial garden is a major event. Just today we had confirmation of attendance from the mayor and a prominent state representative."

"We are not responsible for others' mistakes. We fulfill our orders with what we've been given."

"I didn't spell my last name wrong." This argument was going nowhere fast. "I have my invoice here, which I personally scanned and faxed to you. Somehow, someone, I'm not saying it was you, swapped the *d* and the *s* of one of the paramedics' last names. It's Hudson, not Husdon."

Lindsay stole a glance at Mason's genial face. A muscle in his firm jaw twitched, so imperceptibly that someone who didn't know him as well wouldn't have noticed. Tim had been his partner prior to the accident that claimed her husband's life two years, two months, and six days ago. Not that she was counting.

"Um, I see your point. However, spring is our busy season, and we can no longer guarantee our original date."

"Do you know what this order is?" Lindsay cut to the chase. "The Hollydale Botanical Garden was chosen as the site for a monument to the first responders who've lost their lives in western North Carolina. My boss, who's on vacation at the Outer Banks, chose your company based on your competitive bid. If there's no plaque during the dedication ceremony..."

"It was an honest mistake on our part. We'll rush the revised proof back to you."

"You do that. Have a nice day." Lindsay ended the call.

Mason folded his arms and leaned against her office door, the twinkle in his blue eyes more mischievous than his relaxed stance would suggest. "Remind me never to argue with the head botanical horticulturist. She's feisty."

"*She's* also hungry, but I don't have time for lunch downtown." Lindsay rose from her chair and donned her green blazer. "Before you head out for the sandwiches, I want to show you the memorial site."

He shook his head and straightened. "I know better than to stand between you and your Reuben. I'll be back in a few."

He opened the door, but she ran ahead of him.

"Hmm. It's getting late. Don't want the deli to close before I place my order."

"You don't wear a watch when you're off duty." Pointing out the obvious, she grabbed his arm and tugged him toward the employee exit.

His indigo tie-dyed T-shirt and jeans were

rather casual compared to the average wardrobe of the garden's visitors, but he'd have stood out in a crowd whether he wore a dress shirt or his black-and-blue paramedic jacket.

"It'll only take a couple of minutes. You're coming to the dedication ceremony, aren't you?"

Mason halted, and the door almost collided with her forearm before she scooted out of the way, leaving them inside the administrative building. "I haven't thought much about it."

"You have the same expression as Evan when he's lying." Lindsay faced Mason and folded her arms, beaming the same glare she'd give her four-year-old son.

"I'm not lying. I volunteered to work that day so other paramedics could attend."

"What? I can't believe you'd do that without talking to me first." Her mouth fell open and she marveled at him standing there so cool and nonchalant. "Why didn't you tell me this sooner?"

"Because I knew you'd respond like this."

"You don't know everything about me, Mason Ruddick. You don't know the half of how upsetting this is." She pressed the metal bar with a little too much force and the door flew open.

Bright April sunshine didn't match her

mood at this second. No one else could aggravate her as much as Mason. She needed a new best friend, someone who'd keep her patience on its usually even keel. A field of wildflowers in bloom drew her attention, and she walked that way, appreciating a minute of beauty before she resumed her day.

"What type of flowers are they?" he asked. She'd sensed Mason had followed her even before his low, husky voice had called to her.

Lindsay remained where she was, resolute she wouldn't give in and turn around. Mason needed to get it through his head how important his attendance at this memorial was, and she needed a minute so she'd come up with a logical retort rather than get distracted by his charm.

A visitor to the garden arrived and echoed Mason's question, leaving her no choice but to turn around and answer. "Those blue-lavender stems are crested dwarf irises while the light purple flowers are wild geranium. The white trilliums are particularly striking."

"Those fragile-looking ones? Are they easy to grow? My husband and I just downsized and moved into a new home. I finally have the time to start the garden I've always wanted."

Lindsay faced the visitor, whose green visor shielded her eyes while she held out a notebook and pen, waiting for the answer. "We should be past the last frost of the year, although that's been recorded here in the mountains as late as May. It's important to triangulate the best place in your yard with access to sunlight and a good water source. If you join our annual membership here at the garden, you can show that pass at Farr's Hardware in town for a ten percent discount, the same for Jasper and Jules's Garden Center."

Mason cleared his throat and, despite herself, Lindsay glanced his way. "So those of us who want to impress our neighbors, the ones who are adept at gardening, should grow trillium to get back in their good graces?"

"Notice the other flowers in that field. They balance out the smell. Trilliums are beautiful, but there's a distinctive odor to them, a bit like rotting meat." Lindsay kept her smile calm and determined.

The woman shoved her notebook in her handbag. "Thanks for your help."

She scurried away, and Lindsay glared at Mason. "I wish I could say the same to you."

"What did I do?" His eyes widened, and he flashed that boyish grin that always sent her twenty-month-old daughter Chloe to the moon.

"That woman was excited about gardening and I let my emotions get the best of me."

Lindsay headed for a nearby wooden fence that led to a shortcut to the greenhouse. She intended to spend her afternoon there checking on the progress of the petunias and other summer bedding plants and fixing the ancient irrigation system.

Mason's footsteps beside her proved he wasn't giving up yet. "Do you want extra Russian dressing on your Reuben, like always?"

"Are you coming to the dedication? Tim would have been there for you if the situation had been reversed."

He shoved his hands into the pockets of his jeans, his jaw clenched. "I don't deal in 'what-ifs.' I'll see you later."

Lindsay watched him walk away. Mason rarely made up his mind with such vehemence. What was going on in that head of his? Somehow, she'd find out the answer, while taking care to make sure their friendship remained intact. It was one of the few things that had kept her from staying in bed for the past two years.

MASON FLICKED ON the kitchen light in his rental home and trudged over to the refrigerator. He placed the to-go box holding two pimento cheese sandwiches next to the storage containers of chopped carrots and bell peppers. He hadn't liked the abrupt way he'd ended it with his next-door neighbor and all-around best friend, Lindsay, earlier today, and that uneasiness had carried over to his solitary lunch, where he hadn't been able to savor his one weakness to his organic lifestyle.

Now he had dinner, but no appetite.

Would she still appear tonight at the fence separating their adjoining yards, monitor in hand in case either Evan or Chloe got out of their beds? If so, he'd mend, well, fences with her. Somehow, they'd get through this. He'd work during the dedication ceremony so others in the department could witness her cutting the ribbon, doing double duty as the horticulturist in charge of the garden and the widow of one of the paramedics listed on the plaque.

Problem was, he couldn't bear seeing Tim as just another name and statistic. His throat tightened. This was too much to consider tonight. He took a deep breath and tried to clear his mind. Time with his future chopper would help. Building a motorcycle from the ground up had always been his perfect antidote to the worries lingering within. This was exactly what the paramedic ordered.

Mason ran upstairs, eager to change into his old clothes. Halfway up the stairs, his phone rang, and he checked the screen in case the chief needed him. *Hmm.* What did Bree want to discuss at three in the afternoon Nashville time, four here? She should be at work.

He answered as he reached his bedroom closet. "Hey, sis. Can I call you back? It's my day off and I want to finish part of the bike's electric panel."

He switched to Speaker and threw the phone on the bed, shrugging out of his tie-dyed shirt and replacing it with a long-sleeve shirt already stained with oil.

"Do you have a minute now? This is important," his sister said.

The wobble in Bree's voice was unlike her feisty and fun self, and he sat on the edge of his mattress. Mason reached for the phone and switched off Speaker. "Bree? What happened? Are you okay? Was Tris in an accident or something?"

"Tristan's fine. It's the *or something.*" She paused, and he held the phone pressed next to his ear.

"You don't sound happy."

She and Tristan were married four years ago, with college graduation one day and their wedding the next.

"Bree?"

A sniffle turned into wailing, and his brother-in-law came over the line.

"Hi, Mason." Mason heard his sister still

crying in the background. "Bree found out she has thyroid cancer. The doctors think they discovered it early."

Mason's heart stuttered, and a wave of nausea roiled his stomach. He clenched his phone and listened to his brother-in-law trying to sound optimistic while outlining the course of treatment, but the worry in his voice came through. Mason's mind wandered, knowing too well what Bree was facing. Most likely, they'd remove her thyroid and then scan to see if the cancer had spread.

Bree came back on the line, and Mason composed himself, tamping down the concern for her sake. "Have you told Mom and Dad yet?" They'd lost one child to cancer already. How they'd take this development was beyond him.

"I've only told Grandma Betty and you." Bree blew her nose, and he waited for her, itching to do something when he was three hundred miles away.

"Do you want me to fly to Nashville? It might be easier to deal with this if I'm at your side." This meaning all of it: telling Mom and Dad, the surgery, the recovery. He hadn't asked for any vacation time this year. He could pop to Nashville for a couple of days to start with, and no one would miss him.

"I love your visits, but no, I'll be okay for

now. We'll visit later. I've got the treatment to get through and…when I'm on the road to recovery, that's when I want to see you." Bree sounded more like her usual self the longer she kept talking. "I'm glad I could get the words out. Thanks for listening. Really glad you answered. I'll talk to you again soon. Love ya."

"Right back at you, sis."

He held onto his phone and sat there remembering the day she was born and the day he served as an usher at her wedding and many of the days in between. He couldn't bear to lose someone else close to him. Everything blurred, and he forced himself not to drive to Nashville that second. The prospect of deserting his next shift and his new partner held him back.

He didn't know how much time had passed when he eventually tugged on his oil-stained shirt. Mason headed for the garage; an image of Bree laughing merged with the faint memory of his other sister Colette during her brief battle with leukemia from so long ago.

He switched on the light and stared at the motorcycle. Processing Bree's news with a wrench in hand might be for the best. After Tim died, he'd dismantled the original bike until little piles of parts surrounded him. Since then, he hadn't even cracked the door to his workshop for six months. Tonight, though, he couldn't wait to install that breaker box underneath the transmission. Ever since he'd finished constructing his first bike way back in high school, he'd been hooked. Too often, on the online loops for fellow enthusiasts, he read about bikers starting similar projects only to give up and move on to easier pastures. He hadn't put the past eighteen months of his life into this for it to grace someone else's garage or be scrapped for parts.

Mason gathered the pieces for this next step, a welcome distraction until he'd talk to Lindsay later tonight. He stopped and breathed out the shakiness from Bree's news. Once his fingers were no longer trembling, he started working on the electrical system.

Perhaps this would be his therapy in light of Bree's diagnosis. Motorcycle sessions, along with confiding in Lindsay, the steadiest woman around, kept him together in a profession where burnout was legendary and stress propelled many paramedics into other careers.

He'd lasted eight years already.

Putting the thought aside, he concentrated on the intricacies of the panel. Mason crossed the length of his garage and picked up his drill, giving it a whirr for good measure. He examined the circumference of the bit and found it too wide. He rifled through the box until he located a smaller bit and then tightened the chuck. In no time, he'd mounted the breaker box and examined the plans tacked to the wall of his garage. The gray lines of the sketch reminded him of the charcoal flecks in Lindsay's serious eyes.

Those eyes had reflected hurt at his decision not to attend the dedication ceremony. While Tim was alive, they'd shared barbecues and birthday cakes, her on Tim's arm and him squiring a different woman every couple of months. Back then, she'd been gracious and greeted each of his dates as a long-lost friend. Then came the helicopter crash that rocked both of their worlds.

He regretted not being the person who informed her of Tim's death. Instead, he'd been the one who held her while the baby still inside her kicked lively unaware she'd never lay eyes on her father. About six months after Chloe was born, he'd spotted Lindsay on her patio trying to uncork a wine bottle with a screwdriver, muttering to herself. That was their first real one-on-one conversation. Since then, he'd come to appreciate how much of an open book Lindsay was, much more than himself. He let people see what he wanted them to see, whereas she wore her heart on her sleeve.

Mason found the signal flasher and checked

the plans again. This was a tricky part, requiring he use his welding skills for sure. After donning his protective gear, he installed the rest of the switch housing hardware and stepped back, blinking at the quiet surrounding him. How long had he been lost in his work, anyway? He searched for his phone and couldn't find it anywhere.

His neck ached, and he rubbed it. The garage windows no longer had light flooding in, and he crossed the path leading to his house. Entering the back door, he then found his phone on his bed with four text messages waiting for him. If one of them was his boss…

Nope. They were all from Lindsay, wondering where he was, a sign she was still upset with him since she'd normally have knocked on the garage door. Checking the time, he winced. He should have been on his side of the fence thirteen minutes ago.

His stomach rumbled, and Mason stopped at the fridge. He tucked a bottle of beer and Lindsay's favorite Riesling under his arm before grabbing the to-go container of pimento cheese sandwiches and heading out the door, closing it afterward with his foot.

He hurried to the fence and found Lindsay going inside, about to close her patio's sliding door.

"Wait!" Mason ran up to the fence separating his yard from hers.

Lindsay halted, raising her head so her short honey-brown hair framed her face. She came forward to open the gate for him and then retreated to her patio.

Seconds ticked by as she seemed to be composing herself. She stood, a good eight inches shorter than him, the difference more pronounced since she wore her flip-flops while he was in his work boots.

"When you're done counting to twenty, I could use a chat with my best friend." Mason kept his voice soft enough so as not to possibly wake Evan and Chloe.

Lindsay sent him a slow-burn glare. "Best friends don't ignore text messages."

"I forgot to bring my phone in the garage with me. I left it upstairs in my room."

"What if you'd hurt yourself while you were working on your bike?"

That slow burn became a forest fire, and he squirmed.

He placed the container and beer bottle on her patio table flanked by two yellow Adirondack chairs, his last anniversary gift to her and Tim.

"But I didn't." He held up the Riesling. "Are

we sitting tonight instead of talking at the fence?"

She disappeared and returned a second later with a corkscrew. She twisted it until the cork came out with a soft pop.

"I should take this bottle inside with me and share it with Aunt Hyacinth, who's reading Evan and Chloe bedtime stories." Lindsay pursed her lips together, but then her expression relaxed. "I sometimes lose track of time, too, while I'm gardening, but I'm out in the open. No one would have seen you if the motorcycle had fallen on you...or something."

She scooped up the bottle and her glass and took two steps toward the sliding glass door. He jumped to his feet.

"Bree has cancer."

Once again, she halted. Slowly, she returned and placed the wine with his offerings. She hugged him then, her lavender and freesia scent a change from the oil and other stinky fumes of his garage. He melted into her softness. As soon as he realized what he was doing, he jerked back. He had no business finding Tim's widow soft, even if Lindsay was his closest friend.

"How long have you known?" Her pink lips formed an O. "Was that why you wanted to have lunch with me today?"

"No. I didn't find out until I arrived home and got lost in the garage so to speak." Speaking of food, his stomach grumbled again, loud enough for her to arch her brow. "Sit awhile?"

"Of course. It'll help to talk to someone about your sister. She's my friend, too."

While she poured the Riesling, he devoured one of the sandwiches. Once he swallowed it down with a sip of his stout, he updated her on Bree's condition until a bark interrupted him.

He glanced at Lindsay, who paused with her glass halfway to her lips. "Did your aunt bring her boxers with her?" he asked.

"Her dogs are at her house." She rose and scanned the area. "The noise sounded like it came from your driveway."

Out of nowhere, a small black dog appeared and snatched the second sandwich from the to-go container.

"Goliath!"

His grandfather's voice reached him, and then he came into view, puffing and holding a bright green leash. "There you are."

"Grandpa Joe?" Mason reached in his pocket for his phone.

"Nine thirty. You really should start wearing a watch on your days off," Lindsay said.

Grandpa Joe boomed out a hearty laugh and clipped Goliath to the leash. "That'll be the day."

Yeah, the day I settled down, which would be never. "What are you doing here this late?" He frowned. "Does Grandma Betty know you're running out to the store for a pint of ice cream again?"

Ever since Grandpa Joe had a touch of angina last year, his grandmother had placed him on a strict diet of heart-healthy foods. But every other week, Grandpa Joe showed up with a pint of butter pecan from Miss Louise's Ice Cream Parlor for himself and rainbow sherbet for Mason. Mason still hadn't worked up enough courage to tell his grandfather that nine-year-old Mason loved the stuff while he only consumed it now to not hurt his grandfather's feelings.

"Your grandmother is the reason I'm here."

Mason folded his arms and huffed out a breath. "Your concern is really kind, Grandpa, but I'll be fine, and Bree will be fine. I'm not four anymore."

"Exactly. That's why Betty sent me here after we talked to your sister." His grandfather glanced at Lindsay, then at him. Mason could have sworn he saw a glimmer of a smile, but it must have been the moonlight that was throwing him, especially since the corners of Grandpa Joe's mouth now turned downward.

"My wife is overly worrying of me and thinks I can't live without her."

That sounded ominous to Mason on several levels. If his grandparents, who'd celebrated their fifty-sixth wedding anniversary last June, were splitting up, what hope did any couple have of making it in this world? Just one more reason he stayed the course of being a confirmed bachelor.

"Where's Grandma Betty, and why aren't you with her?"

"After she arranged for a leave of absence from the community center, she caught the first plane to Nashville to be with Bree. I stayed behind for my job and for Goliath, but she's worried something might happen to me, so she made me promise to stay with you until she returns." Grandpa Joe came over and slapped him on the back, the impact of which sent Mason stumbling. "I bought groceries. Nachos, pizza and ice cream. It's going to be great. It'll be like I'm thirty again, until Betty comes home. We'll be bachelors together."

Lindsay let out a sudden burst of laughter. She held up her glass in Mason's direction. "Two bachelors out on the town. I'm glad I have a front-row seat. I wouldn't miss this for the world."

CHAPTER TWO

LINDSAY ENTERED FARR'S HARDWARE STORE, the next-to-last stop on her morning of errands. A quick visit with brief contact with others suited her fine. Then she'd go home and construct the trellis, which had been on her long list of gardening tasks for her backyard.

The smells of paint and peat enticed her as they entwined with the heavy scent of oil soap. The Farr family had used the soap ever since they opened the homey shop in the fifties. She grabbed a metal platform dolly and headed toward the lumber stored in the back.

Fabiana Ramirez waved to her enthusiastically and strode toward her. "You're just the person I wanted to see." Fabiana's long salt-and-pepper hair curled around her shoulders. Lindsay braced herself for the inevitable matchmaking ploy that always came from the well-meaning woman. "Someone is attacking my lettuce."

"Someone or something?"

"There are little holes in my leaves. Roberto

is in the pesticide aisle, but perhaps you know something that won't hurt my daughter's new puppy when she brings her over for a visit? That dog's big brown eyes are almost as lethal as my Roberto's." Fabiana winked and laughed.

"Sounds like you have aphids. I have a recipe for an organic, all-natural garlic oil pesticide that will help." Lindsay extricated her phone from the front section of her purse and had Fabiana type in her email address. "I'll send that to you tonight."

Lindsay seized the dolly and began pushing, only to have Fabiana hold her arm. "One more thing. My son Carlos is coming home for Easter. You two would make such a cute couple."

And there it is.

She faced Fabiana, the gleam in the empty nester's dark brown eyes too diabolical for Lindsay's taste. "This is the busy season at the botanical garden. I'd hate to make plans and disappoint him."

"If your adorable children need a babysitter while you and Carlos go out on a date, let me know." Fabiana nodded.

"You're so sweet to offer, but…"

"But nothing, Graciela is an angel with dogs and kids, and Carlos would make such a loving father." She nodded more. "My older daughter

Gisele is also taking her sweet time finding someone. I want my three kids to be happy. That isn't a crime. Don't forget to send me that recipe so I can get rid of those nasty aphids." She sped off, leaving Lindsay speechless.

Making haste since Tim's parents had driven into Hollydale and were watching Evan and Chloe for her, Lindsay hustled over to the cedar planks. *Eight ought to do it*, she thought.

"Need any help?"

Lindsay jumped at the sound of Mason's low husky voice behind her. "You scared me."

"Sorry about that, but you're just the person I was looking for."

Oh no, not again. Her jaw clenched, and she loaded a plank on the platform with a thud and quickly added the rest. "Not you, too? Let me guess. There's a new paramedic or firefighter in town, and you're convinced he'd be perfect for me. No thank you. Even if I wanted to get involved with someone again, and I don't, I would never date a first responder."

Even one as handsome as Mason.

Today's red tie-dyed T-shirt brought out the auburn glints in his thick wavy hair. She caught herself and blinked away that pesky thought.

"How many more planks? Can I do anything to make your life easier? Say the word and it's done." Mason pulled out another plank, and she stopped his hand with hers.

"I also need gravel, which is in a different aisle. See you at the fence tonight."

She glanced behind her and found him following but he soon disappeared. Lindsay hurried toward the bags of gravel on the other side of the store, but Mason arrived at the display two seconds ahead of her. "Do you want the twenty- or thirty-pound bag?" He flexed his arm muscles and grinned. "Or one of each?"

She tapped her watch. "Tim's parents drove here from Wilmington this morning to take Evan and Chloe to the new nature preserve, and I'm running out of time to finish my errands. I'm finally building that trellis I've been talking about for months." After stepping around him, she loaded her favorite brand of pea gravel on the empty side of the dolly. "So, whatever's on your mind, just ask."

"You're right about one thing. There is a male involved in my request. Actually, two males."

"No."

"Hear me out. You have a guest room. How would you like a boarder?"

"While moving in with me might keep the matchmakers at bay, Evan and Chloe would get the wrong idea." A gallon of exterior deck stain was next on her list. Some preferred to let the cedar planks weather, but she liked the rhythm of painting the trellis and the shiny finish afterward. She started for the paint aisle.

She'd loaded her preferred brand and noticed Mason steadying the cart for her. "Not me. Grandpa Joe and Goliath on the nights when I'm at the fire station for my twenty-four-hour shifts."

Lindsay remembered too well the small area designated for paramedics at the station.

"With Evan's asthma, a dog in the house wouldn't be such a good idea." A stop at the pharmacy for her son's new inhaler and spacer with a mask was next on her list.

"Studies show early exposure to a pet may decrease a chance of allergies or asthma. Goliath might be more help than a hindrance to Evan. You know I'd never ask you to do anything that would endanger Evan or Chloe."

Lindsay wasn't worried about him endangering her kids as much as her sense of well-being. She needed to stem this one-sided attraction before it grew. "Nice try, but he'll be more comfortable at your house without two young children underfoot." Lindsay made her way to the checkout counter. He continued to tag along and so she faced him. Something was wrong with this picture, but what?

"You're empty-handed. You always buy something when you shop at Farr's."

She wasn't so predictable that he knew where to find her on her day off, was she?

They reached the front of the cashier line, where Mr. Farr's well-known granddaughter Missy checked out customers. "Mason!" Missy held up her index finger. "Grandpa said to look out for you. We have your special order at customer service. I'll only be a sec."

Missy hurried away, and Mason pulled out his wallet. "I ordered a new planishing hammer for the metalwork on my motorcycle. That's why I'm here."

Lindsay examined the side display of batteries, key chains and energy bars as if her life depended on a new LED flashlight. "That's nice."

Missy returned and rang up his purchase. "Thanks for the special order. We're trying to expand this service so we can keep up with the times but still provide that extra touch for our customers."

The young woman handed Mason's credit card back, and Lindsay caught herself staring at the lingering touch of Missy's fingers on Mason's hand. Lindsay blinked and turned her attention toward her purchases. In no time, she transported her paid order out to her truck, where Mason helped open the tailgate.

"Can I hitch a ride home with you?"

She glanced at him, picking up the cedar planks as if they were Lincoln logs rather than long, heavy pieces of wood. Her gardening clogs allotted her an extra inch of height, but he still had a good six inches on her average frame. "Where's your car?"

"I drove Grandpa Joe into town, and he bought me lunch at the Holly Days Diner since he wanted a piece of lemon meringue pie. Some of his buddies were heading to Sully Creek. When I saw your truck in the parking lot, I told him to go ahead in my SUV."

Lindsay slammed the tailgate shut. "Pretty sure of yourself, huh? It'd serve you right if I made you walk home, especially after eating a big lunch," she teased.

"Take pity on me. This planishing hammer's big and heavy. I can't lug it home by myself." He jutted out his lip and raised his hands as if surrendering. "Besides, Goliath hogged my side of the bed, and my three-day shift starts tomorrow. I'm exhausted."

She busted out laughing at his plaintive expression. "He's a slip of a dog."

"Chiweenies are long and feisty. He curls up right in the middle, and I can't tell him no."

"Oh, you poor thing. Tsk, tsk. If you get dark circles under your eyes, how will you keep your title of Hollydale's Most Eligible Bachelor?" She waited while he loaded his hammer next to her purchases, then jerked her thumb toward the passenger door. "This ride will cost you."

He turned toward the retro diner across the street. "I'll run over right now and buy you a slice of lemon meringue pie, if they're not sold out already."

"That's not my price." Although she wouldn't have minded a piece of pie from the Holly Days Diner. Lemon meringue happened to be her favorite, as Mason well knew. "I have one quick stop before heading home. I hope that's okay with you?"

"Beggars can't be choosers. Thanks for the ride." He settled into the passenger seat.

Lindsay started her truck, and the speakers began blasting a Taylor Swift tune. Her hand touched Mason's as they both rushed to turn down the music.

He chuckled as she reversed out of the spot. "Pumping up the volume when the kids aren't in the car?"

"I can listen to what I like as loud as I like when I'm alone. My kids prefer the newest Disney tunes, especially Chloe, who sings along much to Evan's dismay." She hated her defensive tone as she passed the brick storefronts of downtown. It wasn't about leaving her music on full blast and all about becoming more predictable than bees pollinating the spring flowers.

"I can't believe she's old enough to sing already," Mason said. "It seems like yesterday I thought you wouldn't make it to the hospital, and I'd have to deliver her."

There'd been five minutes where she'd been mortified Tim's former partner might have to deliver Chloe. They were waiting for her aunt to arrive to take care of Evan in the middle of the night after Lindsay's water broke. Fortunately, they'd made it to the hospital in the nick of time, and Mason stayed in the waiting room.

"She and Evan are even old enough to argue now. Evan complains about her music, and they bicker."

"Sisters can be the biggest pains, but big brothers will do anything they can on their behalf. Evan will step up. You'll see."

Without a doubt, Mason must be thinking about his own sister. "Any update on Bree's prognosis?"

Mason tapped his fingers to the beat of the song playing on the radio. "Bree got through her initial shock and reaction, she's regrouped and is ready to kick cancer to the curb and beyond. Having Grandma Betty there for moral support helped when they called our Mom and Dad together."

Stopped at one of four traffic lights in Hollydale, Lindsay let Mason's words sink in and she focused on the lush purples of the petunia planter on Cobb Realty's upper level. Chloe would especially love the shades from lavender to violet.

Next door, the personality of the outfitting store was on display with spring succulents gracing the window box. Still, the tulips surrounding the gazebo were her favorites, their long stems and bright variety of colors marking the transition from the muted stark browns of winter to the rainbow surrounding them.

The light turned green, and she found a parking space on Main Street in front of the pharmacy. Mason waited in her truck while she paid for Evan's inhaler.

On the way home, Mason read Evan's prescription label. "How's Evan doing since his asthma diagnosis?"

"Better now that we know the cause of his breathing issues."

She turned onto their street and backed into her driveway so it'd be easier to unload the wood.

"So, what's your fee for the ride? Unloading the wood? Buying your next bottle of wine for

our nightly talks? Your wish is my command."
Mason performed a mock bow from the passenger side of the truck. "Except for gardening, of course. I'm not big on standing around and waiting for something to sprout and grow."

"In that case, I'll have to do something to change your mind about my favorite hobby." She used the remote control on her key chain and raised her garage door. She hopped down and opened the tailgate, then removed the first plank.

"Come on, Linds." Mason grabbed two planks at once, and she rolled her eyes at his showing off. "Anything but gardening. Double the usual babysitting?"

"But I thought you love spending time with Chloe and Evan." She paused near the grid lines she'd drawn on the garage floor with chalk before plopping down the first cedar plank and leveling a look at him. "You care about them, don't you?"

"Lindsay." All traces of levity disappeared, and his gaze bored through her. "I'd never lie or joke about that. Chloe and I bonded the minute I first saw her and she held my finger. I love Evan and Chloe as though they were mine. As a matter of fact, they're my beneficiaries."

He laid his two planks near hers, muffling out her shocked "What?"

Mason wiped his hands and moved toward her shelves crammed full of fertilizer, buckets with gloves and trowels, loppers and other gardening tools. "Do you want the gravel inside or outside?"

Dumbfounded, she stood there, her feet planted to the concrete. "Repeat what you just said."

"Do you want…"

Lindsay shook her head. "About Evan and Chloe being your beneficiaries."

"It makes sense, plus, I'm too ornery for anything to happen to me." He headed outside and wiped his brow with the back of his muscular forearm. "Hey, if I'm going to help you garden, the least you can do is offer me a glass of water."

Mason wasn't getting off this lightly, she thought.

"Why didn't you tell me? You have a sister, parents and grandparents, not to mention a legion of cousins scattered here in North Carolina and out in Colorado."

Her question came as he gripped the first bag of gravel. He dropped it on the driveway, and Lindsay stared him down.

"A straight answer, please."

The muscles of his jaw clenched as seconds ticked by. "Because I didn't want it to be awkward between us…like it is right now. If something happened to me, you'd have found out then. I live in the present. It's easier that way."

Easier than what? Letting go of memories wasn't her style, but maybe he was right. There hadn't been this type of uncomfortable silence between them since Tim had introduced them, and they milled about while searching for common ground.

She scuffed the driveway with the tip of her clog. She wasn't sure how she felt about his revelation but let the beneficiary matter drop for now. "Gardening isn't all about planning for the future."

A bit of the challenge and spark she always associated with that chin tilt of his returned. "How is something that takes forever interesting? It takes forever for seeds to grow to fruition."

Lindsay tugged on his hand and led him to the side yard that bordered her other neighbor's house. Bright sunshine warmed the deep pink peonies flourishing in the rich brown mountain soil, unlike the red clay that predominated most of the state. "I transplanted those when they were fully grown last year." She looked down, her hand still holding his, she released him. "Sorry about that."

"You don't have to be embarrassed for caring about something you're passionate about. I've put people to sleep at parties talking about my favorite brand of motorcycle helmets. One thing's always puzzled me, though."

Lindsay almost sighed with relief since he'd assumed she was flustered about her hobby. Talk about awkward. Her stomach fluttered when she dropped his hand as if she was making some sort of mistake in letting him get away. "What's that?"

"How can you spend all day at the botanical garden and then come home and relax by doing the same thing? There's no way I could finish a three-day shift and then only read medical thrillers. I'd get bored if I didn't have my motorcycle."

"Help me build the trellis for my new morning glories then, instead of digging in the dirt as payment? Your electric saw will make quick time of those planks."

Mason waved his arm with a flourish along the length of his torso, the bright sunlight turning the red locks of his hair into burnished gold. "That's the deal? You could have asked for anything from me, and you want my electric saw?"

"Driving you home wasn't that big of a deal." Unlike the tingles still pricking her fingertips.

This was Mason, she reminded herself, her husband's partner and her best friend. She'd already lost too much to also lose her cool over a man who'd kept her together after Tim died. Everyone else, including her parents, had coddled her and thankfully taken care of Evan while she hid in bed, until one afternoon when he stormed into her room, opened her drapes and let the sunshine in.

"Your wish is my command." He smiled and turned, marching toward his garage with that determined gait of his, the one that made women in Hollydale stop and take notice. Just as attractive was the respect he'd earned from his fellow first responders.

Flicking her fingers, she absorbed the spring warmth and willed all thoughts of him as anything other than a friend aside while reviewing her strategy for building a trellis.

In LINDSAY'S GARAGE, Mason drilled the screws on the back side of the cedar plank. Constructing this trellis was right up his alley. Give him a project that involved building something or his tools, and he was content.

Lindsay understood that, and that was why

she was his best friend. Although in the past couple of months he'd caught himself wishing they were more than friends. The delicate arch of her eyebrows when she was animated. The lush pink of her lips when she finished her one glass of wine. The soft sway of her hips as she slid the door closed at night. These were not attributes he should notice about Tim's widow. Losing her as a friend? He'd do anything to prevent that from happening. Even tamping down his feelings while spending the day with her.

Lindsay came into the garage, and he pushed his safety goggles atop his head. She deposited a gallon of exterior stain at his knees, her hands stained with dust and dirt. "When's your grandfather coming home?"

"My best guesstimate is sunset." He exhaled at the mention of his grandfather. Right now, Goliath was safe in the confines of Mason's backyard, chewing on a beef bully stick. For the next three days, Mason would work twelve-hour shifts, something that must have slipped Grandma Betty's mind when she entrusted his grandfather's care to him. "About Grandpa Joe…"

Before he could ask Lindsay about Grandpa Joe moving in with her, car doors slammed in the driveway. Evan ran up to them with a container of plastic birds. "See what I got?"

Lindsay smoothed his fine blond hair plastered to the sides of his face. "Nice."

Chloe bounded over to Mason in that toddler run of hers, clutching a stuffed turtle. "Pick Chloe up?"

The way she uttered her name sounded so much like the way Colette had said *Coey*, his pet name for his firstborn sister. He obliged and grinned. "I like your turtle."

He touched it, and she snatched it away. "My turtle."

"You won't share?"

"Your cheek feels funny so Chloe share." She rubbed the stuffed animal's green fur against his stubble and then giggled. He couldn't imagine loving a daughter of his own more. Lindsay's family was his family.

Tim's father headed his way and reached out his hand. "Mason, good to see you again."

Mason gently lowered Chloe, and she went over to show Lindsay her new toy. "Mr. Hudson."

He accepted the handshake.

"Call me Tom. Donna stayed in the car. She's feeling a bit wound down after a day with the kiddos, and it's a long drive back to Wilmington." Tom's blond hair was now liberally streaked with gray. Tall and still lean, he was the image of what Tim would have looked like in thirty years. "It's hard on her since Evan's the spitting image of Tim at that age. Sorry we can't stay, Tim talked so highly of you. We'll catch up more at the dedication ceremony."

Despite Tom's comment, Mason had no intention of making an appearance. "Maybe, maybe not."

A long blast of the car horn prevented Tom from asking the questions written on his face. He patted Mason on the back. "It's a relief for us both to know Lindsay has Tim's partner looking out for her. You're a good man, Mason."

Tom's throat bobbed, and he hurried away. Lindsay came over, and Mason cringed at whatever she was about to say. He spoke first. "I'm still not coming to the ceremony."

"I have a feeling you'll be there." She turned toward Evan after he threw a smooth stone between the slats of the trellis lying on the ground. "What are you doing?" she asked.

"Playing hopscotch. This is great, Mom!" He jumped and hopped the length of the trellis and back again.

"Fun is over." She faced Mason, her pretty features a mottled shade of pink, the same as her peonies. "I'll take the kids inside, could you move the trellis to the backyard by the fence?"

She tapped her chin, leaving a smudge of dirt, and he had the funniest urge to wipe it away and kiss the clean spot.

He quickly cast the thought aside. "Sure, but what else is on your mind?"

"I have another question, but I'm not sure I want to know the answer."

He glanced over at Evan dumping out the container of birds and Chloe plopping beside him with her turtle. "They're keeping busy."

He tried his special smile, the one reserved to calm patients, especially female patients. However, Lindsay, typically patient herself, was having none of it. "That'll only last for about a minute."

Seconds ticked by, the air growing thick between them. He started to panic. Something was changing between them. At the very least, something was changing in him. Every day when he woke up, he counted down the moments until he'd see her again. *No.* He couldn't be attracted to Lindsay. He'd keep this moment light, keep the friendship bond between them.

"C'mon. Tell me. I'm all ears." He used his fingers to wiggle his ears.

She leaned in close enough for her lavender

scent to catch him and drive him crazy. "Earlier you said something about two males. Were you matchmaking?"

"Never." That wasn't quite what he expected, but he'd take anything right now to break the tension. "I need help with Grandpa Joe and Goliath while I'm working my three-day shift."

"Just help? At Farr's Hardware, it sounded like you wanted Joe and Goliath to move in with me until your grandmother came home." That intense gaze saw through him every time. "Don't forget who you're talking to."

"Okay, then." His palms became sweaty, not a result of the physical labor but because of this woman who sometimes knew him better than he knew himself. "The fact is Grandpa Joe doesn't listen to me."

"What're you talking about?" She looked at Evan, who was hopping around, making the plastic birds swoop and fly, and Chloe, who toddled over to her brother and picked one up under Evan's careful brown gaze.

The similarities between himself and Evan at that age, when he and Colette did everything together, struck him, and he fought the urge to flee. "Grandpa Joe does what he wants to do and won't accept my advice."

"That's not true. Why would you think that?"

"His diet, for one thing. He doused my low-fat turkey chili with sour cream, guacamole and cheddar cheese." He shook his head remembering how his grandfather's first of three servings had resembled a heart attack in a bowl.

"Is that the recipe you tried out on Evan and Chloe last week? The one where you snuck in carrots and zucchini?"

He nodded and kept watch over Evan and Chloe, seeing how they were the closest he'd ever come to having kids. "Anything two kids under five demolished that fast has to be good."

"True. But it's sweet you're worried about him so I'll invite him to dinner for the next couple of nights. I'm glad he's staying with you. You need this time with him. Someday you'll realize just how much."

He opened his mouth to protest he already appreciated his grandpa's visit, but one look at Lindsay's resolute face told him to save his breath. Instead, he just smiled. "What time should I tell him to arrive tomorrow night?"

She narrowed her eyes and stared at him. "Was that a compromise or your intention all along?"

He smiled again, a genuine one that had everything to do with the way she made him feel. "I shared my chili recipe with you and

Grandma Betty. I'll let you stew over this one and decide."

Lindsay groaned and threw her gardening gloves at him. "With puns like those, I don't know why I keep you around."

Sometimes he wondered the same thing.

CHAPTER THREE

GLEEFUL SHOUTS OF JOY from the Children's Play Zone carried over Sully Creek and the tree-lined bridge, which separated the heart-shaped Hollydale Botanical Garden into two halves. Lindsay knelt in Sycamore Station, testing the soil for pH levels one last time before the flower planting commenced. She reveled in the Carolina sunshine, the wide brim of her canvas hat shielding the harmful effect of the rays but not the caress of the breeze on her cheeks. Spring days like today made her job as head horticulturist seem more like play than work.

Sycamore Station with the center's most famous tree was in the southwestern quadrant where she'd lobbied for this memorial. The noise from the children's area was the primary reason she supported this section over Rose Blossom Way, where four squares of roses and gardenias converged upon a fountain into which visitors tossed a penny and made a wish.

She stood and stretched. Where were the volunteers she was expecting? A glance at the chart confirmed they were running late, but she groaned at the sight of the name of Heather Schmidt, her boss's gossipy wife, as one of the morning helpers. Nothing she could do or say about that. Finishing her stretch, Lindsay drank in the peaceful sight until something amiss with the sycamore caught her eye. Her focus narrowed in on the spot.

Her boots imprinted into the loamy brown soil as she examined the leaves of the sycamore, one of the few planted in the state from seeds taken up to the International Space Station. Visitors to the garden were always asking to see the space tree, as many referred to the garden's most famous landmark. Folks often claimed they traveled here for the sole purpose of having a look at it. Some leaves appeared as though they'd been covered in baby powder when in actuality the tree had powdery mildew fungus.

"You noticed that blight, too." Lindsay's boss, Phillip Schmidt, came up behind her.

"Fungicide should clear it up in no time." Lindsay released the limb. "No doubt the cool, wet spring is the culprit. Before I leave today, I'll apply the first dose."

As well as check the weather forecast again and take any precautions if the expected storms showed signs of worsening. This morning, the meteorologist had predicted only a soaking rain for later tonight, but this close to the mountains the forecast often changed.

While she had been buckling in Evan and Chloe for day care, Joe and Goliath had met her in the driveway at the end of their walk. Joe confided his rheumatism was a sure sign tonight's storm would be a real whopper before shuffling away, muttering how much he missed Betty. Right there, she'd invited him over for dinner for the third night in a row.

"Now that I'm back from my vacation, I talked to the plaque company." Phillip wasted little time in getting to the point.

"I thought my report showed that I'd handled that." She removed one glove, then the other, while counting to ten. She went to her rolling cart and dumped the gloves in a bucket.

Phillip tucked his clipboard under his arm. "The president of the company called me personally."

Lindsay grabbed her reusable water bottle that Mason had given her last Mother's Day, the one with flowers and the slogan "You're never too old to play in the dirt." She took a long swig of water. "They spelled *Hudson* wrong and then had the audacity to insist the order would take longer than promised."

"I'm friends with the president. He apologized and guaranteed the plaque would be here two weeks sooner and reduced the price by ten percent. I went ahead and contacted the media outlets, along with our web designer and moved up the opening. Several local celebrities who were unable to come with the original date said they'd attend."

The water went down the wrong pipe, and she coughed at her boss's sudden announcement. Every perennial on her site rendering and every detail on her meticulous chart had involved realistic preparation time. She'd allowed for five built-in days for delays, but not fourteen.

After her coughing attack subsided, she stared at her boss as if he'd sprouted branches and dogwood flowers. "You didn't consult me first to make sure this is even possible."

"You've worked here since your graduation. Your projects always come in on time and under budget."

But none of her previous projects had measured this high of a magnitude. Stunned, she sipped more water, only to have it follow the same path. Another coughing fit marred this beautiful afternoon. She wiped her mouth with the back of her hand. "As it was I left little margin for this significant of a change. Some of the flowers are set to arrive two days before the original opening."

Phillip pursed his lips. "It's done, Lindsay. You'll adjust and make our botanical garden the talk of the state. Last year our attendance numbers were down, and we need this publicity as a selling point."

"Tim and the others aren't a tourist attraction." She whipped out a clean pair of gloves and donned them. "We didn't bid so we can drum up business."

"The mayor rejected the gazebo, and it came down to a few other sites."

Mayor Wes made the right call in the end. The gazebo, located in the heart of historic downtown Hollydale, was a romantic spot and she preferred keeping it that way. Tim had proposed to her there, and she knew couples married on its steps, including her friend Georgie, who'd wed the town's sheriff, Mike Harrison. Now she had to get everything perfect in a mere ten weeks instead of the original twelve.

Tim and the other first responders deserved nothing less.

"I'll be busy with this afternoon's budget meeting, but I trust you'll handle the new date." It was a statement rather than a question, and Phillip walked away without waiting for her reply.

Shaking her head, she gulped down another few sips while keeping a lookout for those volunteers. *No-shows*. Lindsay frowned, knelt by the cart and glanced at the plats of cannas and cosmos flowers awaiting transfer into the prepared bed of soil. Needing little care, these plants would thrive in the area to the left of the sycamore. She checked her watch. She'd have to start without Heather or the others. It wasn't a big deal, just time-consuming.

She examined each plat and considered the order in which she wanted to plant the showier yellow-and-orange cannas and the daintier white cosmos tinged with the lightest of lavender.

"Of course, Phillip brought up Lindsay before they awarded the contract. Why else do you think we got it?" Heather's high-pitched voice caught Lindsay's attention.

From her low vantage point behind the cart, she saw she wasn't the only one staring at Heather and the other volunteers. People near the sycamore gawked in that direction. Boss's wife or not, Lindsay wouldn't let them gossip about the garden in full sight and sound of visitors, possibly Hollydale residents.

Lindsay popped up and motioned to the two volunteers. "Ladies." She silently counted to twenty as she ushered them behind a chained-off area for employees only. "This is a public area, and you're wearing the special green T-shirts that designate you as official volunteers."

Heather pulled to her full height, a good four inches taller than Lindsay's smaller frame. "May I remind you my husband is the director here?"

"And may I remind you people post cell phone videos online?" Lindsay refused to be intimidated. "Are you ready? We have a lot of work ahead of us."

Unsurprisingly, Heather didn't look shocked when Lindsay brought up the revised timeline and dates. After that the morning passed by in no time, and the flowers were transferred to the first arc while others would follow in the coming weeks, completing the circle that would always have one plant or flower in bloom. Already the area looked more colorful, a fitting tribute for the men and women who'd lost their lives serving others.

Heather and her friend left, and not a moment too soon as far as Lindsay was concerned.

She removed her gloves, and noticed her fingers trembled. She gripped the cart and rolled it back to the southern shed.

"Lindsay? Are you okay?"

Lindsay halted and found a very pregnant Natalie Murphy approaching her.

She smiled and nodded. "Natalie, I can't remember the last time we talked." Her friend's wedding to Aidan perhaps. Come to think of it, she'd cut herself off from quite a few of her friendships after Tim died. "When are you due?"

"Not until June though Aidan originally told some people I was due in May. I've asked my obstetrician to make sure I'm not carrying twins, being one myself. But she assures me there's only one Murphy baby in there, who's destined to be as tall as his or her father, I'm sure."

Natalie's husband, Aidan, was the new city manager, having finished serving in the army before finding the position here and marrying her friend.

Should she ask Natalie if Heather had spoken the truth, and the garden received the contract because she was Tim's widow? If that was the case, she'd quit on the spot.

Natalie laid her hand on Lindsay's shoulder. "You look stressed. Do you need to sit down?"

"I should be the one asking you that."

"I could rest for a minute. My mother told me to enjoy some time alone before the baby comes while she watches Danny at the Children's Play Zone. He loves the annual membership Aidan gave him for Christmas, although, at the time, he scrunched his nose like the present was a pair of stinky socks." Natalie laughed, her bangle bracelets chiming like music. She headed for the nearest bench. "Do you have a few minutes to catch up?"

Lindsay glanced at the cart and considered the many afternoon duties awaiting her. Maybe a chat with an old friend would help her tackle that list with more enthusiasm. "I shouldn't, but I will."

They settled on a bench donated by Lindsay's aunt in memory of her husband, Craig Hennessy. "I'm sorry I can't attend the ceremony." Natalie patted her stomach. "Baby Murphy is limiting my engagements."

"You have the best of excuses."

"Speaking of excuses, you haven't responded yet to the baby shower invite from Becks and Georgie." Becks was Natalie's twin sister, and Georgie was her sister-in-law.

"I don't know if I'll be able to attend. Phillip just moved the dedication date up two weeks."

"Is that why you're pale?" Natalie rubbed her baby bump and stretched her back. "Or does it have to do with the reason for the memorial garden itself?"

"Thanks for your concern, but I'm okay."

She'd kept herself relatively isolated, so her friends had no idea she'd come to terms with Tim's death. "It's the prospect of extra work to get everything ready in time. I'll start calling vendors this afternoon, but it's just…"

If Lindsay didn't want Heather to gossip about the way the garden's bid was accepted, she best keep what she overheard to herself. With attendance already down, the last thing she needed was people getting wind of negative talk like this and then staying away.

Natalie nudged Lindsay. "I might be overreaching here, but if you ever need a good listener, I'm available. I know how close you and Tim were. I still think about my best friend Shelby whenever her son Danny laughs a certain way. The hard truth is it took some time after she died for Danny to laugh again. Even though Aidan and I officially adopted him, Shelby will always be his mom in my eyes. I know talking to me won't be the same as talking to Tim, but the offer stands."

"Thank you."

Natalie swept her red hair away from her face and pushed off with her other hand on the armrest and stood. "Time with friends and family. That's the best thing to do as far as I'm concerned. I'm so happy I ran into you."

Lindsay walked alongside her with the rolling cart, the matter of the bid still unsettling. "Natalie, did Aidan ever…?"

Natalie faced her. "Did Aidan ever what? Jump the gun? Act a mite stubborn? Plan everything about this baby to the nth degree, even though I told him the baby won't come with a day planner? Yes, to all of the above."

The redhead laughed, but then winced, placing both hands on her lower back. "The baby must be more like my husband than I thought. He didn't seem to like that."

"Are you okay? You're not going into labor, are you?" Lindsay thought about Evan born six weeks premature but relatively healthy, despite his recent asthma diagnosis.

"Braxton-Hicks, that's all. The hospital's the place where I want this wee one to be born, even though the garden might be my new favorite spot in Hollydale. Such vibrant colors. That butterfly enclosure is simply divine, but I should be getting back."

"There's an employee shortcut to the children's area. Let me take you that way." Although Natalie protested, Lindsay insisted.

Outside the entrance to the Children's Play Zone, Natalie hugged Lindsay goodbye. "At first, Aidan had his doubts about this being the right selection for the memorial though this was the lowest bid, but he's come around."

Lindsay's ears perked. They'd won the bid on its merits. "I'll do my best to attend your baby shower."

"If Becks and Georgie don't end up cancelling the party first, since they can't agree on much," she laughed jokingly. "Except how much they love me, of course." Natalie waved goodbye and passed through into the kids' play area.

There was no use dwelling on the bid process when Lindsay had vendors to call and fungicide to mix. More than ever, she looked forward to comparing notes with Mason tonight at their fence.

WITH ANOTHER SHIFT in the books, Mason shrugged on his jacket. Beside him, Jordan, his new partner of two months, his fourth since Tim died, stared off into space. No doubt the man's mind was still at Timber River and the scene from a few hours ago after a group of teens had flipped their raft. Everyone had made it out, but one teen was in critical yet stable condition in the ICU at Dalesford General while another had already been discharged.

Mason slammed the door of his locker shut and snapped the lock, ready to sleep in his own bed after this long three-day shift spent on call at the station. "Earth to Jordan."

Jordan blinked and shook his head. "How do you handle the stress of the job, Mason? How have you kept at it this long?"

"Because of things like today… we arrived in time, stayed calm, did our job and they survived. The teen with the concussion is already home and expected to make a full recovery, and the girl in the hospital can thank her lucky stars her boyfriend kept performing CPR until we arrived."

Jordan closed his locker but stayed where he was, his chest noticeably rising and falling. Mason worried and wondered if he'd have yet another new partner by the next shift. Burnout was a factor in this profession, and Jordan's hollow eyes told the story of why, even though Mason considered today a success. Days like these did take a toll.

"I'll lay it on the line for you." Mason tapped his partner's shoulder until the younger guy met his gaze. "Your grandparents run the best pizza joint in town, right?"

"I could start working there tomorrow." Jordan's voice sounded cool and distant, and Mason imagined the guy was already drafting his resignation letter.

"Maybe it's better you find this out when you're twenty-one instead of thirty-one, like me." Not that Mason was going anywhere.

"Except." Jordan placed one sneaker on his foot, tied it, then did the same with the other. He looked down and swore. "Wrong feet." He shucked off his sneakers and started over. He huffed out a breath. "I love this job."

"Remember that and take the successes where and when they come. Those can keep you in check and motivated during the hard losses." Mason sat beside him and softly elbowed Jordan. "If you do that, we'll make a good team, partner." He grew somber and handed his partner his other sneaker. "Are you prepared for the day when it turns out differently? We can't save everyone."

Jordan accepted the sneaker and slipped it on his foot. "I know. This is the first time we've handled a call with people younger than me. Is it hard the first time someone really young dies on your watch?"

"Yeah. But it's always hard when that's the outcome. Can you handle that?"

"I'm not sure. I hope so."

"Take the next couple of days and know so." He patted Jordan's shoulder. "Your instincts are good, some of the best I've seen."

Mason waited until Jordan was feeling better. By the time he got to his SUV, dusk surrounded him. The rain started picking up in intensity, and the wind made it almost impossible to open his door. He exerted extra force until the door blew open and then almost slammed shut on his leg. He sat there motionless, raindrops running down his face. Today's scene at Timber River was one that would stay with him for a while, a fun day for a group of teens cut short by circumstances beyond their control.

The rhythm of the rain on his car roof subsided, bringing him out of his memories. He inserted his key in the ignition and waited for his hands to stop shaking. His phone rang, and he wanted to ignore it, except it was Grandma Betty. He never ignored her.

"Hello, Mason. Can you hear me? This is Grandma Betty Ruddick." The lilt in her voice at her usual greeting, a running gag with her five grandchildren, always let him know she was in on the joke.

Only a handful of people lifted his spirits like his grandmother, and most of them resided next door to his house. "Excellent timing. My shift just ended ten minutes ago."

"I know. I timed it so I could check on that roguish husband of mine, who sounded very chipper on the phone today. How's Joe really?" That type of concern proved what fifty-six years of marriage and an abiding love could do for someone.

At moments like this, he wanted that same type of commitment. Then images of Colette and Tim flashed in his mind. He'd seen his parents mourn Colette. Same with Lindsay after Tim's death. He'd never want to cause anyone that kind of grief. The bachelor life was for him.

"As much of a rascal as ever." Somehow, he kept his voice casual. Enlightening her on Grandpa Joe's dietary downslide, however, would only cause her to worry, so he skipped that detail. Somehow, he had to corral his grandfather.

"That's my Joe. I miss him, you know?"

He could only imagine. "He's lonely without you, too, but Lindsay agreed to have him to dinner while I worked my long shift. She's probably spoiling him."

"You make Joe sound more like a dog than Goliath." She chuckled.

Mason heard Bree in the background, and he waited while Grandma Betty relayed everything to her. "How's Bree?"

"Why don't you ask her yourself? By the way, expect some surprises tomorrow."

Shuffling noises came over the line, and the rain seemed to be tapering off so now was as good a time as any to venture forth. He switched to the hands-free speaker for the drive home. He exited the lot, but Bree still hadn't come on the line.

"Bree?" he repeated her name. "Did we get disconnected?"

"I moved into another room so I could talk to you in private."

He braced himself. "I'm driving." As far as he was concerned, he could keep driving until he hit Nashville. "Do I need to call you back? Is this more bad news?" Had the scans showed advanced cancer? How would she cope? He couldn't bury another sister.

"Nothing like that, so stop worrying. My scans were clear. It's localized, and my long-term prognosis is good." With those simple sentences, Bree lifted that iron weight off his chest. "I wanted to talk to you about Grandma Betty."

He smiled. "So, she's driving you to distraction? Some days Grandpa Joe is happy to be on his own, and others he's ready to get on a plane and join her."

"Huh? That's not where I was going at all." Bree's serious tone was unlike his gregarious sister. "I don't know what I'd have done without her for the past week. Thanks to her, Mom and Dad managed to hold it together, although Mom still cried on the videoconference call. Grandma Betty even persuaded them not to fly home from Australia. You know how long they've waited for this opportunity at the university in Adelaide. Mom's hard at work on her doctoral thesis while Dad's loving teaching geology and studying the rift formation nearby. They'll visit over their winter break."

"Hold that thought. I'm almost home." He turned onto his street, his smaller rental next to Lindsay's bigger, homier Cape Cod. Even the rain couldn't diminish the spring colors on full display in her front yard. He parked in his driveway. "So, I'm guessing the great news is Grandma Betty will reunite with Grandpa Joe soon?"

"That's why I wanted to talk to you in a different room. Tristan landed a major coding project, and he wants to turn it down since it will involve extensive travel over the next month, but Mason, you ought to see his eyes light up when he talks about the intricacy of the assignment and the challenges."

He knew where this was going. "And if Grandma Betty stays for a little while longer, Tristan wouldn't have to say no because she'd be here, and Mom and Dad can keep working in Australia." He glanced at Lindsay's windows, lights blazing, the picture of happiness. "Has she told Grandpa Joe she's extending her visit?"

Bree inhaled and exhaled. "I was hoping you could do that."

He'd be a heel if he refused this smallest of favors for his little sister. "Good thing he's at Lindsay's. That might lessen some of the sting of hearing it from me."

"My surgery's next week. After that, my doctor will finish planning my next course of treatment. Grandma being here is making all the difference. We're really bonding. I so appreciate you and Grandpa Joe banding together." Bree's yawn came through loud and clear.

"Go get some rest," he told her.

"Okay, love ya."

"Right back at you." He sat there, staring at his dark house. Suddenly, the empty place didn't seem as appealing as it had when he'd left the station. Besides, he should head to Lindsay's and tell Grandpa Joe this latest twist. He ran for Lindsay's covered stoop. Her front door opened before he formed a fist to knock.

"You're soaked. Wait here." Lindsay must have seen his headlights through her window.

Yips greeted him next as Goliath scrambled forward, his paws clattering against the hardwood of the foyer as he ground to a halt. Mason hurried inside and shut the door behind him. The plump dog jumped on him, and Mason waggled his finger. "Down, Goliath."

The dog wagged his tail before giving in. Mason rewarded him with a "Good dog" and a scratch behind his ears. In no time, Lindsay returned with a fluffy blue towel and gray sweats, which looked familiar. "They're not Tim's." He must have been more transparent than he realized, judging from Lindsay's response. "They're yours from the time Chloe had her little accident. I kept them here in case of another emergency."

He chuckled and accepted the clothes. Goliath leaped up and sniffed. He must not have been impressed since he abruptly left.

Mason held up the sweats. "You forgot about these until just now, didn't you?"

She chuckled this time and tilted her head toward the guest bathroom. "Stop reading my mind and get dry, then join us in the playroom."

"Aye, aye, matey." He lifted two fingers to his forehead in a mock salute.

Lindsay rolled her eyes and walked away. The intriguing smile on her face caused him to sway slightly. This was Tim's widow, and he had no right to think of her in any other light.

In the guest bathroom, he splashed cold water on his cheeks before he swapped his set of sopping-wet navy sweats for the dry gray ones with the faintest trace of the lavender fabric softener Lindsay favored. He left the bathroom and found them all in the living room. With a few strokes, he rubbed his hair with the towel and watched the scene before him. Grandpa Joe was helping Chloe build a cabin with Lincoln Logs while Lindsay and Evan constructed something of their own. The serenity of the setting wasn't lost on Mason, and he credited Lindsay with the toasty atmosphere as opposed to the wet mess of the spring storm outside.

Even the soft instrumental music, something low and sweet with a Celtic flair, brought a sense of repose, something lacking this afternoon when he and Jordan came upon the scene at Timber River.

She'd even found an old blanket and pillow for Goliath, who was curled up on a makeshift dog bed. He didn't realize he needed this. Until now.

"What's that?" Mason asked and settled on the cream carpet. He pointed to the structure in front of Lindsay and Evan.

"It's a greenhouse."

"It's a dungeon."

Mother and son had answered at once, then both burst out laughing.

"I guess we didn't ask each other. It just happened," Lindsay explained.

Lightning flashed, spotted through the window, with thunder splitting the air a few seconds later. Her gray gaze met his, and something connected between them, an arc of electricity as potent as the storm. He shivered, too aware it had nothing to do with the weather and everything to do with this beautiful woman. She scrambled to her feet.

"How about some peppermint tea to ward off any lingering cold from the rain? Or I can put on a pot of decaf?" She turned toward Grandpa Joe. "I bought more of that hazelnut creamer you liked the other night."

"Can we have hot chocolate?" Evan licked his lips.

Chloe separated herself from Grandpa Joe and motioned for Mason to pick her up. He did so, and she reached for his hair and giggled. "Mason's hair scwunchy."

"Crunchy hair? Not exactly the look I was going for, but it should be all the rage next season."

A loud clap of thunder rocked the house, and Chloe lowered her head to his shoulder and whimpered. Lindsay rushed over, but Mason comforted the little girl by rubbing her back. "It's just the air, honey, but it's more fun to imagine a story for it. Some say thunder is someone bowling a strike or maybe banging on a drum." Two rams butting heads with each other also came to mind. Sort of how he'd been feeling around Lindsay these days.

Chloe giggled, faced him and patted his cheeks. The lights in the house flickered, but the power didn't go out. The rain crashed with force against the windows, and again he met Lindsay's gaze. She checked her phone and then announced, "Severe thunderstorm warning and tornado watch. We're moving this party to the basement."

Grandpa Joe rose and clutched his back. "I think I'll stay up here and give the all-clear signal when it's safe."

A tornado siren pierced the air, and Goliath howled. Chloe tightened her grip on Mason, digging her little fingers into his back. He transferred her to Lindsay. "If you take Evan and Chloe, I'll be down in a minute with Goliath and Grandpa Joe."

Lindsay nodded and ushered her children to the basement. Mason went over to Grandpa Joe as the shrieking wind intensified. "Time to join them."

Grandpa Joe nodded. He tried to step forward and winced. "My back medicine's in my bedroom at your house. I can't make it downstairs like this. Take Goliath, and I'll wait out the storm here."

Mason reached for his grandfather's arm and finagled his way under him, so he supported most of his weight. "Goliath will follow you, and I'll get your medicine when it's safe. Come on."

With some effort, his grandfather made it down the stairs. As soon as they reached the finished basement, Lindsay helped with Grandpa Joe. Together they settled him on the sectional. Then she handed out candles and matches. "In case the power goes out."

Lindsay picked up the children's book she'd been reading, and huddled her kids around her. Even Goliath's and Grandpa Joe's ears perked up as her calm voice filled the air. Within minutes, rhythmic sounds of breathing and dog snuffles prevailed, and even Mason had a hard time keeping his eyes open.

What seemed like only minutes later, he opened his eyes. He shifted from his place on the floor and jerked awake, checking his cell's screen only to find it was already Thursday. His gaze went to Lindsay, her arms protecting Evan and Chloe cuddled against either side of her. He'd never seen her asleep before, with her honey-brown hair surrounding her like a soft cloud.

Lindsay was beautiful. The thought rocked him as her eyelids fluttered open. With a start, she blinked and looked around the room. He pointed toward the stairs, and she extracted herself, taking caution not to wake Evan or Chloe. His grandfather rested on the other side of the sectional. In spite of the circumstances, Mason wasn't in that big of a hurry to break this spell.

She rubbed her neck and joined him, her gray eyes still tinged with sleep. His gaze landed on Goliath, who peeked at them before returning to sleep at his grandfather's feet. "How late is it?" Her whisper caressed his cheek, and he stepped backward. Anything to stop this type of reaction to Tim's widow. "Ten, eleven?"

He held up his phone. "More like five in the morning."

Her eyes widened, and she hurried up the staircase. He followed her. Wedding pictures hung on the closest wall. Was it just him, or was Tim frowning at Mason's reaction to his wife?

"Thanks for not waking the kids. I wanted to look at my messages," she said and extracted her phone from her pocket. When she scrolled, her eyebrows creased. "Aunt Hyacinth texted. Her house is fine, and she's meeting her business partner to check on Sweet Shelby's Tea Room."

Mason checked his messages, focusing on the ones from his coworkers detailing the tornado that had touched down outside city limits. His chief hadn't activated him to report for duty, so he texted him he was available if needed. A quick reply informed him everything was covered. He waited as three more dots appeared. He let out a breath as the reply indicated calls were limited to being about power outages and the like, without the need for extra paramedics at this time.

"I'm going home for Grandpa Joe's medicine."

"Oh, no! Your grandfather's back. I totally forgot. I'm so sorry. He needed that medicine."

Mason waved away her apology. "You did everything right. And your house has a basement, so I'm glad we were here. You kept him calm, and we all apparently liked the story you read to Evan and Chloe a little too much."

She chuckled, although her smile didn't reach her eyes. "Is that a polite way of saying I put everyone to sleep?"

"No. It's a polite way of thanking you for the kindness you provided my grandfather. And me."

Without hesitation, he leaned in and brushed

her cheek with a quick kiss. He quickly pulled back and left via the sliding glass door. Outside, darkness surrounded him, his lips still tingling from the contact with Lindsay's soft skin. The rain had stopped, and a mountain bluebird's predawn chirps cut through the silence. Her friendship meant everything to him. Why had he done something foolish, like kissing her cheek?

Mason retrieved Grandpa Joe's medication and brewed a cup of coffee in case he was called in. He poured his first cup and lingered, his normal confidence replaced by doubt. Should he bring up the kiss? Should he apologize?

Taking the last sip, he clutched the pill bottle and headed for Lindsay's, a sliver of orange and pink on the horizon heralding the beginning of the new day. The impact of last night's storm became evident in the light. He stopped and stared. Lindsay's vegetable garden, the one she tended so reverently, looked as though a giant had stomped on it, the row markers shredded like cheddar cheese. Nothing would be salvageable. All that work gone in an instant.

A brief rap on the sliding glass door and he let himself into her kitchen, wondering whether he should begin by telling her about her yard or face up to discussing the kiss.

He found her on her cell phone, her cup steaming on the counter with the tea bag hanging over the edge. As quiet as he could be, he checked on the occupants of the basement, still asleep. Upon his return to the kitchen, Lindsay was looking annoyed, her phone on the counter.

"What's wrong?"

"The tornado. It hit the botanical garden. My boss wants me to stay home until he evaluates the damage, even though there's no safety risk as far as anyone can tell. I hate it when others make decisions for me. I need to see it for myself." She glanced at the door to the basement. "On top of that, their day care center sent out a text. They incurred some damage and are closed today."

Mason checked his phone, and his chief hadn't changed his mind. "I'll watch Evan and Chloe."

"I shouldn't be too long."

He grinned, knowing she'd lose track of time once she was there. "Take as long as you need. If I'm called in, Grandpa Joe is here." He held up his grandfather's medication. "This doesn't cause drowsiness, so he should be fine."

"Thanks." She grabbed her car keys and rushed for the front door.

He cleared his throat, and she glanced over her shoulder. "Is something wrong?"

"I love pink hippopotamus lounge pants, but you might want to change."

Her cheeks flamed and she rolled her eyes. "Where would I be without my best friend?" She grabbed her tea and hustled upstairs.

Where would he be without his best friend was the real question, and one he didn't want answered.

CHAPTER FOUR

THE DAMAGE WAS more extensive than Lindsay had feared. At Sycamore Station, she clenched her stomach, feeling as though she might be sick. Numbness overtook her, her bones weak at the sight of uprooted plants and broken stems. She reached down and rubbed a velvety cosmos petal between her fingers, frowning at the devastation of what was once beautiful and alive now reduced to debris and fleeting memories.

The canna flowers she planted a few days earlier were ruined, their remnants scattered and plastered in the thick, drowning mud. The circle for the memorial garden was destroyed. This was more than her workplace or a garden. It was her sanctuary. She loved these plants. Now she'd have to start all over.

She stood and faced Phillip. Protective goggles covered his eyes. "We have to postpone the opening." Lindsay didn't want to waste a moment driving her point home. "I can't guarantee we'll be ready in time."

Stone-faced, he examined the sycamore, some of its smaller branches lying on the ground, a gash evident just above her eye level. "The gardens are fortunate. With most of the damage relegated to this area and the Children's Play Zone, where Heather is going to oversee the cleanup—"

"Excuse me?" She couldn't believe her ears. "Those are my tasks. Overseeing the volunteer roster is also on my list of duties."

"And I oversee you. My wife is more than capable of simple limb removal and tidying up, so you can focus all your energy and attention on this area and on the damage to the visitor greenhouses on the western side." He moved the goggles to the top of his head and wiped off some sweat. "The tree will be fine. The gash isn't deep and the opening will continue as planned."

"The circle of flowers is destroyed, and I have to begin again." His stony face gave no sign her words were having an impact. "Can you at least postpone the opening date?"

"We're already going to lose visitors for the next two days while we make repairs, and we can't afford that at our busiest time of year. At least the space sycamore was spared from ruin. This is becoming an unnecessary discussion. We're wasting precious minutes. I expect a report with any revised budget estimates and so on by next Monday." He removed the goggles altogether, and his face suddenly softened. "My vacation in Wilmington already seems a distant memory. Heather and I do truly miss the place. Never mind, the fact is we need visitors back here ASAP. We're on the same side, Lindsay."

He strode away, and she surveyed the scene once more before starting out for the supply shed. The buzz of chainsaws whirring to life cut through the silence, so unlike the normal gleeful shouts from the Children's Play Zone. She paused with her hand on the latch of the fence. One of the oaks that provided shade for the giant playground had split in two before falling on the main wooden play structure, and she shivered. At least the tornado had swept through at night, rather than the busy daytime, with no injuries reported so far.

Her phone chimed the familiar ringtone of her mother, and she winced. She knew she'd forgotten someone.

She accepted the call but before she could say a word she heard her mother's voice.

"Why did I hear about a tornado from Hyacinth and not from you? Thank goodness my twin sister texted me and assured me she was safe, but what about you? Are you okay? What about Evan and Chloe? Should your father and I quit our trip and catch the next plane back to the States?" Her mother managed to convey all of that in one breath.

"Good morning, Mom. I'm fine and the kids are fine." Her mother Dahlia and her mother's twin sister, Hyacinth, were day and night. Hyacinth loved Hollydale while Dahlia roamed the globe with Lindsay's father, now retired from chiropractic medicine.

Dahlia and Jonah had sold their house prior to their around-the-world adventure, placing a deposit on a townhome in the new development near Sully Creek, which wouldn't be ready until late summer.

"There's no need to fly back from India. Everyone's fine, and I'd be lousy company seeing as I'll be putting in extra hours at the garden."

"Jonah, start packing the bags. Our grandchildren need us. Oh, Lindsay, those pictures you texted the other day are absolutely adorable."

Her parents' return was the last thing she thought she needed. Her mom had good intentions but in terms of practical help, it would be nonexistent. Same applied to her father.

"Is Dad there?" Lindsay waited until her mother passed her father the phone. "Please don't cut your visit short on my account."

"Oh? Wait a second. Your mother's tapping my arm—"

"Lindsay, are you spending every minute at work? That's not healthy, you know. When we arrive for the dedication, I'll teach you some new meditation techniques. It's the most divine experience." Lindsay listened as her mom went into detail.

Her mother finally stopped for breath, and Lindsay cut in. "Mom, I'm sorry, but Phillip moved the dedication up by two weeks. You'll miss the ceremony, but I'll be able to spend more time with you and Dad when you arrive."

"See, Jonah. I was right about that date. Your father double-checked the garden's website before he made our arrangements just now. It's settled then. We're coming home to Hollydale for the dedication. Hyacinth is having some work done to her bathroom in June so we're staying in your guest room."

Great. Now Lindsay had to air that room out and give it a thorough cleaning that would be good enough for her mother's inspection. In the meantime, Sycamore Station demanded her attention.

"Mom, I have work to do."

"Of course, darling. We'll talk more soon, and I can't wait to see your face when you and the children see your souvenirs. You're going to love them."

The goodbye stretched out for a while before Lindsay pressed the End Call button. She closed her eyes and counted. A tornado and her mother in one morning. She brushed her fingers where Mason's lips had skimmed her cheek. Tingles marked the exact spot, and she wasn't sure if that was a good thing or not, given as he'd hightailed it out of her house the second he'd realized what he'd done.

The first time a man kissed her since Tim had left on the morning of the helicopter accident. It was just a small peck on the cheek that hardly qualified as a real kiss, and yet Mason had run away faster than a rabbit being shooed from her vegetable garden. Hardly flattering, to say the least.

She pushed past the gate and reached the shed. What would a real kiss from Mason feel like? Taste like? She shivered and hurried inside afraid she'd like the answer too much.

TWO SETS OF sparkling eyes gazed at Mason as though they expected him to sprout wings and fly around the room for their entertainment. After he'd fed Evan and Chloe steel-cut oatmeal with blueberries for breakfast while

Grandpa Joe grumbled for doughnuts, they'd colored until his fingers cramped.

Then he'd fed the kids lunch and tucked them in for an hour of slumber along with his grandfather and Goliath. Nap time was now over, their supply of energy replenished, and they clamored for a new project.

The doorbell rang, and he sent silent thanks to whoever it was. He checked the peephole and spied Hyacinth waving and pointing to something that looked like a pie plate.

His mouth instantly watering, Mason opened the door, and Lindsay's aunt flowed inside, her sunflower scarf tied like a hairband around her curly gray locks. "Good afternoon, my sweethearts." She hugged Evan and Chloe, who crowded around her. "Who's ready for some pie?"

"Pie?" His grandfather echoed from the top of the stairs, and he and Goliath hurried down. "Hyacinth, you're a lifesaver. Mason insisted on an organic kale salad for lunch. A man needs sustenance."

What was wrong with kale? Mason was quite fond of it, and the crunch of the vegetable went well with the smoothness of his homemade pineapple vinaigrette. Evan and Chloe hadn't complained once.

Hyacinth patted his grandfather's cheek and

then made her way to the kitchen. Like she was the Pied Piper, everyone, including Mason, followed close behind her.

"Aunt Hyacinth, what type did you make today?" Evan asked.

"Cherry crumble." She waggled her finger toward Mason, who came closer. "I know you like healthy food. This has oatmeal and the cherries are full of fiber."

"But how did you know we were here and not at my house?"

"Lindsay texted me that you and Joe are babysitting." Hyacinth opened cabinet doors, pulled out plates and started cutting the pie.

Mason hooked Chloe into her booster seat and handed her a small sliver of pie at the same time Hyacinth gave Evan his. "Thank you, Aunt Hyacinth." Evan bobbed his head before sitting next to his sister.

"Tank you," Chloe added.

"I've stopped by on my way from the tea room." Hyacinth clucked her tongue. "My business partner Belinda graciously consented to my leaving early so we can begin the gardening my niece won't mind us accomplishing on her behalf. Master gardeners like her are sometimes finicky, but we'll start by removing the debris."

"Since you're putting me to work, make

mine a double slice." Grandpa Joe held out his plate like it was Oliver Twist's bowl.

Mason kept his growl to himself. Or at least he thought he had until his grandfather jerked his thumb toward the living room. Mason followed.

"What is your problem? And it had better be good since you're keeping me from pie," Grandpa Joe insisted.

"You hurt your back last night and could barely get down the stairs. Maybe you and Goliath," the dog jumped on Mason's leg when he uttered his name, "should stay inside so you don't get hurt."

"Nonsense. That nap and medicine worked wonders." Grandpa Joe's mouth snapped shut, and he folded his arms. "I'm not twenty months old like Chloe. If I want to eat pie and garden, that's my choice."

He stomped into the kitchen, and Mason fought the urge to throw his arms up in the air. Hyacinth entered and placed a plate of pie and a fork into Mason's hand. "You look like you need this. I'll keep an eye on your grandfather while we're cleaning up Lindsay's yard. My husband, Craig, was quite obstinate that I not treat him like an invalid after his cancer diagnosis. It was hard to accept change, but we must. That was my gift to him and myself."

After pie and milk, they all headed outside, and Mason's gut wrenched at the devastation, more evident in the bright sunlight than at dawn. Chloe sucked her thumb, and Mason knelt in front of her. "Hey, sweetheart, what's wrong?"

Her big gray eyes, almost violet, filled with tears. "Mommy's gawden. Not pwetty like yesterday."

"Then we'll just have to make it pretty again, won't we?"

She nodded and removed her thumb. Gardening wasn't his preferred cup of coffee, but he'd do this for two of his favorite females and Evan.

Hyacinth assigned the tasks accordingly, and Mason helped Evan with the raking. A while later, they'd filled three garbage bags with yard scraps and stood back while Mason rested his chin on the tip of the rake handle. "Great job, E." He gave the boy a fist bump.

Hyacinth came toward them, holding a tall coppery stake sculpture thing that resembled a bare willow tree with multicolored bells hanging off each metal branch. "I'm so glad Lindsay stored this in her garage so her beautiful birthday gift didn't sustain any damage in last night's storm. This one has an especially significant meaning. You know Lindsay's maiden name is Bell, right?"

"Yes, ma'am." Mason kept from laughing, as he knew the whole story. Lindsay had stashed the metal structure away in her garage three months ago, not wanting to hurt her aunt's feelings by rejecting the gift.

"But Aunt Hyacinth—"

"Lindsay will be stunned when she sees it in the yard. Absolutely stunned," Mason interrupted Evan.

That was as close to the truth as he could manage.

Hyacinth beamed. "Evan, can you help Joe and your sister while Mason shows me where this goes?"

With no other choice, Mason set the rake against the house and picked up a trowel. He led Hyacinth to a spot in the front yard, shielded by some trees, and Hyacinth jabbed the wind chimes into the ground. "A bit of color makes the world that much brighter, don't you think?" Hyacinth pointed to the other helpers. "Spring air is glorious for people of all ages, and this type of activity will be perfect for your grandfather, don't you agree?"

Mason blinked, not sure which statement of Hyacinth's he was supposed to address. Instead, he nodded.

"You know, I really wanted to talk to you away from Joe and the wee precious ones."

He hadn't realized that, and he moved toward her. Since she was a good friend of his grandmother's, he had an idea about what was coming next. "Did Grandma Betty send you to check up on us?"

Did no one trust his judgment? For crying out loud, he was a paramedic. At work, people darn well better rely on him for split-second life-and-death decisions, and they did. Why didn't his friends and family do likewise?

Hyacinth reached out and patted his hand. "No, she didn't. Although now that you mention it, I sense tension in you. If you let it, gardening can be a most relaxing hobby, a chance for a person to get back to nature and allow life to spring up—"

"Lindsay's been telling me that for the past year."

Hyacinth removed her gloves and shifted them to her left hand. "And she's the real reason for this little chat. I'm concerned about my niece. You're her closest friend, so I'm assuming you have her best interests at heart. For the past few years, she's pruned herself by retreating into work and avoiding her friends until there's barely anyone left. She's surrounded herself with what's comfortable and familiar rather than allowing herself to blossom."

"Lindsay's a fighter, and she's doing her best to hold her family together." He dug his sneaker into the moist dirt and clenched the trowel, uncomfortable talking about his best friend behind her back. "I need to check on my grandfather. Leaving him alone with two small kids and a dog might aggravate his back."

Mason walked on.

"One more quick question if you don't mind." Hyacinth's pleading brought him to a halt, and he faced her. "Is Lindsay ready to date again?"

Shocked, Mason dropped the trowel.

He bent over and picked up the garden tool as Lindsay's truck pulled into her driveway. "You should ask her, but I'd wait until after dinner."

Lindsay slammed the driver's door, and Evan and Chloe ran toward her, enveloping her in a big hug.

"What's going on?" Her gaze landed on the bags of debris that Mason had dragged to the curb.

Hyacinth swept Lindsay into an embrace and then broke away. "You arrived home before we could finish our multitude of tasks. Why don't you go inside for a brief rest or shower? Maybe even enjoy a slice of oatmeal cherry crumble pie before helping us decide what you want to plant in your new vegetable garden."

Lindsay's face crumpled for a second before she blinked, her sad smile cutting Mason to the quick. "So everything's gone? The carrots? Snap beans?"

Hyacinth nodded. Mason longed to comfort Lindsay, but it was hard enough not to remember how soft her skin was when he kissed her cheek. A hug would do him in and would probably violate the friend code.

The bachelor track's the path for you, Mason. "Hyacinth mentioned it's not too late to plant zucchini. I have a recipe for zucchini muffins, and Evan and Chloe won't even guess that's the main ingredient," he said.

Lindsay's throat bobbed, and she exhaled a deep breath. "This is so kind. I can't change the weather, but I can change my clothes and help. I'll be back in a few."

Several ticks later, Mason excused himself and went inside. Lindsay was in the kitchen. Pie for dinner sounded good, so he snagged a piece. "Mind if I join you?"

She sent him a death glare. "Are you going to eat or talk to me?"

"If I stop eating, it'll only be to tell you crucial information that might save your life." He pretended to roll the ends of an invisible mustache.

"Save my life, huh?" She stabbed a small triangle of pie and brought it up to her mouth. "Sounds like I missed something diabolical."

"Worse than that. Your aunt wants to play matchmaker for you." He tasted the cherry pie and found this piece even more delicious than the first. It might be the pie, but more likely it was Lindsay's company. Even upset, something about her apple cheeks appealed to him and brought out another side to him. Why did Lindsay's presence suddenly impact him like this? He'd known her since Tim introduced her as his girlfriend and pulled Mason aside with the news she was *the* one, the woman who'd claimed his heart.

He'd lost one sister because of childhood leukemia and one best friend due to high winds taking down a helicopter flight rescue. Losing Lindsay, too, would be devastating. If he ruined this friendship because of his own selfishness? He had to back off and fast.

Lindsay finished sipping her milk. "Can you blame her? She and her group, I think they call themselves the Matchmaking Mimosas, took the credit for Jonathan and Brooke Maxwell's relationship. Here's another plum assignment right under their noses."

She popped another bite into her mouth as he pushed his plate away. Why did the thought of her moving on with anyone other than him irritate him as much as her moving on at all? Why did the first woman to intrigue him like this have to be the widow of the man he considered a brother?

He rose from his place at Lindsay's table and said, "After a day of gardening and kids, my motorcycle's calling me. It's been too long since I've tinkered with it."

Lindsay stood, her mouth agape. "Oh, no, don't tell me she tried to sign you up. I'll be absolutely mortified if she did."

She fell back into her chair, her cheeks flaming red. As much as he wanted to escape, he remained where he was. "She claims it's because she cares about the your future. Something about color and things blossoming."

Lindsay grimaced. "Caring is one thing. Making it impossible for me to meet you at the back fence later is another." She stabbed a piece of her pie. "You let her down easy, didn't you?"

"Hold on a second. What do you think your aunt said to me?"

"Why, she was trying to match us up, of

course! After Jonathan lost his Most Eligible Bachelor status, it was only time before they targeted you. Do you want me to tell her to leave your romantic future in your hands? Isn't that why you said my life depended on this conversation?"

He sat and brought his pie plate closer again. From her gray gaze, Lindsay believed he was the unlucky sucker, although settling down at all prickled his skin. Didn't it?

The fact Lindsay wasn't ready to date again should have cheered him up, yet her mortification at the thought of being set up with him was a distinct blow to his ego. This time he stabbed a piece of pie and brought it to his mouth, the oatmeal cherry cobbler now tasting like sandpaper.

The wobble in her smile let him know she expected an answer.

Mustering his strength, he produced a big belly laugh he didn't feel inside, and she joined in. "You know your aunt. She sees everything through rose-colored binoculars."

She reached across the table and covered the top of his hand with hers. That was the type of woman Lindsay was, warm and open, sweet and sharing. Until now, he didn't know he wanted something permanent, and someone like her. "Thanks for not bursting my aunt's bubble when she tried to set us up. Every once in a while, my ego needs a boost, especially after a bad day like today."

A sucker for punishment. That described him to a *T.* He cast aside his predicament by concentrating on her. "What happened?"

She finished off her pie, licking the fork clean, a blissful expression on her face. "My boss is overestimating my ability as a magician, and my parents are underestimating me. They're cutting their trip to India short just to fly in for the dedication." She winced. "When I put it like that, I must sound awful."

"So, the botanical garden was spared?"

"The tornado skirted the southern part, but the sycamore didn't sustain as much damage as Phillip and I originally thought. The tree will survive, but the rest of the memorial area needs a lot of work." She massaged the back of her neck. "And my boss is still committed to the new date."

"What new date?"

Her eyes widened, and a slow smile finally brought some color into her cheeks. "I haven't told you. This day might get better after all. The ceremony was moved up two weeks. Will you be able to attend now?"

He laid his fork next to his plate. "I won't be there."

"You claim he was like a brother to you, and yet you won't even come to the ceremony." Her nostrils flared, and those pretty pink lips formed a straight line before curling downward. "I don't get it."

Hyacinth burst into the kitchen and motioned to them. "Come outside. You have to see this."

Lindsay wasted no time in rushing outdoors, and Mason scrubbed his hand over his mouth, the tartness of the cherries now leaving a sour taste. Going to the ceremony would open memories better left closed, but staying away might cost him a relationship he couldn't bear to lose.

CHAPTER FIVE

"THAT'S NOT HOW you're supposed to plant seeds." Evan shook his head at Chloe. "Mommy showed us how to press one in the ground and cover it up, 'member?"

"Evan no fun." Chloe threw a few seeds down and then ran along the row, scattering more seeds as she went. Two unique personalities converging in one garden. Only time would tell which tactics yielded the most zucchini.

"You're such a baby," Evan scolded.

"Am not."

Evan popped his hands on his hips and glared at Chloe. Lindsay exhaled and took another deep breath before coming over.

To her chagrin, Mason followed. Never before had her judgment let her down to this extent. How could she be attached to someone who showed no loyalty to what she held dear? Once more, Mason had declared he had no intention of attending the dedication ceremony, and the other day he'd confided in her about

Bree's condition but only when she was half-way in her house, rather than confiding in her outright. How could she still feel the undercurrent of attraction between Mason and herself? It didn't make sense.

Evan unfurled his dirt-crusted hand and showed Lindsay the remaining seeds. "Aunt Hyacinth let us plant the zucchini, but Chloe's doing it wrong."

Chloe's lower lip trembled before she burst into tears. "Am not."

Mason stepped forward and cleared his throat. "Evan, a gentleman should always be respectful of his sister."

Lindsay shook her head. "A gentleman should also honor commitments, don't you think, Mason?"

That familiar face, handsome even, was tinged with sadness. "My motorcycle's calling me. Evan, Chloe, see you later."

Goliath yipped and ran circles around Mason as her neighbor strode across their shared side yard. Joe whistled for the chiweenie, who circled one more time before heeding his owner's call. Joe reached into his pocket and threw a treat to the dog. Lindsay stared at the corner of the house where Mason had disappeared from view. The evening, full of promise and a shelter from the day's events, stretched out before her, longer now since their later fence chat was presumably canceled.

"Thank goodness that a lovely friend tended to the needs of my boxers, Artemis and Athena, after work, but I must get home." Her aunt looped her sunflower scarf around her neck and patted Lindsay's cheek. "My dear, don't let discouragement take root. Last night's storm wreaked havoc in your precious garden, but new plants will bloom and spread joy."

Her aunt left, and Lindsay walked over to Joe, who was clipping Goliath's leash onto his harness.

"I know Mason," Lindsay began. Or she thought she did. His walking away so easily left her doubtful of that. And if she was wrong about that facet, what else was she wrong about? "Once he starts on his motorcycle, it'll be hours before he emerges from the garage. Did you want to eat dinner with us?"

"At my age, I've learned never to pass up an offer like that from an attractive woman." He laughed. "Especially when you know your wife would approve."

Goliath yipped and jumped on her. Lindsay scratched behind his ear until he flopped on his back. She knelt beside him and gave him a good belly rub. "You're invited, too, Goliath.

Joe told me what brand of dog food you eat, and I bought a bag."

Lindsay straightened and found Joe's gaze never wavered from where Evan and Chloe were finishing planting their zucchini seeds.

"Chloe looks so much like my Colette." Tears slipped down Joe's cheeks, and he batted them away with his free hand.

Was Joe having an episode? Who was Colette? He reached out and patted her arm. "I see your look of alarm. My memory's fine, m'dear. Surely you know about Coey. Mason always called her that since he couldn't pronounce Colette."

She shook her head, unsure of everything today. "Who's Colette?"

"My granddaughter and Mason's sister."

Concern overtook her once more at Joe's faulty memory, so she kept her voice as gentle as possible. "Oh, you mean Bree. I forgot to ask Mason if he heard from her during his shift."

Joe sagged against the side of Lindsay's house, and Goliath left her and licked Joe's pant leg before resting at his feet. "I thought you knew Peter and Tara had three children. Colette died of childhood leukemia when she was four. Bree was born two months later, too late to be tested as a bone-marrow donor."

"No, I didn't know that. Mason never talks about her." Lindsay's heart went out to Mason's parents. She'd seen Tim's parents during his funeral and would never forget the grief etched in their faces at losing their only child.

"Don't think he's forgotten about her, though. I'm sure he hasn't." Just then, Chloe ran over to him, and Joe smiled.

"All done," Chloe announced.

"That's a big girl." Joe bent down and tweaked her nose, raising his hand with his thumb tucked between his index and middle fingers. "Look at what I have. I have Chloe's nose."

Her daughter giggled, her curly honey-brown hair bobbing with her. "Want my nose back."

Joe pretended to paste her nose on his face. "But I need a new nose. That way I can smell when Goliath needs a bath." He sniffed his dog, who raised his head and lowered it again. "Ooh, boy. He's getting one tonight."

Laughter erupted, and Chloe fell on her bottom. Evan ran over. "What's so funny?"

"I have Chloe's nose," Joe announced, winking at Evan in an obvious ploy to try to get her son to go along with the joke.

"It looks great on you." Evan grinned until Chloe's lip trembled. He reached up and touched Joe's nose, then Chloe's. "It's back, Chloe. Don't cry."

Chloe sniffled and patted her nose. A huge smile broke over her face. "Yay!" Lindsay reached out to Chloe, who pulled away. "My nose, not yours."

Joe chuckled and gave her a salute. "Aye-aye, Cap'n Chloe."

Lindsay's head ached at everything that had transpired that day. She glanced at the house next door. She'd had such high hopes Mason would attend the rescheduled dedication. For the first time, though, she wondered why she'd set her mind on that. Was it for his grief process? Or was it for her wanting someone there she could lean on?

Would he be letting Tim down if he didn't attend? Or would he only be letting Lindsay down?

And did it matter as much now that she had more insight about why he might want to stay away?

MASON TIGHTENED THE leather washer and bolt for the motorcycle's gas tank. He twisted the wrench once more and made sure it was good and secure so the tank wouldn't scratch the paint, the washer acting as a needed buffer. Stepping back, he swiped his forehead with his arm and removed his noise-canceling head-phones. Then he turned off the Do Not Dis-turb feature on his phone. No sooner did he do so than his phone rang with a call from Bree.

"I just wanted to say hi to my big brother before my surgery tomorrow." Her voice wob-bled, and he understood.

"But I thought we agreed the next time you called me would be to say hi after the surgery." He tried projecting cool confidence while shoving the phone between his shoulder and head. Then he walked over to the supply shelf.

"I changed my mind. If something happens to me—"

He wouldn't let her go there. "Nothing bad is going to happen, only good. The doctors will remove the tumor, and then Tristan will send that group text to let us know you're okay."

An extended silence came over the line. "Tristan and I had a fight."

Seemed he wasn't the only Ruddick to get in an argument with someone today.

He switched the phone to his other ear. "Wouldn't Grandma Betty be better with this kind of thing? She's been married for over fifty years."

"I need to talk to someone who won't make everything glossy and rosy for me. Tris and Grandma Betty have been doing everything for me. It's worse with Mom emailing and asking if she should finish her thesis in the States. I've replied I want her to stay with Dad in Australia. His work at the rift there is important."

So she called her big brother. Did everyone regard him as honest and overly blunt? What if they were wrong? What if he was just a rebel with a chip on his shoulder? Some unidentified caller tried to interrupt, but Bree was more important. "You make me sound like the voice of gloom, but since I'm honest to a fault, you know any surgery has some inherent risks…"

"Thanks, brother dearest."

"But you're young and, until now, you've had no health issues. You've got the best shot there is to beat this. Don't worry, I'll call Mom and Dad and talk them into not asking for a leave of absence." He set the phone on Speaker, grabbed the bar end mirrors and set them on his workbench. "You know I'd be with you if you wanted me there. All you have to do is say the word. But I have confidence in the doctors and you."

"And you're still in Hollydale, where I want you to stay."

"Yep." Intense rapping at his side door jolted him. "Someone's here, Bree. I'm looking forward and you should, too. You'll come through the surgery just fine. I'm sure it'll be with flying colors. Love ya."

"Right back at you." Bree's voice sounded more hopeful and optimistic, perfect for tomorrow's surgery.

"Mason. I have dinner." Lindsay's voice, insistent and loud, reached him.

As if on cue, his stomach rumbled, and he opened the door. The brightness from the garage's interior was a contrast to the darkness outside. He rubbed his eyes and blinked. "What time is it?"

"Well past nine o'clock." Lindsay wove her way around the block with his motorcycle and set the aluminum-covered plate on his workbench. "After you rejected his phone call, he phoned me, worried about you."

He checked his phone. Good grief, that missed call was his grandfather. "I didn't realize it was him—I was talking to Bree. Thanks for the dinner. I'll let Grandpa Joe know I'm fine so he and Goliath can get some sleep on a real mattress. Good night."

Lindsay folded her arms and didn't move. "How's Bree?"

"Her surgery's tomorrow, and she's nervous." A bit of an understatement, and he didn't blame his sister one bit.

He opened the box with the bar end mirrors.

"Aren't you even curious about your dinner? For all you know that plate could contain a double bacon cheeseburger and French fries with a side helping of Carolina slaw." Lindsay moved, blocking his path to his tools.

"I trust you. You know what I like."

"But I didn't know you had another sister." The hurt and sadness reflected in her face cut him to the core.

"I don't talk about Colette."

"Why not?"

His jaw clenched, and he slid the first mirror out of the box. "She died a long time ago." He examined the mirror and muttered something under his breath.

"What's wrong?" She craned her neck.

"The mirror's cracked." He flipped it over for her to see. This setback would cost him a couple of weeks while he waited for the new part, and just when he was so close to finishing. He'd dreamt of feeling the breeze on his cheek as he sped along the curves of the mountain roads. "I'll have to order a replacement. It might take weeks before I can finish this now."

She picked up the plate of food, holding it out to him. "More time with your grandfather. Maybe that's not as bad as you think. Neither is eating your dinner hot off the grill."

He accepted the offering and peeled back

the foil and found his favorite meal, grilled salmon and roasted vegetables.

"Unless you believe that superstitious nonsense about broken mirrors and seven years of bad luck."

"Come to think of it," he said. "Tim introduced me to you seven years ago."

"Ha-ha, hilarious." She rolled her eyes and a corner of her mouth lifted. "And we only met six years ago. You must have me confused with someone else."

Never. "Nope. Tim fell and fell hard." He grasped the fork and ate a bite of fish.

She leaned against the wall and watched him take another bite. "I think you underestimate yourself. You keep from falling so you don't get hurt."

His best friend was too perceptive at times. If he let himself, he could fall for someone like her, but never her.

He needed a distraction and time away from his house, from Evan and Chloe, from Lindsay. He chewed another bite and lost that battle, determined to win the war. "Tomorrow night at the fence?"

She met his gaze, and something crackled in the air. The hairs on his arm were sticking up. "How about earlier rather than later? I want to hear about how Bree's surgery went."

Of course she would. That was Lindsay. Even if she was upset at him, she still cared, and not just about him, but about every member of his family. "How's six work for you?"

"Great. Aunt Hyacinth is picking Evan and Chloe up from day care while I make dinner for the four of us. I'll have time to eat with them and find out about their day before our talk. Looking forward to hearing good news about Bree." She passed him, before turning back. "And more about Colette."

That was also Lindsay. Tenacious. She stuck to what she believed in. The broken bar mirror taunted him from its position on the workbench, and he threw it away.

CHAPTER SIX

LINDSAY KICKED OFF her left gardening clog into her walk-in closet while smiling at Chloe. Her daughter was chattering nonstop about riding in the caboose of the cardboard train at day care. Aunt Hyacinth rushed into the room, the scarf with colorful tulips, one of Lindsay's favorites, flowing behind her.

"There you are, my darling little buttercup." Aunt Hyacinth swooped Chloe into her arms.

"Are you sure you can stick around while I talk to Mason?"

"You only trust me to watch Chloe and Evan when they're asleep? I'll have you know Craig's nephews and nieces visited us often, and I seem to recall a certain little girl who loved playing pat-a-cake with her uncle Craig." Aunt Hyacinth's eyes glowed the way they always did when she spoke of her late husband.

Lindsay gave her arm an affectionate squeeze, and traded her other gardening clog for a pair of slip-on moccasins that would caress her feet. Her silver T-strap sandals with the two-inch heels winked at her next to her Wellingtons, and she caught a glimpse of her favorite green cocktail dress hiding in the far recesses behind her work blazers. What would Mason's reaction be if she showed up at the fence with a touch of glitz and glamour, a far cry from her ripped jeans and soft floral knit shirt?

Would he even notice? And why did she care? It wasn't like she and Mason were destined to be anything other than best friends and next-door neighbors. Although lately she wondered...

Lindsay checked her watch. She pecked Aunt Hyacinth's wrinkled cheek, tapped Chloe's curly head and rushed out, only stopping at the sight of Evan and Goliath curled up together on the living room sectional while Joe rested at the other end with earbuds and a tablet, and one eye open and one eye closed. She hurried outside.

She wasn't too surprised Mason had beaten her to the fence, today's tie-dyed T-shirt a subdued mix of blues stretched out across his chest, drawing emphasis on how he kept himself in shape. From what she'd heard from his new partner's mother, a volunteer at the botanical garden, those hours at the gym had paid off last week in a rescue involving a group of teens who'd capsized while white water rafting. Mason hadn't mentioned it once to her.

For someone who drew the attention of many ladies, he never blew his own horn. His gaze was glued to his phone, and his fingers were flying fast and furious.

"Good news, I hope." She plopped into one of the Adirondack chairs and he settled into the other.

"Yes. Bree's husband, Tristan, is communicating via a group chat. Grandma Betty already called Grandpa Joe and told him everything went well."

"So, your grandmother will be coming home soon?" Although she was happy for Betty and Joe, she couldn't help but feel Mason and his grandfather needed more time together.

He shook his head and frowned. "They're going to do a scan next week to see if Bree needs any further treatment, and then Tristan has to leave again. Since my parents work in Australia, Grandma wants to stay put until Bree is in the clear."

Lindsay started to say something when the sound of car doors slamming from the direction of Mason's driveway caught her attention. "Are you expecting someone?" she asked.

"No." He looked as surprised as she did.

He headed for his front yard and peeked

around the corner of his house. Then he rushed back. "You have to come with me."

She jumped up from the chair, which had been comfy after a day of constant motion. "What's going on?"

"Covered dishes. That only means one thing. Someone's trying to match me up with an unsuspecting female. You have to protect me." Desperation and humor clung to his voice, and he faced her. "Please."

"Since this is no doubt the work of my aunt Hyacinth, I guess it's my duty to help."

"Um, if I didn't make it crystal clear yesterday, your aunt wasn't trying to fix me up. She only has her eyes set on finding someone for you."

What? Lindsay hadn't seen that one coming, but before she could interrogate him further, he pulled her toward the house. "You better do the same for me someday, Mr. Ruddick," she muttered under her breath, but hoped was still loud enough for him to hear.

Mason released her, and her hand tingled where he'd touched her. Alarm skittered through her until a raindrop plopped on her nose. The electricity must be due to the weather, and not Mason. At least, she hoped it was due to the impending storm.

They approached the front stoop where two

women were talking animatedly as if plotting their next move.

"Hello, ladies." Mason's voice flowed with the buttery smoothness of Carolina sourwood honey, Lindsay's favorite for her weekend tea.

The pair turned toward her and Mason. The shorter woman, Mitzi, the owner of the best beauty salon in town, held her hand to her chest, which contained one of the biggest hearts in Hollydale. Mitzi was one of her favorite people.

"Good thing Destinee is holding your grandpa's cheesy bacon chicken casserole instead of me—you scared the whatsit out of me, young man. Evening, Mason, Lindsay." Mitzi nodded at them, her gray bob accented with one bright purple streak, the same color as her bright tunic paired with black leggings.

"Evening, Ms. Mayfield—"

"It's Mrs. Thompson now." She beamed. "You know, every time I correct someone I think of how Owen practically glowed on the stairs of the gazebo on Valentine's Day. That might be, though, 'cause he was freezing. What was I thinking having an outdoor ceremony in the middle of a Great Smoky Mountain winter?" She chuckled and glowed herself before turning to the taller woman standing next to her. Destinee resembled a model with her hourglass figure and high cheekbones.

Lindsay's floral knit shirt and ripped jeans seemed almost shabby next to Destinee's sequined shirt and bright capris and stilettos.

Mason opened his door and unloaded the casserole dish from Destinee's hands. "Let me take that from you."

"Ooh, thank you, dumplin', and just so you know, I'm Destinee with two *e*'s. That casserole was getting so heavy." The younger woman fluttered her eyelashes, thick with black mascara, and swept back her long, bouncy blond curls. "This is my momma's secret recipe, and it's so delish."

"Luanne is having her corns removed from her feet, so her niece Destinee, who's also a certified stylist, is filling in for her for the next couple of weeks before she heads back to Dillsboro." Mitzi entered Mason's house and looked around. "Where's Joe?"

"Grandpa's next door with Evan and Chloe." Mason smiled at Destinee, who flashed her shiny white pearls. "They're Lindsay's adorable kids."

"You love kids, too? I just knew from the way Mitzi talked about you we'd have so much in common. Dillsboro's just an hour away." Destinee leaned over and touched the ends of Lindsay's hair. "Oh, honey, before I leave town, you need to come into the salon. I'll get rid of those split ends in two seconds and shape your hair so it frames your face. You really ought to consider some gold highlights, too."

If Destinee kept talking, Mason might have to protect the blonde from Lindsay instead of Lindsay protecting him. Lindsay blinked back this unexpected twinge of jealousy and tried to ignore Destinee's flirting with Mason. Odd because the only time she ever felt riled up always involved Mason, and this had to stop. "Thanks for the suggestion. I'll keep it in mind."

Lindsay spied Mason fighting to keep from laughing. He wasn't hiding it that well. "Ladies, it was a pleasure." He placed the casserole on his counter and wound his arm around Lindsay's waist. "Lin and I have to get back to Grandpa Joe."

Lin? Before she could challenge him on the nickname, Mason ushered the two women out of the kitchen and his house. As soon as he closed the door, he pressed his back against it, relief written all over him.

"I thought they'd never leave." He returned and picked up the casserole. "This would be the worst thing for Grandpa Joe's angina."

Mason approached his trash can but Lindsay rushed over. "You're right, but it would be an awful waste. My kids might like it, and we can guess the ingredients and report back to you. Sort of make it a game."

"Be my guest." He laid the dish back on the counter.

Lindsay eyed the casserole. "Then again if they love it, and I can't replicate it, I might have a revolt on my hands."

They both stared at the offering, and Mason snapped his fingers. "Wait a second." He whipped out his phone and sent someone a text. A ping made her that much more curious about the recipient. "My new partner, Jordan, is more than happy to have a homemade meal."

The first time Mason had talked to her about his job after Tim's death had sent a ripple of pain through her. Thankfully, that subsided after a few of their fence talks. "What happened to your last partner, Duncan?"

Mason opened his refrigerator, and pulled out a tray. "I made lemon garlic turkey meatballs earlier. Hungry?"

Another reminder she hadn't stopped to eat more than that protein bar with all the activity at the garden. "Yes, but what happened to Duncan?"

Mason preheated the oven and leaned against it. "He wanted a change. We keep in touch. He's now on his way to becoming a physician's assistant."

The doorbell rang, and he opened the door. On his front porch stood another of her aunt Hyacinth's closest friends, Tina Spindler, who held a large tote bag. By her side was Officer Jillian Edwards in her police uniform, carrying an aluminum baking pan, similar to the one Mitzi and Destinee had just dropped off.

Mason waved the pair inside. "Hey, Jillian, Mrs. Spindler. How are you both doing this fine evening? Let me get that bag for you."

Lindsay was beginning to see a theme in tonight's offerings, and it had nothing to do with food. Aunt Hyacinth and the Matchmaking Mimosas had struck again.

But if Lindsay knew one thing about Mason from the past couple of years, it was that he didn't have any trouble finding dates all by himself.

"Drew's mother lives in Florida, and she's a force to be reckoned with, so please call me Tina." She thrust the bag toward Mason, and he accepted it. "There's homemade chicken noodle soup and four other types of soup as well. I had today off, and your grandmother called. How's your sister?"

Mason gave them the good news about Bree while unloading the soups into his freezer.

"And speaking of family, Grandpa Joe is next door. I'm sorry to take your food and run, but I need to check on him."

Lindsay held up her phone. "Aunt Hyacinth texted a minute ago. He's rocking Chloe, and my aunt is making a sun catcher with Evan. You stay with your company while I check on them."

Though she couldn't imagine Destinee and Mason together in any universe, Jillian and Mason had so much in common, considering they both worked as first responders. Her stomach tightened at the thought of him getting serious with someone.

Mason glared at her, but what was she supposed to do? Come to think of it, when he did become serious about someone, would she lose her best friend? It would take a strong woman to accept her and Mason's friendship. Then again, she knew Mason wouldn't settle for less.

Tina bumped Jillian's arm and tapped her watch. "We're not staying. I'm with Jillian's mother tonight while Jillian's on duty. Rhoda has early-onset dementia, you know."

Jillian's face turned grim, and Tina gave her a small hug. "I have appointments next week in Asheville to look at assisted living homes." Jillian passed her container to Mason as if it held a hot potato. "It's baked orzo with chicken. I remember Joe had a touch of angina last year, and it's heart healthy. Time for me to head to work."

Tina smiled and shook her head. "One evening you need to let me stay with your mom so you can go out and have *fun*."

Lindsay didn't miss how Tina's eyes widened at Jillian and she tilted her head ever so slightly in Mason's direction. However, Mason was harder to read.

Jillian shook her head ever so slightly, then whipped out her phone. "Well, Becks Porter has been after me to go to the Timber River Bar and Grill with her and her friends for a fun night with the girls. I've lost touch with quite a few people outside of work since my mom's diagnosis." Jillian glanced up from the screen and over at Lindsay. "Once we choose a night that works for everyone, I'll send you an invite."

"Thanks." Lindsay watched as Mason escorted Tina and Jillian out the door.

Mason huffed out a breath once they were gone. He turned off the oven and removed the hot meatballs, then placed them on a trivet on the counter. "What happened to your promise to save me from the matchmakers?"

"What happened to the guy who brought a

different woman to each of mine and Tim's barbecues? He'd already have called Destinee."

This was a standoff, no two ways about it. Tension lit the air with his blue eyes flashing fire. He stepped toward her, and she hoped this time his lips would connect with hers rather than her cheek. Before either could end the standoff, the doorbell rang again. They both laughed. "You never told me you live at the Asheville Regional Airport with arrivals and departures every fifteen minutes," she said.

He peeked through the peephole before opening the door and waving in Fabiana Ramirez and her daughter Graciela. "Welcome."

The ladies entered, each carrying yet another aluminum pan. Fabiana's gaze went from side to side. "Ah, Lindsay. Thank you for the advice about the garden. My leaves are so much fuller and don't have little holes in them anymore."

"Any time. Glad those aphids got the message." They weren't the only ones, either. Lindsay stepped forward and relieved Fabiana of her offering, the fragrant smells of garlic and rice making her even hungrier. She stopped short of grabbing one of Mason's forks and tearing off the foil. "This smells delicious. What did you bring?"

"It's Graciela's favorite, arroz con pollo. So delicious and full of flavor." Fabiana smiled proudly. "Graciela made those brownies herself. She's a better cook than I am."

Fabiana stared straight at Mason while she spoke, and he reached over and accepted Graciela's offering. Three matchmakers, three different choices with distinct personalities. Lindsay didn't know whether to congratulate him or cringe. Aunt Hyacinth interfering in her dating life wasn't for her, and she was unsure whether Mason would appreciate the attention despite his initial reaction to his first guests.

Mason nodded at Graciela and graciously accepted the dish, placing it on the counter next to the others. "This smells wonderful."

"De nada." Graciela rummaged through her purse and pulled out a form. "I'm selling dog bandannas as a fund-raiser for the animal shelter. I thought adopting a senior chiweenie was so sweet of your grandparents. Can I put you down for a blue one for Goliath, oh, and a plaid one, too?"

Mason got out his wallet while Lindsay held her hand over her mouth, hiding her laugh. "Um, how much?"

She named her price with a wide, encouraging smile. "It's for a great cause. The proceeds go straight to the shelter, purchasing needed supplies and food." She accepted the bill he held out to her and added it to the envelope. "The bandannas should arrive in a week. Goliath will be the best-dressed dog in the neighborhood."

Fabiana folded her arms and craned her neck. "Where's your grandfather? Betty will be upset if I don't send her a positive report. Anything to help one of my best friends, and she and Joe are just the sweetest couple."

Mason hesitated, his hand on the cabinet that held his plates. "Wait a second. You mean, you, Tina and Mitzi have all shown up tonight for my grandfather?"

She walked over to Mason and patted his cheek. "Apparently you aren't feeding Joe enough."

"So I gather. Soups, casseroles and now brownies. Just for Grandpa Joe." Amusement laced Mason's tone, so he wasn't envious or upset this attention wasn't for him.

"Of course. Who else?" Fabiana stood tall, her back straight, her dark eyes fierce.

Graciela met Lindsay's gaze and she grinned. "Oh, Mami. I'll explain it on the drive home." She tapped Mason's arm. "By the way, Jordan speaks highly of you. We baked the dessert together."

"I'll call Grandma Betty tomorrow and

make sure she's well-informed about my grandfather's health." Mason opened his front door for the women and smiled. "And I'll make sure he doesn't go to bed hungry."

Graciela led Fabiana away, and Mason shooed Lindsay out the door, then followed her. "I'd like to escape before anyone else descends on my home. I'll put the food away later."

She held up a finger. "One second."

An advantage of being his best friend was her familiarity with his kitchen, having permission to raid it on his days off if she ran out of something. She piled some of Fabiana's arroz con pollo onto a plate and shoveled in a couple of bites before joining him outside.

She sat on Mason's front stoop. The delicious seasoning and blend of flavors helped her savor this moment even more. He stared at her. "Do you want to eat the rest of this at your house?"

"In a minute. I rarely get to enjoy a hot meal, and this is too good to miss without tasting every bite. Try some." She moved over when he settled next to her and she handed him her plate.

"No fork? Some best friend you are."

From the sound of his voice, his ego wasn't too bruised.

"Here, use mine. You won't be sorry." She

fed him a couple of bites, and her cheeks warmed. "Oh, oops, sorry. Hard habit to break. Of course, you can feed yourself."

Their gazes connected, something different reflected in those depths, and she pulled the fork back. Nothing could change between them.

"I think we both know I'm an adult, Lindsay."

The seriousness in his voice floored her. Apart from his job, where he was professional and more than capable of performing his duty, Mason was often lighthearted and flippant. This new side of him? Caring for his grandfather, helping with her garden? Then again, he was still the same Mason underneath, escaping to his motorcycle the first chance he got.

A little breathless and a lot warmer, she jumped to her feet, taking care not to spill any of her dinner. "I've been away from Evan and Chloe too long."

They trekked the short distance to her house, and she made sure she kept her hands on the plate. Before she entered, though, he tapped her shoulder. "Have a minute?"

"For you? Anytime." She smiled. "That's what friends do for each other."

His brow furrowed, and apprehension, something she didn't usually see in him, appeared on his face. "I hear Grandpa Joe at night sometimes. He's not sleeping well."

"You know how it is. New house. A different mattress. Unusual sounds. It's sweet that you're concerned. Betty will be back soon, and she sent her friends to help. That type of friendship goes far." She hadn't kept up most of her friendships during her grief. Mason was one of the few who held tight and wouldn't let go. The fact that her friends were drawing her back now brought forth another smile.

"I'm your best friend, right?" He flashed a full grin, and her stomach went to flutter mode. "You know you can count on me any time of the day or night."

"Like I'd need to call you at night." She scoffed, keeping her plate steady, and then softened her expression. "I do, however, reserve the right to call you any time of day once my parents arrive."

"Oh, that's right. I remember what that was like when your mom moved in for a month when Chloe was born. Geesh. Still that bad, huh?"

"Worse. You know, I'm an only child and she's always hovered. Sometimes she takes over and does everything herself."

He nodded. "It happens. Are you done with your fork yet?"

"You can get your own from my kitchen." She moved her fork so he couldn't reach it.

"I wouldn't dream of taking something that someone else claimed first. Although it's a good thing Jordan claimed that casserole. I'll take it to him on our next shift."

The reminder of his profession with its inherent danger was helpful as they entered her house, and she guarded her food from Goliath, who jumped up, his little sniffer quite active. She'd do well to guard more than her plate.

What if she acted on her feelings for Mason and lost him the way that she'd lost Tim? In their type of job, especially, there were no guarantees.

CHAPTER SEVEN

SOMETHING SCRATCHED AT Mason's bedroom door. He turned over, pounded the pillow and then placed it over his head. The scratching became more insistent, and Mason bolted upright in bed, the pillow slipping to the carpet. Goliath's persistence must mean he needed a visit to the great outdoors, or...

Grandpa Joe!

Mason rushed down the hall with the chiweenie yapping and nipping at his heels. He threw open the door to Grandpa Joe's room. *Empty.* For the first time, the robust aroma of coffee reached his nose, and he hurried to the kitchen. In front of the refrigerator, his back to Mason, stood Grandpa Joe. He turned and shook his head. "Where do you keep the real bacon?"

Goliath sniffed at his leash, his signal for his morning walk. Mason waited for some acknowledgment from his grandfather of his dog's need for his morning ritual. Instead, the scowl grew deeper.

"Good morning to you, too, Grandpa Joe.

Your dog wants to go outside, and egg whites are healthier for you. They're quite delicious when you get used to them." Mason would never be known for his tact, unlike Lindsay, who'd find out what was wrong with a sweet smile and a snack. In his experience, there wasn't time to beat around the bush.

Grandpa went over and poured himself a cup of coffee and returned to the fridge. "You're out of cream. A man needs sustenance to take his dog on a long morning walk."

"Good thing I bought extra turkey bacon for breakfast then."

Goliath yipped and headed toward the back door. Mason opened it and let the dog have free reign outside in his fenced yard. His walk would have to wait until later.

Maybe food cooked for him would perk up his grandfather. "How would you like your eggs this morning? Over easy? Boiled? Scrambled?"

"In Tennessee with my Betty. Not that I don't like spending time with you."

The problem crystallized, and Mason understood his grandfather's mood better. There was something sweet about how his grandparents' love endured this long. "I miss her, too, Grandpa."

Mason bustled about the kitchen, pausing to let the chiweenie back inside. "How about an egg-white omelet with onions and peppers?"

"How about adding cheese and ham to that? A man needs some protein." The grumbling reassured Mason that all wasn't lost yet.

He cracked eggs, separating the yolks and then whisking the whites. "The egg whites are a significant source of protein, but you convinced me."

His grandfather's eyes lit up, and he licked his lips. "Make mine so the cheese oozes out."

Mason opened the refrigerator and plopped a container of Greek yogurt in front of his grandfather. "Here. This has more protein than cheese, and it's much better for you."

Grandpa Joe shoved it away. "I'm not that hungry, anyway."

Undeterred, Mason cooked two omelets, delivering one to his grandfather. "What time do you need to be at the community center?"

"Brooke gave me the day off since I'm scheduled for all day Saturday." He cut into the omelet and dropped a piece to the floor. Goliath snatched up the morsel. "Good thing, too. It'd be hard to pass the reception desk and not see my beautiful bride's face."

Mason borrowed a cue from his next-door neighbor and counted to ten. "Grandma's not dead, either. She'll be back soon."

"True, but I don't have anything to do today. Chloe and Evan are in day care."

Part two of the equation was now solved. Lonely and bored. He had to get his grandfather out of the house.

Mason took his first sip and spit out the coffee with a muttered curse. "What did coffee ever do to you?"

Grandpa Joe sipped his and shrugged. "Tastes good to me."

The way his grandfather had brewed it, this would strip the paint off his chopper. Come to think of it, Georgie Harrison, the restoration mechanic at Max and Georgie's Auto Repair, had notified him his new bar end mirrors had arrived, and she had personally inspected them to ensure they were not broken this time. A trek downtown was what this paramedic ordered. "How about we walk Goliath together this morning?"

"Come to think of it, he loves walking along Main Street and sniffing all the good food."

His plan backfired, and Mason sighed. "The Night Owl Bakery makes those raspberry Danish you love, right?"

"Only on Thursdays." His grandfather perked up. "Wait, that's today."

"Then we'd better hurry before Paige sells out."

At Sycamore Station, Lindsay extracted a soil sample from under the famous tree and then glanced around. Satisfaction at her slow but steady progress flittered through her. She'd spent most of the previous week cleaning up the damage from the tornado. The greenhouses had occupied most of her time, but they were back up to speed. Now with the tilling and fertilizing of the soil complete, she'd spent the morning with volunteers planting the new cannas and cosmos flowers donated by Jasper and Jules's Garden Center.

Her revised plan ensured something would bloom year-round with the winter irises and early daffodils, the ones that pushed up in January, providing a splash of color when most of the other exterior flowers and plants were dormant.

Lindsay returned to her rolling cart and examined her itinerary. She headed to the larger of the two greenhouses and entered the employee area. Suzie, the assistant greenhouse horticulturist recently back from maternity leave, glanced up from the Venus flytrap.

"Those new screens you suggested are such an innovative improvement. That zipper is so much easier to use than those old clips. Our electric consumption is down, too. We should see some real savings soon." Suzie removed her gloves and sipped from her water bottle. "And thanks for switching weeks with me on the snack schedule. You saved my morning. Elijah finally slept through the night, and I forgot to set the alarm. I wouldn't have had time to stop and pick up anything for tonight's staff meeting."

Snacks? Meeting? Lindsay kept her smile constant, not letting on that she'd forgotten about the switch. "I'm glad the screens are a success. They'll make my case for the new moisture-control monitors that much easier tonight." She glanced at her watch. "Time for my lunch break."

She left her cart behind and hightailed it to her truck. In no time, she parked near the gazebo downtown, a short distance away from the Night Owl Bakery. The gazebo, made with timber harvested for Hollydale City Hall, captivated attention for miles around.

Under normal circumstances, she'd linger and admire the tulips near the gazebo, but she didn't have any time to spare. A selection of petit fours, cookies, mini eclairs and tarts from the bakery ought to suffice for tonight's staff meeting. Mason would cringe at the treats with nary a vegetable platter in sight. The one time she brought fresh celery, broccoli and cherry tomatoes with a tasty homemade vinaigrette, Phillip glared at her throughout the meeting.

She walked toward the Night Owl Bakery

and rubbed her eyes. Sitting at one of the café tables was Mason. He held on to Goliath's retractable leash. The small dog yipped and ran straight for her, jumping on Lindsay's legs.

"Let me guess. Grandpa Joe?" Lindsay ordered Goliath to get down and rewarded him by petting behind his ears.

"I thought this might cheer him up. He's missing Grandma Betty."

"And you're bribing him with sugar?" She cocked her head to one side and frowned. "That doesn't sound like the Mason Ruddick I know."

"A guy has to have some surprises up his sleeve." Mason grinned and reeled Goliath back his way. "Speaking of surprises, shouldn't you be at work?"

"I forgot I'm the designated snack provider for today's staff meeting." Her gaze widened, and she bit her lip. "Hold on a second. I need to call Aunt Hyacinth to find out if she can pick up Evan and Chloe from day care since I have to stay late for the meeting." She slipped her phone from her pocket.

Mason's fingers made contact with her hand holding the phone and she stopped, noticing the shock from his touch. He gave no sign of a similar reaction, a relief, she thought. Instead, Mason pointed toward the window where she saw Joe taking a bite of a Danish. "Let me bribe Grandpa Joe with Chloe and Evan," Mason said.

"Excuse me?"

Goliath yipped at her high-pitched squeak.

"I'm on their approved checkout list, right?" He waited until she nodded. "We'll pick up the kids. Grandpa Joe loves spending time with them. It'll do him some good."

"I can't keep taking advantage of you."

"Nonsense. And besides, before you know it, Grandma Betty will return, and I'll get back to the single life. For now, though, he needs something, something I can't give him."

"Like Danish and other baked goods?" She couldn't resist teasing him a little, considering her heart was wrapping itself around how much Mason already anticipated a return to his old lifestyle.

Goliath flopped down and Mason rubbed his belly. "I'll feed them dinner."

"When you phrase it that way, how can I resist?" Lindsay chuckled and glanced at her watch. "Between the tornado cleanup and the class I'm giving at Jasper and Jules's Garden Center for Earth Day, I'm swamped."

"You're the lifesaver. Literally. This might save Grandpa Joe." He smiled and Goliath leaped into his lap, and Lindsay's heart melted at the sweet sight.

Lindsay hurried into the bakery and grinned at Joe, who held up his Danish, the impishness in his eyes a match for his grandson's. "You wouldn't believe how good these are. There are only a couple left. Make sure you buy one for Evan and for Chloe and one for yourself."

She laughed and nodded. "They're one of my favorites, too."

He smacked his lips and left the bakery. Lindsay went up to the counter and explained her dilemma to the owner, Paige, who assured her she had a selection of goodies the botanical garden folks would enjoy.

Lindsay ordered five cupcakes for dessert as a thank-you to Joe and Mason. While she waited for Paige to box the treats, she glanced out the window at Goliath, jumping on Grandpa Joe, who accepted the leash from Mason. In such a short time, Mason had made strides with his grandfather to the point where he was going out of his way to find what the older man needed. If Mason was becoming more perceptive at reading emotions, she'd need to keep her growing feelings for him close to her vest. Mason made it clear that everything would return to the status quo when Grandma Betty was back, his path on the bachelor track the one for him.

She didn't need another hint he had no intention of settling down.

CHAPTER EIGHT

MASON SNIFFED HIS WRIST and frowned before transferring the salmon from the prep board to the grill. That new cologne Grandpa Joe had insisted he try on at the Smoky Mountain Emporium this afternoon was really pungent. It even overpowered the seasoned fish. Shuddering, he closed the lid and went inside, only to find Lindsay crossing into the kitchen and peeking into her oven.

"Do you like what you see?" He snapped the tongs for extra effect.

Lindsay clapped her chest with one of her hands. "You scared me."

He gestured to his apron and flip-flops. "I'm scary? I like to think I'm quite lovable. A real sweetheart, if I do say so myself."

She rolled her eyes and pointed to the oven. "You know I was talking about you sneaking up on me."

"I could say the same. I thought you'd arrive home much later."

"Short staff meeting."

He laughed. "I didn't think there was such a thing."

"Me either, but after a long day, I'm not complaining. Besides, I never criticize anyone who's cooking my dinner. What's in there?"

"Oven-baked jasmine rice. Since Grandpa Joe had a Danish today, I thought it might be a way to slip some cauliflower and zucchini past him." He spotted the famous pink box from the Night Owl Bakery on the counter. "And what's in there?"

She blushed a becoming shade of pink. "Red velvet cupcakes."

"Did I hear red velvet cupcakes?" Grandpa Joe and three other smiling faces popped into the kitchen.

Evan and Chloe licked their lips while Goliath wagged his tail. The timer pinged, and Mason used an oven mitt on the rice. His grandfather stared at the casserole dish as if it had two heads. "What's *that*?"

Mason recited the list of ingredients. Chloe folded her arms and plopped on the floor. "Unh-uh."

Lindsay reached for her. Chloe scrambled into her arms but wouldn't meet her gaze. "You know Mommy's rule. Try at least five bites or no cupcake."

Chloe held up three fingers. "Four bites?"

Evan came over and raised her pinky finger. "That's four."

"He's right." Lindsay moved Chloe's thumb. "But I said five and I mean five."

"Except for anyone who gets the senior discount at the Holly Days Diner, right?" Grandpa Joe grimaced and kept a wary eye on the rice dish.

"Those special people don't have to eat five bites." Mason nodded and clapped the tongs for effect once more as his grandfather broke into a grin. "They have to eat ten bites."

Lindsay's laughter followed him outside while he removed the salmon from the grill. Throughout dinner, Goliath went from person to person, looking for morsels of fish. Evan snuck him several pieces, and Goliath parked himself next to the four-year-old.

After dinner, Lindsay shooed everyone into the backyard. "Mason cooked, so I'll clean up."

Evan faced Mason. "Mom signed me up for T-ball. Can you teach me to catch?"

Guilt flittered through Mason. Tim should be the person Evan was asking for that honor. Still, it would be his privilege to fulfill Evan's request. He moved toward the boy, when his grandfather picked up one of the gloves on the patio.

Grandpa Joe touched Evan's shoulder. "I

used to be pretty good with a baseball and glove. I taught my son Peter a trick or two, enough so he was the star shortstop on his high school team."

Mason stepped back and let Grandpa Joe take the lead.

Evan and Grandpa Joe made their way to a grassy area with Goliath on their heels. Mason stayed with Lindsay. "I'd be more than happy to help since you worked all day."

"I'll be fine." Lindsay pushed him and Chloe outside.

With some reluctance at leaving Lindsay's side, Mason escorted Chloe to the patio and settled next to her. Grandpa Joe was less than a yard from the young boy and tossed him the ball, obviously building his confidence with some easy catches. Then he lengthened the distance between them and tossed one with a little more force. It flew past Evan, who backtracked and fell. Goliath trotted over and began licking the boy's face.

Evan took his time getting up, and Mason left Chloe's side.

"Evan?" Mason didn't like how disoriented the boy's brown eyes looked.

Evan blinked, his pale face matching the blond hue of his hair. "Sorry, Grandpa Joe. I should have caught that one." His giggle didn't have its usual pep. "Goliath, I can't taste that good."

Grandpa Joe whistled, but the dog stayed at Evan's side. "Goliath." His grandfather neared, the annoyance of his tone matching his expression until he took a long glance at the little boy. He neared Chloe. "Come on, little girl. Let's go inside."

"Cupcake?" Chloe licked her lips and patted her stomach.

"We'll see. Mason needs a moment with Evan." Grandpa Joe's clear concern proved Mason wasn't imagining something was wrong. "I'll tell Lindsay."

Was the boy having an allergic reaction to something? Or was this an asthma attack? "No need. I'm taking him inside."

Mason swooped him into his arms over Evan's protests with Goliath hovering around the bottoms of Mason's jeans.

"I'm not little like Chloe. I can walk."

"Hey, you're practice for me. I have to stay in shape. Next month, I have to show my boss I can lift a hundred pounds and drag fifty. Your mom wouldn't be happy, though, if I dragged you inside." He pretended Evan was a barbell for a brief second. "So, you're the one doing the favor for me."

A slight giggle turned into a noise that

sounded like Evan was whistling. Lindsay met them at the sliding glass door, and Goliath squeezed through before Lindsay slid it closed. "Joe said something was wrong. What's happening?"

Mason mouthed the words "asthma attack" and Lindsay grabbed her purse and extricated one of Evan's inhalers. Mason deposited Evan on the living room sectional. The whistling was now replaced with a harsher, wheezing tone. Goliath jumped up and stayed near Evan's side.

Lindsay handed Evan's inhaler and spacer to Mason. "I'm getting my phone and calling his pulmonologist."

She left while Evan curled up on his side, away from Goliath, his eyes closed. Mason's paramedic training took over. He tapped the boy's shoulder, and his eyelids fluttered open again.

"I know it seems natural to want to take a nap, but when you're having an asthma attack, it's best if you sit upright. Can you do that for me?" Mason said in a firm but gentle voice. He tamped down his nerves. This wasn't just another case; he loved Evan very much.

Goliath thumped his tail against the cushions.

"I don't like asthma. Chloe can have it for me."

Mason chuckled and shook his head. "It

doesn't work like that. We get what we're dealt with." Ironic, since he'd been thinking along those same lines not even an hour ago.

He checked Evan's pulse, which was about eighty. As long as it kept under ninety, medical attention at home would be sufficient. Evan's fingertips turned blue, and that sent off alarm bells. Mason uncapped the inhaler and gave it three firm shakes. He reassured Evan and then covered his face with the mask connected to the suction part of the spacer. Activating the measured-dose inhaler, Mason instructed Evan how to breathe and had him hold his breath while Mason counted backward from five. Lindsay appeared next to Mason on three, nibbling her thumbnail, while her gaze didn't leave Evan.

Evan repeated the deep breath as Mason relayed soothing instructions, waiting for the medicine to take full effect. After a few minutes, Mason removed the mask and spacer away from Evan's mouth. "How are you doing?"

"A red velvet cupcake would get the yucky taste away."

"Humor and a complete sentence. I think you might get that cupcake soon." Mason glanced at Lindsay, who sat next to Evan, her arm tightening around his shoulders.

"I just called your pulmonologist. She knows Mason and says he's a good judge of whether we need to take you to the ER." She met Mason's gaze, worry clouding her gray orbs. "Do I need to arrange for a babysitter for Chloe?"

"Grandpa Joe would gladly volunteer, except Evan doesn't need to go. I'll monitor him for the next hour and continue taking his pulse, but as of now, the rescue inhaler seems to be doing its job."

Goliath swiped Lindsay's fingers with his tongue, and Lindsay pulled back. Her face turned almost as ashen as Evan's, and she glared at the dog. "Certain triggers exacerbate asthma, don't they?"

Mason moved his fingers to Evan's neck and calculated his pulse again while Goliath nudged closer to the boy as if he could sense Lindsay's disapproval. "Yes, but Evan has been around Goliath for a couple of weeks now. Surely Goliath isn't the trigger. He'd have had a reaction before now."

Almost on cue, Evan's breath sounded as though he were blowing through a whistle. Lindsay stood and glanced around the room. She walked over to Goliath's leash and called for the dog. Grandpa Joe appeared at the doorway, a cupcake with half the wrapper removed near his mouth. "What's wrong? I thought Evan was okay."

Mason approached Lindsay and kept his voice low enough so only she could hear. "I'm concerned, too, but the medication is working. Evan's recovering. And he's learning to manage his asthma well."

"Goliath could be the cause. I don't think he needs to be around Evan."

But everywhere his grandfather went, Goliath wasn't far behind. "Can we talk about this later? Grandpa Joe'll be flustered to think any of this was on account of his dog. Please don't embarrass him like this. He loves these kids as though they were his own. It's the only thing that's kept his spirits up since Grandma Betty went to Tennessee."

She glanced at Evan, whose breath was coming in more natural spurts, the whistling diminishing with each second, and then faced Mason. "As soon as the dog moved away, my son started breathing normally. I think that's obvious proof, don't you?"

Mason found it hard to dispute her logic, but Evan and Goliath had been best buddies for the past few weeks.

"I'm old, but I can hear perfectly fine." Grandpa Joe's voice sounded from behind, and they turned to find him there, crumbs and icing around his lips. His back hunched, he clipped Goliath's green leash to his collar. "I'd never do anything to hurt these two little ones. I'm sorry, Lindsay. I'll keep Goliath away from the kiddos. Come on, Goliath."

With that his grandfather moved toward the door, and the evening came to a halt. While Lindsay hadn't directly called out Grandpa Joe, her rejection of Goliath seemed too quick, a gut reaction rather than a measured examination of the facts.

This was why it was better not to get too attached. Good things always seemed to come to an abrupt end.

"Evan should be good, but if his pulse rises above ninety, call his doctor. If it goes about a hundred and ten and stays there for over five minutes, text me and we'll take him to the ER immediately."

"Mason."

He shook his head. "Later. I have to check on Grandpa Joe. He's my responsibility."

Mason couldn't look at Lindsay as he followed his grandfather and left for home.

CHAPTER NINE

LINDSAY STUCK A BOOKMARK in the gardening journal and turned out her lamp, before burrowing under the thick duvet cover. After all, what else was she supposed to do about Joe and Goliath? If the dog triggered Evan's asthma, Goliath would have to stay away. She hadn't meant for Mason and Joe to take the rejection personally.

She turned over and exhaled. When had every conversation with Mason evolved into an argument? At the botanical garden, she had the reputation of staying calm in any crisis. She could coax plants, which others were ready to gut for dormancy, back to life.

Yet lately, the air around her and Mason buzzed with the expectancy of something different on the horizon, some change too ominous to ignore. The awful part was she liked that too much. She squeezed her eyes shut even tighter, determined to rid herself of any feelings crossing over the friendship line.

A squeak in the floorboards of the ceiling

snapped her eyes wide open. Then something scurried above her, and she flicked on the lamp once more.

Light flooded her bedroom, bathing the soft blue walls in a peaceful glow. Everything was tranquil and orderly, the way she liked it, from the picture of her wedding day on her bureau to her trundle seat at her bay window. With nothing out of place, she assured herself she was hearing things. Her hand reached for the lamp, but more overhead noises alerted her to the fact that something was invading her attic. Her heartbeat accelerated, and she spied her phone on its charger by her bed.

Mason had invited her to call day or night, but that was before he trailed his grandfather out the door. Besides, it might just be something small frolicking in the attic. Lindsay was a competent woman, and she'd check the attic tomorrow. Then she'd call the appropriate company to remove whatever was up there.

She pounded her pillow and went to turn out the light. Ignoring the unwanted sounds would be for the best tonight.

Except tossing and turning didn't help any. Whatever was scurrying around up there had invited friends and it now sounded like they were having a party. She flopped onto her other side and the duvet slipped off the bed.

Out of reach of the cover, she huffed and got out of her warm sheets, only to find the temperature in her bedroom had plummeted.

Glaring at the ceiling, she didn't have a choice between taking action or snuggling deep under the covers. Whatever animal sought refuge in her attic might have damaged something. If she investigated now, she could determine whether it was loose insulation or some sort of stray animal. Then she'd be back in her nice, warm bed in mere minutes.

With a sigh, she swung her feet onto the carpet, the plush fiber cushioning her toes. A chill nipped the air, and she shivered. She grabbed the flashlight Tim had insisted on keeping in the top drawer of their dresser in case of emergencies and tiptoed into the hallway, taking care not to wake up Evan, who was her light sleeper. It would take a bullhorn to wake up Chloe. At least the attic door was on the opposite side of her house from their bedrooms.

A check of the thermostat, four degrees cooler than her preferred preset temperature, elicited a groan. Was the furnace broken or was some animal nibbling on the wires?

She pulled down the squeaky attic door and the stairs descended into the hallway. A quick glance confirmed neither of her children was out of bed. She fought the flutters in her stomach. Flashlight in hand, she entered the unfinished attic, the beams and insulation daunting. She quelled her fears and found the problem, her laugh of relief tamping down those pesky nerves. Somehow, the flap of the furnace filter had opened and was banging against the metal, leaving the air filter exposed. She exhaled at the simple solution. Balancing on the wooden beams, she crossed over and closed the flap. The furnace clicked on, and she all but cheered. To think she'd almost called Mason over something like this.

Halfway back to the stairs, something long and furry with a big bushy tail caught her eye and scampered across her feet. She screamed and dropped the flashlight, the clatter on the wood echoing in the night. Stumbling, she pitched forward and reached for something, anything, to regain her balance. Instead, she lost her footing, falling into scratchy pink insulation. The floor below her gave way. Her bare feet broke through the wood while bits of dust and plaster went up her nose. Falling, she cried out and her heartbeat accelerated. Until she realized she was wedged in a hole. Trapped, her chest was above the hole, and her legs dangled below. She was stuck and couldn't pull herself up. She tried not to panic. The flashlight was close enough where a beam slipped through the crack and illuminated the guest room below. Now was time to panic.

"Mommy?" Evan's voice came from the direction of the stairs and he coughed.

"Stay down there." She didn't want to think about what the dust and insulation would do to his asthma. "Do you remember how to use Mommy's phone?"

"Yes." He coughed again, and she hoped this wasn't the beginning of another asthma attack.

"Call Mason and then release the bar from the sliding glass door so he can come inside." Gripping the beam with all her might, she tried not to think about falling to the floor. "And hurry."

IF IT WEREN'T for the panic in Evan's voice over the phone, Mason would have thought he was dreaming. He hurried next door, where Evan grabbed his arm and dragged him upstairs.

"Mommy's legs are in the ceiling."

He'd heard of minor reactions to the measured dose of asthma medication, but this type of vivid dream was one for the books. Once he reassured Evan everything was fine, he'd wake up Lindsay and warn her she might want to keep better tabs on her phone in the middle of the night.

Mason stopped short outside Lindsay's guest

room. A most attractive pair of legs were dangling from the ceiling. His chest heaved at the sight until he realized the rest of her must be holding on in the attic. This nightmare wasn't a dream. "Hold on, Lin."

He found the stairs leading to the attic and rushed up them, then pulled her to safety. She clutched him close, her chest puffing in and out, a classic sign of hyperventilation. He grabbed the flashlight and then helped Lindsay down to where Evan waited at the bottom of the steps.

"Mommy!" He clutched her leg before she was even off the staircase.

She sent him a shaky smile. "Thank you, Evan, for being such a great helper."

Her voice was also shaky, and she leaned against Mason. "Thank you for coming over."

"Any time."

She brushed his cheek with her lips, the kiss imprinting itself into his stubble. She stumbled, falling back. Her shiver alarmed him, and even the dim light didn't hide her ashen face.

"I could have fallen straight through to the floor."

He pulled her close, and she leaned into him. He kept still, giving her as much comfort and time as she needed. He longed to kiss her, to reassure her everything was all right, but he'd settle for being here for her. Anything else would cross the line.

Eventually, he let go of her. "What happened?" he asked.

"A squirrel, I think."

Why hadn't she called him earlier? He'd save that question. "Let's get you warmed with a cup of tea and then I'll stay here in case Evan or Chloe need me while you take a shower."

He started for her staircase, and she rested her hand on his arm. "I have to see the damage to the guest room first. My parents are planning to stay there."

For the dedication. She didn't have to say the words. They hung in the air like the faint dust coating the carpet. Even this attraction wouldn't change his mind about attending.

"Hello, is everyone okay? I heard Mason hurrying out of the house and came to check up on everyone," Grandpa Joe called out and then appeared at the foot of the stairs. "Chloe? Evan?"

"Chloe would sleep through the zombie apocalypse, and Evan's fine." Lindsay's voice still sounded shaky, a sign she might be going into shock.

Mason escorted her to the kitchen and settled her at her table. Then he started the stove top for some peppermint tea while she told

Grandpa Joe what happened. By the time he found the tea bags, Evan's head rested on the table, his even breathing reassuring after last night's episode and the dust particles that could have brought about another asthma attack.

Lindsay's teeth chattered, and he knelt by her and gazed into her eyes, searching for dilated pupils, or even ones that weren't equal in size. "Do you have a headache?"

"No, and I didn't hit my head so I don't have a concussion."

He realized his grandfather was nowhere to be found. "I'll track down Grandpa Joe and ask him to watch the kids while I take you to the ER for observation."

"There's no need for that, and I'm not scaring Evan again. What I have is little bits of insulation pricking my arm, and I'm cold because a squirrel or mouse was in my attic and was messing with my furnace causing it to turn off."

"You should have called."

The teakettle whistled, and Evan stirred before falling back asleep. Mason started for the stove, but Lindsay passed him and prepared her cup of tea by herself.

"Things ended badly between us tonight," Lindsay said, pouring steaming water into her mug.

"We're both looking out for people we love."

"Yes, but well, I have to stay strong for me. I don't like other people handling everything for me. Take my mother, for instance. First, she wanted me to move in with dad and her. Then she wanted me to stay in bed and let her wait on me hand and foot."

"Which she did for a while."

Lindsay dunked the tea bag until water sloshed out the sides of her cup. "And now my boss believes his wife can handle the volunteer roster, which is on my list of duties, and effectively do my job. I'm not some fragile flower like the ones blooming at the garden."

Her eyes blazed and he nodded his head. "I never said you were fragile."

"Good news!" Grandpa Joe entered the kitchen.

"I thought you'd gone home." Mason glanced at the sliding glass door, then at his grandfather.

"While you've been checking out Lindsay, I've been checking out her guest room and the furnace. It's working again."

Mason's chest tightened. If his grandfather figured out Mason's feelings for Lindsay were growing stronger, he'd have to do better at hiding them closer to his heart.

Lindsay groaned and closed her eyes. "Give

it to me straight. How much damage did I do to the ceiling?"

"You'll need some special drywall, wooden cleats, mesh tape, and compound. That won't set you back too much. Thank goodness you don't have popcorn ceilings. Then I'd have to turn you down."

"I'm not following."

"I'm going to fix your ceiling." He grinned and tilted his head toward Mason. "With his help, of course."

Her eyes widened. Then she pulled Mason into the living room. "I thought your grandmother wanted you to monitor him because of his angina. Won't working on my ceiling be the worst possible thing for that? Should I let him do this?"

"He's been in construction and the like all his life. He's great at repairing things. I'll tell him if he feels any dizziness, fatigue or nausea he should stop immediately." Although he and Lindsay were now in need of repair, too. He just wanted their easy friendship back. He was beginning to think it was too late for that. "This project is exactly what he needs. And he's offering himself. He wants Evan and Chloe around."

She looked unconvinced until she peeked into the kitchen. Her face softened, and he kept himself from staring at her pink lips. "He's looking at Evan as though he misses him already. I know you think I overreacted, but I'm not convinced that I did. Goliath must have been the cause. For some reason, though, this past month you've been getting under my skin worse than this insulation." She cringed and ran her fingers through her hair, disheveled and cute with a chunk of the fiberglass insulation sticking out.

"Let me." He reached over, brushed it away and tried not to notice how soft her hair was, even with bits of plaster and dust turning it from honey brown to white.

He folded his arms over his chest and added distance between him and Lindsay, whose compassion was becoming a distraction that had nothing to do with the late hour. She tried rubbing some of the pink fiberglass fragments off her skin.

"You and Joe will keep an eye on things, or in this case, the ceiling, while I take a shower?"

He nodded, and she gave him a grateful smile. "Looks like the Ruddick men are riding to my rescue tonight."

"You didn't need rescuing, just a helpful hand." He grinned, happy to get this conversation back on safe ground. "Apply some antibiotic ointment liberally to those scratches. An infection is the last thing you need."

"A literal hole in my ceiling is the last thing I need, one I hope will be fixed before my parents arrive. Joe will ask for more help if he needs anything, right?"

"Yes, ma'am." He tapped his wrist, the one that remained bare unless he was on his shift. "Um, I have to report in the early morning hours."

"Then I'll hurry. Be back in two shakes."

Mason waited in the kitchen, watching Grandpa Joe, who watched Evan lovingly. Lindsay was true to her word, returning in no time with a smile.

"All fresh again." She hugged Grandpa Joe, and a light whiff of lavender caught Mason's senses. "Thank you for the offer. I know you'll do an outstanding job with the ceiling. Just make sure you let us know if you need anything, and I'm sorry about Goliath."

With that, she nudged Evan, who trudged upstairs. Next, Lindsay waved and closed the sliding glass door behind him and Grandpa Joe.

Mason flicked on his phone light, illuminating the path between his and Lindsay's houses.

Grandpa Joe chuckled. "Wait until I tell Betty about this. Just when I thought nothing interesting would happen."

A longing swept over Mason. His grandparents shared a special bond which distance nor anyone else could ever break. What would it be like to open himself up to a powerful love like that for his very own? Did he even dare try?

CHAPTER TEN

WAS IT JUST Lindsay's imagination or was the cart Joe pushed through the aisles of Farr's Hardware getting more weighed down by the second? Drywall, wooden two-by-fours and fiberglass tape already rested there. Who knew so much was involved in fixing a gaping hole in her ceiling? Chloe tugged at Lindsay's capris, and she picked up her daughter.

"When's ice cweam?" Chloe stuffed her fingers in her mouth, and Lindsay removed them.

"Soon." Lindsay was also anticipating the trip to Miss Louise's Ice Cream Parlor. "Joe's finding stuff to fix the guest room for Mimi and Pop-Pop's visit."

Lindsay's mother didn't like the usual grandparent names and chose something she believed had more flair.

"I love Grandpa Joe." Chloe reached for the older man, his delight as plain as the wire glasses resting on his nose.

He accepted her, and she nestled her head on his shoulder. "And Grandpa Joe loves you."

Mason moved toward the rolling cart with Evan on his heels, taking care around the other Saturday shoppers. With hero worship in his eyes, Evan asked questions about every power tool in sight. To Mason's credit, he was taking it all in stride.

Lindsay kept her gaze on Mason, seeing what a lot of women in Hollydale saw in him, and more. That grin of his was charm personified, and he made you feel like you were the only person in a crowd of thousands. Yet he rarely showed people that other side of him, the one that craved solitude with his motorcycle, valued honesty and being forthright, the side with a strong core of steel.

Who was the real Mason? The charmer? The rebel? The paramedic next door? As far as she could tell, those were all facets of his personality. To her dismay, she found herself thinking about him more than she should.

"Is this the right one, Grandpa Joe?" Evan turned his attention to the containers of joint compound and pointed to a white tub with thick green letters.

Mason's grandfather shook his head. "I like the one with the red writing better. It's more expensive, but it lasts longer. Can't go wrong with quality. I knew the minute I met Mason's grandmother, she was the one for me.

Her spunk and spirit are quality stuff. Same as your mom." He smiled at Evan, who was struggling with the heavy tub, and handed Chloe back to Lindsay.

Then he grabbed one side of the handle and indicated Evan to get the other. "Next time I'm sure you'll be old enough to load it on your own." He helped Evan swing the tub into the cart and then gave him a fist bump. "Good job."

Little beads of sweat popped onto Evan's forehead. The smile faded from Lindsay's face as Evan's breathing became staggered, more of a whistle sound than his normal quiet intake of air. Joe must have noticed, and his face became ashen. "I didn't think about animal dander."

Neither did she. If Evan had this severe reaction when he hadn't even been around the dog, how could she allow Joe over at all?

Joe backed up and jostled a pyramid of paint cans. Mason reached over and lifted two fingers to Evan's neck. No sooner had he done so and Evan started coughing and raised his fingers to his neck, obviously struggling for breath. Mason glanced at Lindsay and shook his head. "I came here to meet you straight from the station after I finished my two-day shift."

"Hold that thought while I get his inhaler."

Lindsay's fingers rattled against her purse, and she grasped Evan's canister. If she banished Joe from her house, Mason might take that as a personal affront. That would be two more gaping holes to the ones already marring her life. She shook the canister, and placed the mask over Evan's mouth and squeezed, counting aloud.

"Lindsay, I wasn't even near Goliath."

"Don't make me say it out loud." Her voice sounded ragged and she focused on Evan, refusing to look at Mason's face lest she lose her nerve. "Please."

"How can this be a reaction to animal dander? I haven't been around an animal for forty-eight hours."

Chloe took that opportunity to run off. "Chloe!" Lindsay glanced at Evan, needing to be with him.

"I've got her." Mason sprinted down the aisle and grabbed Chloe. He carried her back like a sack of potatoes.

Chloe wrinkled her nose and wriggled as if trying to escape from his grasp. "Smelly. Ick."

"Gee, thanks. You know how to bruise a guy's ego, don't you?" Mason sniffed his wrists and held out his palms to the toddler. "So, you don't like the new aftershave and cologne Grandpa Joe bought me last week?"

"What?" Lindsay almost dropped the canister of asthma medication before gathering her composure. She gave a reassuring nod to Evan and counted backward calmly once more, giving the medicine a minute to take effect. Then to Mason she said, "What new aftershave?"

"The day we went out for Danish, and oh…" Mason whooped and swung Chloe around in his arms, receiving a glare from a nearby customer. "Chloe, sweetheart, you get extra sprinkles on your ice cream!"

Grandpa Joe straightened, that pyramid of paint unsteady for a brief second. "It's not Goliath, then?"

"Highly improbable if you ask me." Mason laughed and then grimaced when he caught sight of Evan. "Sorry, not trying to be insensitive to your asthma attack, Ev, but this is awesome news. It's this new brand of aftershave, not Goliath at all."

The plastic mask didn't hide the smile lighting up Evan's face. For the first time in a long time, in Farr's Hardware of all unlikely places, those gaping holes didn't feel so deep.

CHAPTER ELEVEN

LINDSAY WINCED AT the hole in the ceiling. It hadn't seemed quite so big when she missed the rafter and slipped through, but in full daylight, with Joe and Mason next to her, it was enormous. If she had actually fallen through the ceiling onto the floor, she could have sprained her ankle or even broken her leg.

Or worse.

She brushed her cheeks with the back of her hand. At least she hadn't heard any scurrying noises at night. After the trip to the hardware store, they'd celebrated at Miss Louise's Ice Cream Parlor and Joe decided on an impromptu weeklong trip to Nashville before he started the repair project. In her spare time, she'd cleared away the debris and vacuumed the cream-colored carpet. Between her work schedule and Mason's extra shifts, every minute had rushed by, but now it was time to deal with the aftermath.

She lowered the goggles over her forehead until they rested comfortably on her nose.

Mason and Joe moved the bed against the wall and placed a blue plastic tarp over the furniture. Prepping the room and configuring the workspace would be the first step toward patching the hole. Gloves in hand, she glanced at the ceiling once more. It all caught up with her, and she shuddered. Her breathing became shallow, and her heartbeat accelerated.

Mason came over and reached for her shoulders. "Excuse us for a minute, Grandpa Joe. We'll be right back."

Mason escorted her downstairs and out to the backyard. The vivid pinks of the azaleas seemed to drive home the life around her after the flat dullness of the dust and tiny particles coating the guest room.

"You won't go there." Mason sat in one of the Adirondack chairs, and she sagged into the other.

"The only place I was going to was back to my guest room to start getting everything under control."

"I meant back into the grief."

How did he read her mind like that?

"I'll be all right. It just caught me for a second." She breathed in and rose. "Each spring I have to prune the crepe myrtles in the front yard and then they bloom again. I have to do the same in a way." She took a step forward. "Evan and Chloe ought to be waking up from their naps. I need to make them a snack. There'll be enough for you and Grandpa Joe, too."

"That reminds me. Last night I found Grandpa Joe's snack stash. He needs to eat healthier foods again. I've got something that'll be perfect for everyone."

Lindsay gnawed her lip while he disappeared via the fence. Somehow, she had to put some distance between them. One first responder had already been taken from her; she didn't want to fall for another, who'd made his position as a confirmed bachelor all too clear, anyway.

She went inside. Evan was in the living room, already awake from his nap, playing with the plastic birds. She went and checked on Chloe, who held out her arms for her mother's embrace. Lindsay obliged and cuddled her daughter.

"Sugar and spice and everything nice." She carried Chloe into the hallway. At the open doorway of the guest room, she moved Chloe's arm up and down in greeting. "Look who just woke up, Grandpa Joe. How about some fresh air and a snack, and then we'll start again?"

"You won't have to repeat that offer twice." Grandpa Joe came over and tweaked Chloe's cheek, a spring in his step.

They headed downstairs, where she repeated her offer to Evan, who put the plastic birds into the container and followed them out to the patio. Mason wasn't back yet, and Joe, as the last one through, closed the sliding glass door behind him. Chloe toddled over to him. "Pick Chloe up?"

Joe reached for her hand and sat in the other Adirondack chair, bouncing her on his knee. "How's this instead?"

A giggle served as her daughter's affirmative answer. Evan picked up a plastic bottle of bubbles and started blowing them around the yard.

A clatter at the fence brought her to her feet. The gate swung open, and Mason had something tucked under his chin and both hands occupied with platters of food. Before she could reach him, Goliath darted through Mason's legs and headed right for Evan, who dropped the bubbles. He fell backward in the grass, laughing as the dog licked his face. Her heart thudded as she ran over, joined by Joe, with Chloe a distant third.

"Evan, are you okay?" she asked.

Joe called Goliath, who moved away with some reluctance before he sniffed the air and followed Mason to the patio table. Lindsay looked to Evan, but he ignored her and scrambled to his feet. "Hey, boy. I'm glad you're back. I missed you when you were in Nashville."

Pulled in two directions, Lindsay didn't know what to do. Part of her wanted to trust it was the aftershave while the rest of her didn't want Evan to suffer through another attack. Evan ran to the table and scrunched his nose.

"What's this?"

"Hummus and pita bread." Mason dipped a triangle of pita into the creamy golden mixture and ate it. "Delicious. Homemade, too."

Goliath tried jumping on the table, but Mason had placed the food out of the dog's reach. Lindsay went over and put her hands on her son's shoulders. "How are you feeling?"

"Sorry about spilling all the bubbles."

Bubbles. Though Lindsay could have used his peak air meter, this might be a better way for unofficially measuring his reaction to Goliath. "Why don't you try a bite of what Mason brought us while I run to the garage?"

In no time, she returned with two bottles of bubbles, one for Chloe and one for Evan. "Hey, mom. Hummus isn't half bad," Evan said, waving a pita.

Mason chuckled and passed a plate to his grandfather. The man's blue eyes sparkled when he winked at his grandfather. The breeze ruffled Mason's thick auburn hair, and Lindsay's insides melted. "Want to try?" he asked Grandpa Joe.

That charisma of Mason's was a little too potent. When she became involved with another man, it would be someone unlike Mason. Someone who didn't push her or tempt her with that dimple in his left cheek.

"Maybe later." Joe kept his eyes on the kids while Lindsay opened the caps on the bottles.

Soon Evan and Chloe ran around the backyard, blowing bubbles with Goliath, yipping on their heels and trying to pop them with his snout. So far, it would seem as though Goliath wasn't the culprit of any asthma attack. Seeing her children happy with the chiweenie, she didn't mind, although she did feel foolish about how she'd jumped to conclusions.

She sidled next to Joe. "Mason would love it if you tried some of his hummus." She dipped a piece of pita into the creamy concoction and handed it to him. "And I'd love it if you'd accept my apology."

"Nothing to apologize for, m'dear." He accepted it with a grimace. "You know I think the world of Evan and Chloe."

"Can I ask a personal question?" Lindsay ate a delicious bite while Mason chased the two kids, tickling Chloe before releasing her and going after Evan.

"As long as you don't mind a personal answer." He chuckled and came close to eating the pita before lowering it to the plate again.

"Why are you here rather than staying in Nashville? I know you miss Betty."

"I came back to keep an eye on things while Betty helps Bree. Our home is in Hollydale and I check on our house on my way home from work."

Lindsay reached for a napkin and brushed off the hummus on her lip. "You and Betty have lots of friends. Someone would do that. There must be more to it than that."

His gaze went to Mason and the children running around the yard, having fun on this bright spring day, Goliath's yips in chorus with the chirps of the cardinals and the giggles of her kids. "Ah, but I also have my regular cardiologist check ins, and besides, jobs at my age aren't easy to come by, and the new director's done a bang-up job. I don't want to desert my post."

"Or your grandson?" Lindsay's gaze went to Mason pretending to fall on the grass while Evan and Chloe piled on him.

"Betty and I worry about him, all our grandkids, really. Right now, Bree and Mason need us, and it's nice to be needed. Bree knows it and is thankful for it. Mason, though?"

"Stubborn like his grandparents, huh?"

Joe laughed. "Only his grandfather. Betty's patient yet feisty. She keeps me on the up and up more than anyone knows."

He jutted his chin at the cheerful group and chewed the pita and hummus. "Same recipe as Betty's."

"What a coincidence."

"Not really. Mason gave Betty the recipe." He winked at Lindsay and turned back to the antics. "And let's just say I exaggerate a bit. Betty knows I sneak out for ice cream, but it's an excuse so I get to spend more time with Mason. He doesn't push me away when I bring over the sherbet."

Joe chuckled and Lindsay did the same as he left her side and joined the others.

MASON REMOVED THE bar end mirrors from their box. Georgie and Max's auto shop always ordered the best products. Pure steel was pricier than some of the alternatives, but it was worth it. With everything he'd need at his fingertips, he moved the plug away from the left handlebar and used a smaller expansion sleeve for a tight fit. Losing a mirror during a lane change would be disastrous. He tightened the nut with his wrench and stepped away from the bike.

His phone rang, and he laughed as his grandmother, who as always went through her elaborate ritual of identifying herself. "Bree is doing so much better. Her eyes almost show that Bree spirit again. You and I both know that type of spunk goes a long way in the fight."

If anyone had spirit, it was Bree.

"Glad to hear it." He had regretted not going with Grandpa Joe to Nashville, but duty had called and his sister insisted he should stay in Hollydale.

"Speaking of spunk, how's Joe?"

"Ornery as ever. He's lonely without you." Although this afternoon with Lindsay and the kids had done them all a world of good. So much that Grandpa had even eaten the creamy vegetable risotto for dinner without a complaint. Afterward, Grandpa had headed out to walk Goliath while Mason tackled this next step on his bike.

"While he was here, he didn't make much sense, talking about holes and cologne and pretty ladies hugging him in the middle of the night."

Mason explained everything and reassured her once again that he was keeping an eye on his grandfather. When he hung up and started to pick up his wrench, once again, that feeling that someone cared that much clutched him tight, and he left the right bar end mirror where it was. He needed to get away from this garage, away from the gardener next-door.

After crossing the walkway to his house, Mason grabbed his wallet and jacket. He searched for his grandfather so he wouldn't wait up for him. He checked the hook where Grandpa Joe kept Goliath's leash. *Still empty.* That must have been one long walk.

Or they went over to Lindsay's. He hurried outside and there in his spot on her patio, resting in Mason's favorite Adirondack chair was his grandfather, bouncing Chloe on his knee and laughing while Goliath and Evan played Frisbee.

Orange and pink hues dotted the horizon, and dusk was beginning to claim the day. Lindsay caught sight of Mason and waved him over.

"Evan hasn't had an attack all evening, and Goliath's been here the whole time. Isn't that the best news?"

The happiness on her face caught him off guard. He wished he hadn't become so close to her. It seemed wrong to think that, but he had to listen to his head from now on and not his heart. How else would he keep himself or her from getting hurt? He couldn't stay, not tonight. "It is. Since things are under control, I'm heading over to the Timber River Bar and Grill."

He started to stride away, glad he had his keys in his pocket. Then he felt Lindsay's hand on his arm. He wanted to acknowledge the touch, but he refused to let himself.

"Mason, what's going on? Did you get some bad news about Bree?"

"No, but I feel like the walls are closing in." The huskiness in his voice came off harsh, yet it took all his resolve to not join in the cozy evening.

"Sure, but you seemed happy earlier playing with Evan and Chloe—now you're acting…" She pursed her lips and her gray eyes darkened to the color of a turbulent sky. "Just so you know, sometimes you get me all mixed-up. You're shaking us off like I shake dirt off my gloves." She stepped back.

If she thought she was mixed-up, it was nothing like the confusing mess of emotions swirling around him. He wanted nothing more than to have what his grandparents laid claim to for the past fifty-six years. And yet?

He couldn't claim anything with Tim's widow. No matter how attractive she was, inside and out. No matter how his heart raced when that scent of lavender came his way, acting on the attraction? That would belittle Tim's memory.

He resisted the urge to kiss her, though it was the very thing he longed to do. "Maybe the best way I can honor Tim is to leave and get that drink."

"Huh?" Confusion lurked in her eyes, and she folded her arms over her chest. "If that's not the oddest excuse I've ever heard, I'll eat those morning glories."

As much as he'd like to take her in his arms and throw away all the excuses in the world, he couldn't. "Lindsay, trust me on this one, okay?"

"What do I tell your grandfather, the kids?"

"The truth. Sometimes people need space."

"There's something else going on, something under the surface." The glow of dusk surrounded them, highlighting the golden streaks in her short honey hair and the glint in her gaze. "Something neither of us wants to admit."

She was right. They were both flirting with danger, something below the surface that could undermine their friendship and threaten to rip apart everything he held dear.

If he stayed another minute, he'd kiss her. Then there'd be no more laughter while they built trellises together, no more sunsets with his beer bottle clinking her flute of Riesling, no more evenings by the fence. The air crackled around him, and she licked her lips almost as though she wanted him to kiss her, but she herself said she could never fall for another first responder.

He wouldn't want them in a position where she had to go against her own words. He nodded and pointed toward Grandpa Joe. "Tell him not to wait up for me, okay?"

"I've seen you run before, but I didn't think you would run from something that should be out in the open." Her expression accused him of the very reason he needed to escape.

Those gray eyes would be the undoing of him if he let them.

"Friends should give each other space. We're friends, right?"

What if she said no, that they were more than that? He held his breath. What if they were on the verge of something special?

"Since you've made it clear you don't want to be here, go." She glanced down and scuffed the grassy dirt with her sneaker. "And you're right. There's nothing going on here."

With that, he turned on his heel and left.

CHAPTER TWELVE

FLIPPING ON THE portable fan, Mason turned and assessed Lindsay's guest bedroom. He hadn't liked how he'd left things with her a week ago. Since then, he'd filled in for a sick colleague for five days. Then on his two days off, Lindsay stayed at the garden later than usual. Grandpa Joe mentioned how hard she was working on the display, only taking time to eat and tuck in her children. It was hard to get back in someone's good graces if they weren't around.

From the looks of things, she and Grandpa Joe had made little progress since Mason had made for the bar and grill.

Was he doing this for her, or was he trying to win back their friendship by facing this gaping hole?

No, he wasn't here to regain her favor. He was here because he'd made important realizations that night, nursing his lone beer alone for hours. First, he and Lin made a great team. As friends. If one of them had to get things back on the right footing, he'd volunteer and some-how stop looking at her kissable lips.

So for now, he'd tackle the ceiling. He'd used his spare key to enter Lindsay's house. He'd fix this and save his grandfather from extra exertion and prevent Lindsay from receiving a litany of questions from her mother about her middle-of-the-night slip.

With his keyhole saw in hand, Mason climbed the ladder, which was positioned over a drop cloth so there wouldn't be more damage to the carpet. Taking care there were no wires in sight, he cut an eighteen-inch square in her ceiling. Then he pushed away the excess insu-lation. He descended and collected the wooden two-by-fours he'd insert into the attic opening.

Then he heard footsteps.

"What are you doing here?" Grandpa Joe asked from the open doorway, his white cov-eralls a clue he'd come for the same purpose.

"Fixing the ceiling."

Grandpa Joe harrumphed and checked the consistency of the joint compound Mason had mixed. "A little watery, but it'll thicken before you apply it."

Mason climbed the ladder and positioned the wooden strips where he wanted them. "I've got it covered, Grandpa. You can take Goliath for a walk or maybe have a nap. Can you hand me that drill and a couple of those coarse dry-wall screws?"

"I don't need a nap." Grandpa Joe har-rumphed and passed the screws to him. "Why do young whippersnappers always think old people need naps? Why do you think you need to do everything for me?"

Mason whirred the drill and screwed the strips into place. Satisfied, he descended and found his grandfather waiting for an answer. "This whippersnapper would never underes-timate you—it was only a thought. And as for the ceiling, I had some free time. End of story."

"End of story, you mean end of discussion? Not quite." Grandpa Joe took the drill and picked up the premeasured drywall square. He climbed the ladder and scowled at the open space. "I thought Peter and I taught you better than this. Never cut corners. Anything worth pursuing is worth a little effort. Where are the arrows?"

Mason went and located a pencil and made the appropriate marks on the ceiling and the square. Then he removed the two screws from his pocket and drilled one in, followed by the other.

His grandfather checked his work.

"All I meant is you could go and have some

fun, Grandpa. No use in the both of us hanging out in here."

"This isn't drudgery for me."

Come to think of it, it wasn't for Mason, either. It had been a long time since they'd worked together, like when Mason was young and Grandpa Joe taught him how to construct a treasure box for his mother's birthday present. "Sounds like you're telling the wrong person to go home." Grandpa glared and flipped the fan to the next-highest speed, the wind rippling the curtains.

Once again, his grandfather wasn't listening to him. He loved Grandpa Joe and only wanted the best for him. Instead, his grandfather was like a force of nature Mason couldn't come to grips with. What would Grandma Betty say when she returned if Grandpa Joe wasn't the same as how she'd left him? "Aren't you supposed to be at the community center?"

Grandpa Joe examined the different size putty knives. "Brooke didn't schedule me for this afternoon. I've been doing overtime on the weekends, same as you. Keeps my mind off Betty and Bree, but I'm here now spending time with my grandson."

Since he crossed into adulthood, Mason had thought he no longer needed these bonding moments with his grandad. Maybe he did after all.

"Any word on when Grandma Betty is coming home?"

"Not soon enough, but Bree's progressing nicely. Love is what matters. But enough about me. Why are you avoiding Lindsay?"

"I'm going to put the tape around the perimeter, okay with you?" Without waiting for acknowledgment, Mason climbed the ladder. "And I'm not avoiding Lindsay. My extra shifts aren't about me. My new partner, Jordan, is getting his feet wet. He's the one filling in while Gina and Darius are out. I'm just monitoring him."

Mason ripped off a chunk of the tape with too much force, and the roll landed on the drop cloth. His grandfather tossed the roll up, and he caught it. "Thanks."

"And I suppose you skulking away to the Timber River Bar and Grill last week had everything to do with Jordan and nothing to do with Lindsay?"

Mason taped the other three sides of the perimeter and smoothed them flat against the ceiling. He had to come down off the ladder sometime. "Okay, that did have everything to do with me and Lindsay."

"Glad you can admit that. It might be time

you make some other admissions to yourself, too."

"Admissions are only worthwhile if you intend to act on them." Which he wouldn't.

"You should act on your feelings before someone else does, but you need to realize that for yourself."

Grandpa Joe slathered joint compound onto a three-inch putty knife and climbed the ladder, muttering something under his breath as he went.

Mason stirred the remaining joint compound, making it an even consistency. Grandpa Joe had been right about it being too watery before. "Are we tag teaming this job then?"

"Guess so. That ought to give me enough beauty time to prepare for my date."

Mason's jaw dropped, and his hand slid, causing the joint compound to spill onto the carpet, rather than the drop cloth. He tried to scoop the sticky substance back into the container, fuming that his grandfather had the nerve to stand there, smiling.

"I heard you wrong. Did you say *date*?"

"Yep." His grandfather came down the ladder. "Your grandmother even knows about the date and is quite supportive."

Mason had missed something, or he'd wake

up any minute now. He pinched himself and cried, "Ouch."

"Don't look so appalled. The date's with Chloe, and we're planting a flower tonight at Jasper and Jules's Garden Center for Earth Day. Lindsay's teaching the workshop." He guffawed and stirred the compound. "Like I'd mess up a good thing. Your grandma's the best."

Grandpa Joe laid the putty knife on the makeshift table.

"Grandpa." Mason wanted to prepare him for what would happen when his grandmother returned. "Shouldn't you pull back from Chloe and the Hudsons before you get too involved? Once everything's back to normal, you'll be spending your time with Grandma Betty. Chloe might get attached, and then when you don't come around as much anymore, she'll be devastated."

"Who says I plan on abandoning them when Betty comes home? They'll gain a grandma instead of losing a grandpa." He rearranged the tools on the table. "You can never have too much family. Lindsay, Evan, and Chloe are part of ours now. The demonstration at the garden center starts at six thirty if you want to see Lindsay in action."

Grandpa left, and it was Mason's turn to mutter something under his breath. His grandfather made him wonder who was taking care of whom here. Mason might be the person Grandma Betty enlisted to watch over Grandpa Joe, but it sure seemed as though he was taking care of Mason instead. Still teaching him a thing or two. Maybe it was time to listen and learn.

JASPER AND JULES'S GARDEN CENTER might be one of Lindsay's favorite places. Their selection of native plants of Western North Carolina, along with Jules's eye for container design, brought fans from as far away as Raleigh and Charlotte. With Joe's kind offer to take Evan and Chloe home after Lindsay's presentation for children and their guardians about how to grow flowers from seeds, she now had ten minutes for window shopping before ending her day.

Customers milled about the shop, chatting and choosing various plants and equipment to purchase. Lindsay eyed the long lines waiting to cash out with carts filled with trees, annuals and every garden implement available. She approached the fairy garden display and considered whether Chloe might be old enough for it yet.

"Lindsay, I thought you'd gone."

She turned and there was Jules, patting down a strand of her pixie-cut white hair. An inch shorter than Lindsay's average frame, Jules was a dynamo of energy.

Jules reached into her apron pocket and pulled out an envelope. "Here's the small token of appreciation we gave our workshop leaders. I wish it could be more."

Lindsay pushed Jules's hand back. "Can you donate that to the botanical garden instead?"

"It's a gift card, or else I would. Why don't you use it to buy the materials for a fairy garden for Evan and Chloe? Kids love them. We do a thriving birthday-party business on the weekends where each child leaves with an aquarium that has all the trimmings and a mini display." Jules picked one up for Lindsay's examination. "For those with younger siblings, we include a mesh lid that's childproof."

"I'll bring Evan and Chloe back after the dedication ceremony. They enjoyed tonight's class and especially planting the marigold seeds in the little clay pot they painted first." Almost as much as Joe had, from the look on his face.

His smile had widened when he told her Betty had called with good news right as he'd pulled into the last available parking spot at the garden center. She was finally coming home this weekend.

A timer pinged, and Jules smiled. "Time to award a door prize." She thrust the envelope at Lindsay. "Better yet, use this for a gift for yourself. Considering how many extra people you squeezed in for the workshop, I'll make a special starter fairy garden that's childproof and pretty for your kids. It'll be in my office the next time you drop by."

Before Lindsay could dissuade her or return the fee, Jules disappeared in the crowd. Lindsay marveled over the different fairy gardens in the different aquariums, each unique, each beautiful.

"Which is your favorite?"

Lindsay glanced over and there was Mason. That urge to brush the thick auburn lock of hair from his eyes, just to touch him, swelled in her, and she steadied her impulse. She should be mad at him about how they parted a week ago, but she had to be honest with herself. He called her bluff and, in doing so, it cooled anything going on between them. She should feel relief, but instead she struggled with everything he forced her to feel once more.

"You know this is Jasper and Jules's Garden Center and not the local auto parts store, right?"

"Grandpa Joe said you had a presentation tonight. Is it over?" Mason picked up one of the aquariums. "What does a mermaid have to do with gardening?"

"Yes, it's over, and that's a terrarium fairy garden. Later this fall, the Children's Play Zone at the botanical garden is going to have a display with gnome houses and more. It's a great way for parents to introduce their children to gardening and talk about the natural world around them." She stood on her tiptoes and tried not to inhale his fresh scent of soap and sandalwood and spring that was as aromatic as a bunch of roses. "The typical fairy garden also recycles materials available on hand. It's particularly appropriate since today is Earth Day."

"Is that why it's so crowded and why someone gave me a blue ticket when I entered?" Mason replaced the aquarium on the shelf and pulled out the ticket.

"Good evening to our customers who stayed with us until the end since you must be present to win our grand prize." Jules's voice came over the loudspeaker. "The winning number is two-four-six-eight." Jules chuckled. "Who do we appreciate? Mother Nature. Don't forget to plant a tree, go green and recycle. Make every day Earth Day."

Mason pocketed his ticket without looking at it, and Lindsay scowled. "Aren't you going to see if you won?"

"No. I'm sure someone else did."

"I haven't heard any shouts of glee. Give me your ticket." He rolled his eyes but handed it over anyway. There they were, the four correct numbers. She grabbed his arm and shrieked. "You won! Come on—Jules has been bragging about that basket every hour. I want to see what's in it."

Without thinking, she launched herself into his arms for a hug. The full contact with his hard chest sent alarms ringing through her. Not because there was anything wrong with the hug, though, but because everything was right. She jerked away and glanced at her clogs, too conscious of him and the undercurrent still between them.

"Will they give it to someone else if I don't claim it?" His expression gave no sign the embrace counted as anything but a congratulatory hug. Instead, he bent over and examined the closest display, which happened to be a coordinated group of houseplants. "I need a plant in my house. Something to welcome me home after Grandma Betty collects Grandpa Joe. Is this one easy to maintain?"

"It's a philodendron. It's great for removing

toxins from the air, but it's toxic to pets." Vetoing his selection, she went over and picked up a calathea instead. "This will be perfect in your living room. It likes a bit of shade and you only have to water it every week or two in the spring and summer. It's perfect for a bachelor. Now let's claim your prize."

"I'm not a gardener, Lin. Let someone who loves gardening win the basket." He examined the calathea from every angle and returned it to its spot.

"It's a basket, Mason, not a lifetime commitment."

He scoffed and tapped the terra cotta pot. "Trust me. I know the difference, and yet it seems all this is better suited to someone who has their yard mapped out."

"This isn't about the basket, is it? Are you saying people shouldn't branch out and try new things? And bachelor or not, we can still socialize." Her nostrils flared, and she reached for the calathea. "I'm buying this for you as a present."

"What I'm saying is you need someone like you." Mason glared at the calathea. "And I don't need a gift."

"Everyone loves gifts. It's like breathing. Besides, it'll add some color to your life. Your living room is monotone brown. A little green will go with the scheme just fine." She started walking to the end of the checkout line before changing direction for Jasper and Jules's office.

He followed her, and said, "I don't love gifts. It means you're obligated to someone."

She halted, and a cart skimmed her leg. "Don't stop in the middle of the aisle when it's close to closing time," muttered the woman who bumped into Lindsay and who now rushed toward the checkout.

Mason stared at the cutest display of gardening boots in a variety of prints from chickens to flowers to bumblebees. Next to it were a variety of wooden racks for boot storage. Lindsay stood in front of him, moving the calathea leaves aside so she could see his face better. "Gifts aren't obligations."

"Everything's an obligation."

"Family's not."

They glared at each other, and she kept hold of the ticket next to the terra-cotta pot containing the calathea.

"If I claim the basket, can everything return to the way it was?" he asked.

"If you claim the basket, will you let me buy this for you?" she asked.

The intercom crackled. "We are closing in fifteen minutes. Please take your purchases to the nearest register and thank you for shopping at Jasper and Jules's Garden Center. We open tomorrow at ten."

Lindsay blinked first. "This calathea needs a home. Chloe will name it for you, but she's twenty months old so you'll probably be stuck with a plant named Greenie."

"I'll accept it if we start talking at the fence again."

"Isn't that one of those obligations you just claimed to hate?" The electricity between them zinged, and she stared at his body language, the vibes coming off him spellbinding and strange. Well, not really, but she hadn't seen him like this around her, only around women he brought to social occasions or the like. Women he was interested in romantically.

"Our talks aren't obligations, Lin. They're fun. Both of us went into them needing a little levity and a shoulder to lean on during a tough time. I knew that's all they were, same as both of us know you'll end up with an extra houseplant if you buy this for me."

Did he think she only talked to him as an escape?

The fence talks were more than a way to end her day. He'd become her best friend. They'd shared everything over those countless hours. She'd assumed those times meant as much to him as to her, but had she been wrong? She'd best retreat before he bruised her heart.

Though it might be too late.

Still, she couldn't believe the meaningfulness of those talks was one-sided.

"It's a risk I'm willing to take."

"You always make it tough to say no to you." He reached for the plant and grinned. "Don't say I didn't warn you, though, when this ends up in your kitchen."

And, just like that, he'd given himself an out when he thought he needed it. That was Mason in a nutshell. She wouldn't give up. Not yet.

"But you'll claim the basket?"

"Will it make you happy?"

You'd make me happy. She discarded the thought. Being happy by herself and for herself was an adjustment, and the last time she loved someone, the fall had come without warning, breathless and hard, leaving her broken.

"Surprises make me happy." She hedged, wanting to be careful and cautious. No use getting burned by someone who had no intention of forming a commitment to a plant, let alone a person.

"Okay. We'll claim that basket before they put the merchandise back on the shelf."

On the shelf. Had she been on the shelf for the past few years? Or had she been going through the motions, playing at living so she could stay where it was safe, a place where she couldn't get hurt?

Jules was using the intercom to announce the store was now closed when they found her. Mason presented the ticket to Jules, and Lindsay peeked at the overloaded basket, and it was even better than she'd expected. Inside, there was a window box that held glistening metal tools and sharp shears. A green-and-gold reusable tumbler sat on a cozy green-and-gold blanket; a watering can, packets of seeds and an envelope nestled out of reach under the protective plastic wrap fixed with a bright green bow.

"What's in the envelope?" Lindsay asked.

"A one-hundred-dollar gift certificate with an added consultation for his yard with a design and maintenance plan." Jules accepted the ticket from Mason with a smile. "Glad one of Hollydale's first responders won the basket."

"Thanks. Is the yard consultation transferable? I'd like to give that to my grandparents."

Jules nodded. "Joe and Betty? For them, sure."

Mason pointed to the calathea. "And I'd like to buy that now if it's still possible."

"Actually, it's a gift from me." Lindsay reached into her purse and pulled out the envelope with the gift card Jules gave her earlier in the evening. "You sure have been handing these out tonight."

Jules reached over, clipping the tag off the houseplant. "People come in and spend three times as much when they bring a gift certificate. Besides, your presentation brought in customers, most of whom purchased something afterward, and we only awarded one grand prize. The rest of the door prizes were small, like a free flower, and only given on the hour."

Mason tried to hand the basket to Lindsay. "Grandpa Joe told me what time I was supposed to be here for the workshop. Since I missed it, please have this."

She nudged it over to him and picked up the calathea plant instead. "No, you won that fair and square. I'll help you spend the gift card, but it's time to bring some color into your yard, and I'm just the person who can do it."

CHAPTER THIRTEEN

MASON OPENED HIS back door and carried the bag of groceries into the kitchen. Something was wrong, but what? He had the answer almost as soon as he asked the question. There'd been no greeting. Not one hello, nor a dog racing up to him.

What was going on? Where was Grandpa Joe? Where was Goliath?

He lowered the groceries onto the counter and called out their names.

Checking the hook where his grandfather kept Goliath's leash and spying it empty and that Joe's jacket was gone told Mason what was up. Until now he hadn't realized how he'd grown accustomed to having the two of them greet him when he came home from shifts or errands. How had he never noticed the silence before?

Probably because Lindsay and the kids lived next door.

He'd placed the last container of yogurt in the refrigerator when the creaking of the front door signaled someone's return. The chiweenie flew to his side, greeting him with jumps and swipes of his tongue on Mason's jeans. His grandfather wasn't far behind, his grin stretching from ear-to-ear.

"Excellent timing. I just finished putting away the groceries. Is that why you're smiling?" Mason teased and bent down and gave Goliath some attention. Grandpa Joe peeked in the freezer.

"Any chance you bought butter pecan? And I'm not smiling because I got out of helping you. I talked to my beautiful bride during our walk." His grandfather's eyes glistened with love. For a moment, Mason was a little jealous.

"I didn't buy any ice cream, but how's Grandma Betty?" Mason straightened and folded the reusable bags. "And Bree?"

"Tristan's going to California for a business trip." Grandpa Joe's smile faded. "Betty's not coming home for another two weeks."

The normally jovial tone Mason loved hearing was missing, and he felt a need to cheer his grandfather up. "Why don't you visit her again and stay until you both come home? Surely they can do without you at the center for a couple of weeks."

"Trying to get rid of me that easily?" His grandfather nudged Mason's ribs.

Far from it. "I want what's best for you, Grandpa."

Was that a tear in his grandfather's eye? It must be the light.

"Ah, that makes this old heart proud to be your grandfather."

Mason gulped and shrugged. "I can keep a watch on your house if that's the problem."

Grandpa Joe shook his head. "Goliath has a vet checkup this week, and I have a couple of doctor appointments myself." He unclipped Goliath's leash. "And then there's my job. It's something I love doing."

Where did Mason see himself at his grandfather's age? A fair question, and one he'd never asked himself. Did he really want to be alone or on his own that far in the future?

Last week at the garden center, Lindsay had hugged him, her softness and excitement melding into him. Every spark of him had come alive for those brief seconds while they connected. After, she'd skirted away from him, giving him enough space to come to his senses.

"There are other jobs." Mason poked at the tile floor with his sneaker. "Why Hollydale? Why not move somewhere else you might like and enjoy?"

Although the question was finally out in the open, Mason was almost afraid of the answer.

"For one thing, you're here. So are our friends, many of whom are my family. They need me too." His grandfather arched an eyebrow and shook his head. "I'm seventy-five, Mason. I want to be useful to the town I love. Hollydale is special, it's my home."

His grandfather never ceased to amaze Mason.

"All right, Grandpa. Good to know. I suppose it's time for me to make dinner."

"It's too nice of a night to sit at home on a recliner eating a boring old supper."

They looked at each other and burst out laughing. "Is that a hint that you don't want me to make my legendary barbecue tofu bowl?" Mason exclaimed.

"*Legendary* is a word I wouldn't place in the same sentence as anything you made."

Mason flipped his grandfather's phone over and noted the time. Almost seven on this Saturday night. "I hear Mark at the Timber River Bar and Grill introduced a new veggie burger that's as good as beef ones."

"How about you try that while I order the real thing?" His grandfather perked up, so did Goliath. "Sorry, boy. You'll have to stay here and guard the house."

More laughter bubbled on Mason's lips. Goliath would merely lead a burglar to the refrigerator and wait for a snack. "It's a date then?"

Grandpa Joe nodded. "My calendar hasn't been this full in years."

A date with his grandfather on a Saturday night. Bachelor-track Mason would have once scoffed at the idea, but so what? This was what he and Grandpa Joe needed.

MASON MOVED THE pager around in his hands. A half-hour wait for a table in Hollydale?

"Do you feel like waiting that long?"

"If it's this or tofu, we'll stay here," his grandfather grumbled.

"There are nights I don't have time to eat on my shift, so a half-hour wait is nothing."

"Do you know that's the most you've ever said to me about your job?" Grandpa Joe leaned against the brick exterior of the bar, the late sunset and this sudden spring warm spell allowing them to wait outside rather than in the crowded interior.

"That can't be right. Surely I've mentioned details to you and Grandma Betty over Sunday dinner."

Grandpa Joe arched those bushy eyebrows of his and shrugged. "Name the last time you've eaten with us on a Sunday."

Mason searched his mind and couldn't remember when until he stumbled onto a memory. "I brought Lindsay and Evan and Chloe with me between Thanksgiving and Christmas."

"More like she brought you." Grandpa Joe chortled as he zipped up his jacket. "Not to mention that was months ago."

What was this? Attack Mason Week? First Lindsay accused him of not being grateful for gifts and gave him a hard time about their friendship, and his lawn, and now his grandfather was arguing with him after that heart-to-heart talk back at the house. Was Goliath the key to his getting along with Grandpa Joe? He couldn't take a dog everywhere, could he?

His grandfather shivered, and Mason fingered the buzzer once more. "Do you want to go somewhere else? Or should I check to see if they can seat us at the bar?"

"I'm not Evan or Chloe. I closed my jacket because I was cold, and I'm already warmer. I can wait like everyone else."

The tension between them lingered, and Mason relented. "Grandma Betty would never speak to me again if anything happened to you."

"And what about you?" His grandfather folded his arms across his chest. "How would you feel if something happened to me? Would you volunteer to work so everyone else could mourn my loss instead of you?"

That punch out of nowhere hurt more than the time a confused, angry patient clocked Mason's jaw. The buzzer lit up and vibrated before he could respond. Not that he knew how.

They remained silent as his grandfather opened the door for him. Still stunned, Mason handed the glowing buzzer to the hostess, unable to hide his trembling fingers. Grandpa Joe laid his hand on the back of Mason's hand. "I'm sorry. What I said was cruel and over the line."

Mason didn't know which was worse, the fact his grandfather's statement was blunt, or that it rang true. "Sometimes the harsh truth is a good wake-up call."

"Nothing excuses unacceptable behavior. Not age, not hunger, nothing." His grandfather followed the hostess, who seated them at a table next to a group of four women who were sharing a basket of wings.

"Joe!" His grandfather's boss, Brooke, jumped up with a smile. "It's wonderful to see you. When did you get here?"

His grandfather rose and stepped closer to the others. "A while ago. We waited outside." Grandpa Joe's cheeks reddened as the other three ladies joined Brooke in bragging over him.

"How's Betty?" More questions about their family followed.

At his earliest opportunity, Mason grabbed a menu and inspected the offerings. He peeked around the menu and spied his grandfather smiling and joking thanks to the attention from Betty's friends and the community center's director.

His grandfather had hit too close to home with his question. Tomorrow night at the fence he'd have to talk to Lindsay, make her see why he didn't want to attend the plaque ceremony. If he could convince her, maybe they could talk to Grandpa Joe together. His decision had nothing to do with mourning or grief, and everything with how he wanted to remember Tim. She'd understand. Deep down, he believed that, as much as he believed Grandma Betty would be home again when the timing was right.

Mason decided what he'd have to eat just as his grandfather, his ruddy cheeks glowing, finally pulled up his chair. Their server tapped Grandpa Joe's shoulder. "Where have you and your pretty bride been hiding lately?"

Despite the size of the noisy crowd, she listened while Grandpa Joe recited his story. Then she wrote their orders on her pad and scooted to another table. Brooke came over, leaned in and hooked her arm through Grandpa Joe's. "Mason, would you mind if we borrowed your grandfather for a minute? We'll return him—we promise."

"Be my guest." Mason rose and pointed to the other room. "If I'm not back when my order arrives, throw me a line and come get me. I'm going to see if anyone's up for a game of pool."

LINDSAY TESTED A dart in the back room of the Timber River Bar and Grill. Behind her, someone broke a rack of balls, and laughter ensued from the crowd surrounding the pool tables. She'd always preferred darts anyway, especially since her uncle Craig had taught her how to cast them. Even though she hadn't played for years, throwing something with a sharp point suited her mood.

An order for Asheville's Botanical Garden arrived at their facility today, only compounding a lousy week that had started with discovering that a contractor installed a subsurface drainpipe near the Children's Play Zone, rather than the Azalea Pathway. After a week of back-breaking work, she'd jumped at her aunt's offer to babysit Evan and Chloe so she could come here with Jillian and her friends for a fun night.

Except Jillian had deserted the table when the owner of the local outfitter appeared at the bar and Lindsay took that opportunity to escape to the back room with the pool tables and dartboard.

"Need a teacher?" Mason's voice sounded from behind her, and she faced him.

The low lights of the room glinted off his auburn hair, her gaze lingering on the black T-shirt, different from the tie-dyes he usually favored. It made him look even more attractive. She retrieved the bar's dart case from a shelf and handed it to him. "A bit presumptuous, don't you think?"

"That you want to learn to play darts? Why else would you be in here? Unless you're escaping people." Mason strolled toward the table and opened the case. "Hmm. Good quality."

He removed three darts from the case and then explained the rules and the scoring. After the rough week she'd endured, teaching him a lesson about presumptions was going to be fun.

Mason stood behind her, close enough for his breath to graze her cheek. The spicy scent of his cologne made her senses go haywire. Missing his friendship at the fence was only part of it. She'd missed his deep laugh and his ready wit. She'd missed him period.

He guided her shoulders and lifted her arm. "Balance your weight forward and keep a good grip on the dart, but make sure it's not too tight."

She nodded as he closed his hand over hers, the dart between her fingers, ready to throw. A sudden noise from behind caused the dart to go off course and into the wall, missing the dartboard completely. He shook his head and stepped back. "Then again, this might not be a good idea."

Already she missed the close contact. It was the best thing about her week so far, apart from the brief snippets of time she'd spent with Evan and Chloe at bedtime. "What? Are you worried word might get out that you're not an excellent teacher?" She leveled a challenge, knowing he wouldn't back down from that.

He laughed, and the server approached with a tray of beer mugs with frothy tops and several bottles. She delivered a bottle to Mason, and Lindsay ordered the same. There was something about the back room of a bar with a pool table and a dartboard that cried out for a beer rather than her usual Riesling.

An older man came up to them, his scowl visible in the dim light. "You two playing a game or what?"

Lindsay held her hand out to Mason to shake

it. "Come on. I promise no one will get hurt in the course of our friendly game, and it might do us both good."

Mason nodded. "Sorry, mister. One game, but it shouldn't take long."

Lindsay smiled wryly and nodded in return. The man grumbled into his beer and signed his name on the waiting list. "I'll be back in twenty."

The server brought Lindsay her beer, and she sipped it for courage. There was something distinctive and nutty about the taste that she rather liked. She could get used to the flavor.

"How about we just play a simple version called three-oh-one where we start with that many points and work down? To start, you have to shoot a double bull's-eye, that's one in the exact middle, and then the points are deducted from there." He proceeded with his first throw. "We each get three practice throws. Watch to see how it's done."

The first dart landed under the twenty in the double-score section, the second in the single bull's-eye zone and the last was a perfect bull's-eye. He might give her a run for her money. "That's some serious casting. Have you had the same type of week I've had?"

"Just a terrible night." He approached the board and yanked out his three darts, not blinking at her slip of the tongue that gave away she knew something about darts. "It seems you're not the only one who's taken note of my intention to skip the dedication ceremony," he said.

She wasn't surprised he hadn't changed his mind. "Who said something upsetting to you?" She stepped to the line and purposely threw them in the single-score range of the one, two and three. "That's good, right? I hit the board."

"Not quite, unless you're playing a game called Around the Clock, where you start with one and end up at twenty. Grab your darts." He sipped his beer and motioned to the board. "My grandfather thinks I should go to the ceremony and spoke his mind about it."

"How about you tell me the real reason behind your decision not to be there?" She went to the board and gripped the darts. "And not some convenient excuse. I want the truth this time."

"The person who did better in the practice round usually gets to go first. Does that work for you?"

She nodded. She only had one intention: closing out the game on her first turn. Once Uncle Craig had joined Aunt Hyacinth and their guests, Lindsay would spend hours practicing her throwing technique, enjoying the time away from her overprotective mother.

"As long as you come clean." She sipped her beer and settled on the stool next to the table.

He sat next to her and took a long moment to finish off his beer. "Grandpa Joe might have to drive me home." He set the bottle on the table and looked at her. "I don't want to remember Tim as a name on a stone or on a nice plaque. He was more than that, you obviously know that. Seeing him in that sense when he should be here with you and Evan and Chloe…"

The raw voice matched his bare honesty, revealing the real reason he didn't want to be at the botanical garden.

"It's about how he lived his last moments, Mason. Doing his duty. This isn't reducing him to a line on a plaque—it's a way for his memory to live on," Lindsay tried to explain.

"You believe in this. Your voice, your stance. And that's a good thing. But for me, this is different and personal." He glanced at her, and something like regret flickered in his blue eyes.

He stood and they resumed their game. He hit a bull's-eye. Twenty points. But her confidence in the dart lessons her uncle taught her remained, although at this rate she worried she wouldn't get a chance to prove herself.

On his next throw, he hit another dead center. Here he was, running the board before she even had a turn.

"I understand your point, but I don't understand—why don't you tell Joe that? The same way you just told me."

"I could use the moral support when I do." He threw another dart and reduced his points by eighteen.

Maybe a distraction would help. "How about this? We'll make our game a little more interesting. If you win, I'll talk to your grandfather for you."

"Great. Seeing as I'm ahead and having seen how you throw, that's a done deal," he said in a teasing tone.

"What if I win? What do I get?" She kept her tone light enough for him to believe there was no chance of that happening. Sure, she was playing him a bit, but she wondered what he thought would match an honest heart-to-heart with Joe.

He eyed her and then removed the three darts from the board. He returned and shrugged, that gleam a little too sparkly for her taste. "You've worked eight days in a row, haven't you?" She nodded. "If you win, you do something that doesn't involve gardening. Try something new."

She sipped her beer, considering his offer. "I won't have time for that for about seventeen more years."

He squinted at the dartboard and then at her. "I remember those barbecues where we had so much fun and there was music and games and… What happened to that woman?" He turned bright red. "Not that I saw you as you then."

"You saw me as Tim's wife then."

He relaxed his shoulders. "Exactly."

But did he see her in a different light now, the way she noticed everything about him? She couldn't pinpoint what quality she first saw in him, but his unexpected layers drew her in and fascinated her. The same man could gently explain something to Chloe one minute and then his blue eyes could turn navy when his gaze made contact with Lindsay's the next.

She sipped her beer, growing more and more accustomed to the full richness of the taste. "I understand."

"Do you?"

They were dancing around something they'd started by the fence a year ago. This attraction went deep down to her bones.

"I understand more than you know."

"Well, you should have more fun in your life. You need people."

"And you don't?" she asked.

"Trust me—I'm learning to navigate the boundaries with my grandfather every day."

To Mason's credit, he'd been working on his relationship with Joe, something neither of them realized needed the same fine care as an orchid. A beautiful flower, but one notoriously difficult to grow, requiring a delicate balance of sunlight, temperature and water.

"What are we waiting for, then? We have a bet, and that guy will be back soon."

Mason cast another dart and reduced his score by ten just as the pool players burst into loud cheers. In the process of throwing the next dart, he missed.

"Oh, that's a hard break."

He removed his darts and settled on the stool. "Then again, I can't get too comfortable. I'll put you out of your misery soon enough," he said.

Except this wasn't misery.

She set down her beer and grinned at him. "Hold that thought." Extra pressure rarely bothered her. She hefted one of the darts and then rolled it in her fingers to gauge the weight of it and how that would affect her throw. She stepped to the line and let the first bull's-eye land in the middle of the board. She flashed him a smile. "Wow, you're a brilliant teacher."

She concentrated on her next aim and went on a run before throwing her last dart, another bull's-eye to end the game. She wiped her hands and pulled the three darts out of the board.

His mouth gaped, and his eyes narrowed. "You've played before."

"You assumed I hadn't. Never presume." She placed the darts in the case. "Sometimes you can tell someone you're capable, but sometimes you have to batten down the hatches and just deliver."

"Message received." His lips twitched before let loose with a laugh. "And I thought I knew everything about you."

"I hope there's still a lot to learn." He nodded and smiled at her. "What are you going to try that doesn't involve gardening?" When she put his darts away too, he asked, "Are you secretly a pool shark or do you want to come back next week for a game?"

The grumpy man returned and arched a brow.

"That's our cue to leave." She started to walk away. "Besides, I have to get back to my group of friends I deserted. See you tomorrow night at the fence." She waved and returned to the booth in the back corner with Becks Porter and the others.

Becks smiled and introduced Lindsay to Penelope and Kris, who looked familiar.

"I was wondering if you'd walked home,"

Becks said. "I ordered several appetizers, and they should be here any minute. I was just telling Penelope and Kris about my recent investment, a couple of abandoned buildings by Sully Creek. I'm starting a soccer complex, which should keep me busy for a while. Penelope's reviewing the contracts for me. She's my lawyer." Becks placed her glass on a coaster and scooted over on the bench, making more room for Lindsay. "Jillian's still at the bar, but, in the meantime, the rest of us single ladies have to stick together."

After a hard divorce, Becks had moved back to Hollydale. The food arrived, and the evening passed with jokes, stories and laughter. Sitting back after a last bite of bread pudding, Lindsay spotted Mason helping his grandfather with his jacket.

She noticed Kris watching him as well, and then Kris faced Lindsay, her brown eyes highlighting her flawless skin. "I know I should know you, but I just moved back to Hollydale. Have I seen you around the elementary school? Perhaps one of your children is in my class." Kris reached for a peanut and popped it in her mouth.

"Evan's four and Chloe's not even two yet. Somewhere else maybe?"

"Most likely I've seen you at The Busy

Bean. My mom owns the coffeehouse. Wait a minute! You live next door to Mason, don't you? That's where I know you from." She snapped her fingers. "Mason and I went to one of your barbecues ages ago."

"Oh, that's right. I'm sorry I didn't recognize you. It's been a while." Lindsay felt bad she hadn't figured out the connection quicker.

Kris gestured in Mason's direction and then broke into a chuckle. "We dated a couple of times, but that ship sailed away ages ago. He let me down gently, and then I met my daughter Gigi's father. In the end, it all worked out. I was never sure Mason was the serious type about relationships, anyway."

Lindsay had seen how Mason treated his romantic relationships, making it clear all along he wasn't that interested in something permanent, but this confirmed it. Who was the real Mason Ruddick? The grandson who fretted over his grandfather and took Joe's criticism to heart? The paramedic who reassured Evan after his asthma attack? The genuine guy who held her close after she almost fell through the ceiling, so close she could feel his rapid heartbeat?

There were obviously more layers to him than the one he cultivated as the fun, footloose, single guy about town.

She could fall for the man if given half the chance, but then what? He'd simply tell her the same thing about not wanting to settle down once he was ready to move on. And she'd risk their friendship in the bargain.

No, she had to keep her feelings to herself, not only for herself, but for her children, who'd be devastated without Mason in their lives.

And wouldn't she feel the same?

CHAPTER FOURTEEN

SPRING WAS IN full force, beautiful one day with a hopeful promise of summer, the next overcast and cold. The cooler temperature was more than enough indication Mother Nature had some surprises in store before the gardenias bloomed in June. At Sycamore Station, Lindsay shivered and rose from the flower bed. She brushed the soil off her gloves and glanced around. The memorial circle was now 60 percent complete, a mere two weeks until the ceremony.

"You're the person I've been searching for." Her boss's authoritative voice boomed and she joined him at the base of the sycamore tree.

"The fungicide worked well." Lindsay examined the tree for any further signs of deterioration but found none. "By now, we'd have known if the gash caused more damage, so I think the tree's in the clear."

"Good, good, but that's not why I'm here," Phillip said.

If this was about her reminding Heather

she was planting the hostas too close together, Lindsay might take the rest of the day off. As it was, this was now the tenth day in a row she'd worked.

"Excuse me, but we'd like to take a selfie with the sycamore." Two visitors, one with a selfie stick, were polite in their request, and Phillip ushered Lindsay over to her rolling cart.

"I've been talking to Heather." Phillip picked up a spray bottle and examined the nozzle.

"I spent hours that day replanting hostas—"

"No, no, I'm speaking personally, not professionally." Phillip flashed a smile before examining the cannas in the circle. "What are your plans here?"

She looked to the lamb's ears for the border to go along with the creeping phlox.

"I'm planting these, deadheading those flowers and then checking on the greenhouse filtration system."

The two visitors left the area just as new people arrived.

"Well, I'm checking in with employees. Nice to see attendance is good today. That lovely sycamore's one of our biggest attractions, isn't it," Phillip said, as if Lindsay didn't already know this. She could almost see the dollar signs in his eyes.

"We should have closed it off until the grand

opening." She placed the water bottle he'd taken back in the cart. "Can this discussion wait?"

"Let me rephrase my earlier question. What are your long-term plans?"

"Continuing on like always." She loved her job, so much so that she and Tim had argued days before the accident about her continuing to work after Chloe was born. Lindsay sipped from her water bottle and considered why Phillip would ask something like that. One possibility hit her like falling timber. If attendance figures continued to free-fall, Phillip could be looking to downsize the staff. "Is there something wrong with my performance? My evaluation's not for another three months."

"You're right, it's not, but didn't you mention something about Tim's parents driving here from Wilmington for the dedication?"

Phillip came all the way from the main administrative offices to the southernmost tip of the gardens to ask about Tom and Donna?

"I did, and they are." She liked her home and being near Aunt Hyacinth in Hollydale, and the kids loved the mountains and their friends. That precluded any possibility of a move. "What do my in-laws have to do with my schedule or job performance?"

"Didn't you see that email I sent you from

the director of one of the largest botanical gardens in the state? He and I happened to meet during my recent vacation to Wilmington and hit it off, having adult children and being the alumni of the same college. He called me this morning to let me know he's retiring."

"Good for him. If he's looking for a mountain cabin, Robin at Cobb Realty is amazing. Comes highly recommended."

"You haven't responded yet about whether you'd be interested in the Wilmington posting, the one with the larger salary and better benefits. Closer to Tim's family, too."

"I'm sorry, Phillip. I still don't think I'm on the same page. I didn't think I needed to answer that email since I wasn't planning on applying." She rubbed her eyes and reached for her pruning shears. "If that's all, I have lots of things to do before the greenhouse filtration system."

"But you'll look at the email and give the job some consideration?"

"Only if you do the same." That slight exasperation in her voice was unlike her, but she couldn't help it. "Now that you also have a tie to the area, Phillip, and your youngest started college, a new challenge might be right up your alley."

"Heather wouldn't hear of it, but it would be

a raise and advancement for you, something you're not likely to find here."

"Oh, ok-ay. Thanks for telling me." Satisfied he'd leave her in peace, she set about her duties and he hurried away.

MASON ATTACHED A manual block sander to a pole in Lindsay's guest room. Then he climbed the ladder. Grandpa Joe walked in, whistling a Beatles tune.

"Good afternoon. Lovely day, isn't it?" His grandfather came over and inspected the joint compound, which Mason had already prepared for the next step. "Perfect, absolutely perfect. I just got off the phone with Bree."

Mason laid the pole across the top rung of the ladder and rushed down. "Did she get her scan results?" *Please let her be in the clear.* Otherwise, the doctors would have to order chemotherapy or radiation or both. He whipped out his phone. He checked his texts. "Hmm, no update."

"There aren't any yet. It was a simple grandfather, granddaughter chat, that's all."

It must be the day for that type of talk as he'd spoken to Grandma Betty earlier, reassuring her he was looking after Grandpa Joe. They'd laughed over his grandfather's first taste of turkey bacon, which he'd proclaimed pretty good.

"Okay, then." Mason climbed the ladder once more, not wanting the joint compound to set. Sanding the ceiling first would allow for a more even coat of mud.

"Are we still on the second coat?" Grandpa Joe asked.

"Yep." He'd half expected his grandfather to have done this step by now. "You won't be able to tell anything ever happened by the time Lindsay's parents arrive for the dedication."

No sooner had he said the words than he wanted to take them back. He'd opened a hornet's nest. If only he'd won that bet with Lindsay, she'd be beside him for moral support or even be the one doing the talking. Although the way she'd surprised him and thrown a darn good dart curled his lips into a smile. Just when he thought he'd known everything about her, she kept him on his toes. Made his toes curl, too.

His smile faded. Losing that dart game was probably for the best. Lindsay shouldn't be the one dealing with his grandfather. He needed to speak up.

"Most people wouldn't know anything about their neighbor's parents." Grandpa Joe glanced around the room. "You and Lindsay are close, aren't you?"

"We've been friends for a long time, but our patio and fence conversations didn't take off until a year ago. Now she's my best friend."

He'd arrived home one night and found Lindsay in her backyard, staring at the stars; at first, he'd thought something had to be wrong, but there wasn't. Apart from a woman trying to come to terms with what life had dealt her. And not just for her own sake, but for the sake of Evan and Chloe, too. She waited until he finally came over and spoke to her, then she opened up about her day. Pretty soon the floodgates gaped, and he found her the easiest person to talk to. When she glanced at her watch, they laughed at how three hours flew by so fast.

Ever since, he'd discovered an appreciation for how she held everything together. And how her beauty radiated from within.

Grandpa Joe stirred the compound and whistled more of the song, moving his hips in time to the rhythm. "There's not a doubt in my mind that you never noticed her as a woman while Tim was alive, but now you have. What's next?"

Nothing. It was obvious she was still in love

with Tim. She was so committed about the dedication.

"We go on with our lives." Mason finished sanding the ceiling and descended the ladder. "As friends and nothing more."

"You won't get anywhere with that type of attitude. Sometimes you have to go for it. Did you two have a fight when you played darts? I noticed you were a trifle cross when you came back. I, on the other hand, had a fantastic time that evening." He started whistling an old Stones classic, moving his shoulders in time. "Don't wait up too late for me tonight. I've got a miniature golf game with friends, and then tomorrow it's Karaoke Night at the Timber River Bar and Grill. I'm thinking about 'Born to Be Wild.'"

Taken aback by his grandfather's sudden full social calendar, Mason located the three-inch putty knife on the makeshift worktable and added enough mud for the application of the second coat. He climbed the ladder once more, wondering if his next call should be to his grandmother. "Isn't it time to act your age?"

With broad strokes, Mason covered the lines of the fiberglass tape with the joint compound, taking care to trace the rectangular perimeter. He came down and swapped out the smaller putty knife for the larger version, scooping up enough mud for the interior of the rectangle where Lindsay had fallen through. Like a yo-yo, he stepped up to the plate once more.

"You left a glob at the corner. Smooth it out." Mason glanced at his grandfather, who stopped whistling and folded his arms. "I'd say you were the one acting younger than Chloe with this attitude."

And now back down again. There wasn't anything else Mason could do for the ceiling until this coat dried, then he'd apply the third one before sanding everything and painting it smooth.

He faced Grandpa Joe. Maybe he should just be honest with the man.

"I leveled with Lindsay about the real reason I don't want to attend, and she seemed to accept it. I don't want to feel as though I'm reducing Tim to fine print on a plaque. The ceremony is for those who want one. I can understand that." Mason rubbed at his jaw.

"I see where you're coming from. Don't think I agree with you. Showing respect to Tim should be embraced no matter what the circumstances." His grandfather leaned in and patted his shoulder. "But you're my grandson and I want to make sure you're feeling alive and living life to the fullest."

Mason blinked. Of course, he was living

life to the fullest. "That's what I do. Live for the moment."

"Without anyone at your side."

Life was easier that way. "Makes it a lot less complicated to hit the open road whenever I want."

His grandfather looked at him hard. "That works up to a point. I love you, Mason, but is it that you're afraid you might end up on that plaque? And if so, you're wondering who'd make sure they spelled your name right? Who'd keep your memory alive?"

Had that been the problem all this time? It could easily have been Mason on that helicopter. Was it guilt for Tim dying? Or was it guilt about being the one who lived? Was that the reason he didn't want to go to the ceremony?

Mason placed the lid on the compound. "You and Grandma would keep my memory alive. Mom and Dad. Bree." He'd also like to think Lindsay would remember him.

But that would be selfish of him to expect her to mourn him.

"What about Jordan?" Grandpa had been listening.

Mason gathered the putty spreaders so he could wash them. "I see what you're doing."

"What I'm doing is living." Grandpa lowered his hands and performed a smooth putting motion. "Eighteen holes of fun surrounded by a group of kind people. Can't beat that at my age."

Grandpa Joe crossed the threshold, and Mason called out. "Grandpa Joe!" His grandpa turned to him. "Can you understand why I don't want to go?"

"Oh, I understand perfectly, but remembering someone by honoring their service shouldn't be an issue." He returned, reached up and patted Mason's cheek. "It's all in how you see things. For instance, there was once a gaping hole in that ceiling. Now it's being repaired. It doesn't mean it wasn't there. It means hard work and effort fixed it up, and that took time and sacrifice, but it was worth it. Think about it, Mason."

His grandfather left, whistling once more. If Mason went to the dedication, he'd be seeing how much Lindsay still loved Tim. He clenched his fists, unwilling to hold on to hope he had something to do with the spark of life reignited these days in Lindsay's eyes.

But if he didn't attend? He'd risk losing the respect of some people he cared about most in his life.

LINDSAY CARRIED THE tray of homemade guacamole and chips, her thank-you to Mason for the work on her ceiling earlier today, to the small table between the Adirondack chairs. Then she rearranged her glass of wine and Mason's beer before she sat and looked to the west.

The silhouette of the Great Smoky Mountains provided the perfect backdrop for the full moon, rising high. In the distance, a barn owl screeched, starting its nightly hunt. She settled back and let her neck muscles relax against the headrest. Comfortable, she closed her eyes for a minute, only to open them when a chill descended on her.

A quick peek at her watch bolted her out of her chair. She'd fallen asleep for an hour. She checked the chair next to her. No Mason. Then she checked the guacamole. No indentations there. He'd never arrived.

Hustling inside, she reached for her coat, needing warmth as the nights were colder in the mountains than other parts of the Tar Heel State. She also grabbed the nursery monitor she kept for such occasions.

She knew where Mason was.

She knocked on his garage door. Sure enough, he opened it, a narrow gap that wasn't an invitation to enter. "Lindsay."

"I know my name. Funny how you forgot about tonight."

He ran his hand through his rumpled hair. "Who says I forgot? I finished my bike."

His shiny motorcycle took center stage in the middle of the garage. She squealed and elbowed past him. "It's beautiful!" She glanced at him, his excitement radiating from him. "Can I say that?"

He covered the rearview mirrors with his hands. "He's sensitive. Handsome at the very least." He winked, and she grinned.

"And thanks for your work on my ceiling, Mason. It looks great." Only ten days until her parents arrived. A series of yips caught her attention, and she glanced around. "Is that Goliath? Where's Joe?"

Mason looked surprised now. "I lost track of time, and Goliath needs to go outside. Grandpa Joe is fine, but he's sort of embraced the bachelor life."

"Goliath can run around my backyard while you explain what you mean by your grandfather acting like a bachelor when he's devoted to your grandma Betty. This might take a while, and I need to be closer to my house." She raised the nursery monitor.

Within minutes, they settled on her patio, and the active dog begged for a tortilla chip. She couldn't resist the little fellow.

"Now he'll keep wanting more." Mason

scooped some guac in a chip and downed it. "I didn't eat dinner. Thanks."

She rolled her eyes and went inside, checking on her kids before grabbing a plate of leftovers for Mason and returning. Mason picked up the chicken quesadilla and bit off a good chunk.

"What's this about Joe?" she asked.

He polished off the first quesadilla and washed it down with a sip of beer. The second and third disappeared in a flash. Goliath ran over to her feet once more. She slipped him another chip.

"When you and I were playing darts, he accepted an entire month's worth of engagements." Mason reached for the last quesadilla and chomped on it.

"Isn't that what you wanted?" She loaded a tortilla chip with guac and ate it before tossing another to Goliath.

"Maybe at first, but things change."

She reached for another chip, and her fingers brushed his, that electric spark almost making her jump. Her gaze met his, and that intensity jarred her. Yanking her hand back, she blinked when Goliath jumped onto her lap and licked the salt off her face.

"Calm down, Goliath." The dog settled, his eyes heavy. "Good dog," Mason said.

She petted Joe's dog until gentle snuffles of sleep overtook the little chiweenie.

"So, you don't want your grandfather having fun while your grandmother's out of town? And, in case you forgot, we have a date with Joe tomorrow at Jasper and Jules's Garden Center to spend your gift card." She kept her voice as soft as possible; Goliath's snuffles were quite adorable.

"When you put the question like that, I sound rather controlling if I stand in his way." He laughed and ate another chip, the intensity of a minute ago gone, replaced by that laid-back goofy grin she loved so much.

"There are words to describe you, but *controlling* is not one of them."

He met her gaze once more. "And how would you describe me if someone asked?"

Caught off guard, she wanted to make an excuse and retreat to the house, but the weight of the dog prevented that. The Mason of a month ago wouldn't have asked that, assured in himself and his reputation. Now it was almost as if he was allowing her in, valuing her opinion of him.

"I guess it would depend on who asked and why. Take the other night. Destinee would have loved it if I'd pulled her aside and told her something personal that would get you to notice her."

A wry smirk crossed his face, and he scooped more guac and ate another chip. "And what would you have told her?"

"For me to have said that, it assumes you've noticed me."

His soft gaze confirmed what they both knew and couldn't avoid anymore. He'd noticed her, not as Tim's widow but as Lindsay. Her heart skipped a beat. Mason stood, his hands reaching for her, then pulling her up, much to Goliath's dismay. The dog snorted and curled up on the deck. Mason cupped her face, his hands warm.

"I think we both know I have."

"Hello?" Joe's voice called out from Mason's yard. "Goliath? Mason?"

Goliath's ears perked up, and he yipped a welcome to his owner. The chiweenie zipped through the open gate.

"Goliath!" Joe's voice sounded panicked. "Come back here!"

Mason hurried after the dog. "Goliath!"

Lindsay grabbed the bowl of chips, hoping food might aid in bringing back the dog. A noise from inside the house stopped her, and she opened the sliding glass door. Evan was standing on the step stool, reaching for a cup.

"I was thirsty and heard Grandpa Joe. Is Goliath okay?"

Her phone pinged a text with one word appearing on her screen. Safe.

She nodded and poured Evan some water. "Mason let me know he's okay."

If only she could say the same for her heart.

CHAPTER FIFTEEN

MASON DROPPED THE tailgate of Lindsay's truck. "Was all of this necessary?"

She gave one emphatic nod and started removing his myriad purchases. "Your lawn has been in serious need of TLC for years. I've been itching to help you plant perennials and hostas and more, but you weren't ready until now."

Until his grandfather had moved in with him, that is, and began sharing his wisdom daily, he'd never considered himself ready for everything life offered most people. Maybe it wouldn't be selfish forming attachments even with the risks associated with Mason's particular career.

"I think we bought out the store this morning. Do they have new stock to replace all the plants and flowers we purchased?"

"Jasper and Jules have been at this a long time. They're experienced at inventory." Lindsay handed Evan a small bag of soil, so he'd feel useful, but nothing too heavy, while giving Chloe a box of sidewalk chalk. "Jules was right when she said the gift cards pay for themselves. I'm just glad everything checked out with the sycamore, and I was able to join you at the nursery earlier than planned."

His phone rang, and he looked at the screen. "Can you carry on without me for a few minutes?"

After she nodded, he connected with Bree. "Hi, sis. What news?"

"I must have the wrong number. You have the same voice as my brother, but you're what I would call chipper." She laughed, perhaps the first genuine laugh since her diagnosis.

"And you're sounding more like the—" he caught himself before he said the word *old* "—like Bree. So how was your scan?"

"I'm on the mend. No chemo, no radiation. My margins are clear."

He closed his eyes, gratitude washing over him, and he fell into one of Lindsay's Adirondack chairs. "That's amazing, Bree. I'm so happy for you and Tristan. And Grandpa Joe too."

"About that."

Hesitancy was back in her voice, and he was glad he was sitting down. "Why do I have a feeling Grandma Betty hasn't booked her return flight yet?"

"Because she hasn't. I have more news. You remember Tristan went on a month-long work trip." Excitement now dominated her tone, and he let out the deep breath he'd been holding. "He received a promotion."

"And, let me guess, more hours, so more responsibility, and more time Grandma Betty will be spending with you?" Would he have to be the person who'd convey this message to Grandpa Joe?

"You're only mostly right. The reason I need Grandma Betty is we're moving to Atlanta! We'll be closer, and after we're settled in our new house, we're driving her back and Tristan and I will visit with you and Grandpa."

"What about your treatment in Nashville? Your doctors?"

"They have those in Atlanta, too." That teasing note he hadn't heard in a long while also reassured him. "By then, I'll even be finished with the scarf I'm knitting you."

"Scarf?"

"It started as socks and it still might end up as a blanket. I'm not sure yet. Grandma keeps clucking at me, and she says I'm already a pro at dropping stitches." Voices sounded in the background. "Gotta go. Realtor's here. Give Grandpa Joe a great big hug for me. Love ya."

"Right back at you." Mason stared at the silent phone. He rubbed his temple before standing and placing it in his pocket.

He found Grandpa Joe helping Hyacinth unload the last supplies from the back of the truck. The two of them appeared deep in conversation, so Mason glanced at the sky, the dome a perfect blue with nary a cloud in sight. Once everyone scattered for lunch, he thought, he'd head out for the first time on his motorcycle and figure out how to break the news of yet another delay in Grandma Betty's homecoming to Grandpa Joe. Albeit a temporary one. For now, he wanted nothing spoiling this moment.

Goliath barked and ran over, nipping Mason's heels. Mason moved toward Lindsay, but first paused and watched her nimble fingers. She knelt by the row of bushes at the side of his house, her face shielded with a light blue wide-brimmed hat.

He approached, and she glanced up. "Was that work or family?"

He wasn't sure there was a difference. As far as he was concerned, his fellow paramedics and first responders in Hollydale were like family to him.

"That was Bree." He knelt beside her.

She placed the trowel on the dirt and focused on him. "How's she doing? Any updates?"

Lindsay leaned in toward him as though her whole day pivoted around his answer. This wasn't simply casual interest. She cared about Bree and Grandpa Joe and Grandma Betty as if they were members of her family.

While Lindsay's lopsided smile and soft curves accounted for the physical pull, he found himself in a deep hole of attraction for this intelligent and intriguing woman.

"There's a fresh problem on the horizon."

"Did something else show up on her latest medical test?" Lindsay reached out and touched his arm, her instant support another quality he found endearing.

"Her prognosis is good." He glanced toward Grandpa Joe, his face animated as he described last night's golf outing to Chloe, his voice exaggerated for extra effect. "However, there's news on the Grandma Betty front, and it isn't great."

"Make yourself useful and dig with me as you fill me in. This is your yard we're making beautiful."

They worked in sync and talked about Tristan and Bree's latest update. He couldn't help but peek at Grandpa Joe, Goliath at his feet, playing with Chloe. "We're growing closer, but I'm concerned about him moving back home before Grandma Betty's return."

"Aw, that's sweet. So, it's his possible reaction to yet another delay and not the move that's worrying you."

"It's both, and hey, I'm not the worrying type." Mason reached for the next plat of impatiens and lifted one from its nesting place. He then planted it, smoothing the mound in the same manner as Lindsay had.

"You're so cute sometimes."

"Only sometimes?" He grinned.

"You're insufferable all the time, and cute most of the time." She grinned back, her sly smile wide enough for conveying she was in on the joke.

"The lady thinks I'm cute." He collapsed backward in the grass, and Goliath ran over and licked Mason's face.

Lindsay laughed and reached for his hand to pull him upright. "And insufferable."

"Well, you're cute all the time." He tapped her nose affectionately, the shock sparking through his body, too aware of her as more than just his neighbor.

It took a herculean effort not to kiss her right in front of everyone. More and more, every time he did anything with her, he was finding it harder and harder not to kiss her.

Her eyes widened, and she rose as if the

change in their relationship was now irrevocable.

Goliath yipped once and then returned to Grandpa Joe's side. "Abandoned by a dog."

"You'll live." Lindsay gathered the gardening implements and stepped back. "That looks a sight better, doesn't it?"

Even though he knew she meant their handiwork, he only had eyes for the woman standing beside him, her honey-brown hair glinting in the spring sun, her wide cheeks blooming pink. "Yes."

She faced him and tapped his arm with her gloves. "We need a cold drink. Follow me."

She went over to the small refrigerator in his garage and handed him a bottle of water. "Now that we've stopped for a break, you can fill me in on the rest of that phone call. For someone whose sister is moving closer to him, you don't seem that excited."

"She'll have a different set of doctors, and her support system in Atlanta won't be the same. I just want her to stay confident. She's gotten such good care in Nashville."

She sipped from her reusable water bottle. "So, you think a support system in place outweighs job advancement? Is one more important than the other?"

"I didn't say that. Bree's situation is unusual." He uncapped the bottle. "For the most part, though, I believe if there's something you want, go for it."

Why couldn't he go for it with Lindsay?

Tim, Colette, my job. All of that held him back. If he gave all of himself, he wouldn't be able to run anymore.

But the spark between them soared again, warming him from head to toe. For a second, he considered pouring the bottle of cold water over his head. Then a calmness came. Taking a chance on her would be worth everything. "Lindsay—"

"Have you ever been to Wilmington?"

"Of course. It's a great surfing town. Love the A-frame barrels there."

She paused and took another drink. "Tim's parents live there, you know."

"No, I didn't." Or at least he didn't remember that. "But Bree is moving to Atlanta, not Wilmington."

"Their botanical garden is searching for a new director. I don't think Bree would be qualified for that."

No, but Lindsay would. Suddenly he felt as though that cold water had drenched him. "You're definitely qualified, probably over-qualified."

She sighed and focused on her aunt Hyacinth who peeked at them for a second, but she backed away. "As far as support systems go, mine is here, but Phillip thinks I should apply for the job and go for it, as you said."

"Is the job right for you?" His heart thudded while awaiting a response. Hiring Lindsay would be the best thing any organization could do for itself. Dazed, he bumped into a row of waiting planters.

"The pay's great as are the benefits, including an extra week of vacation, plus Tim's parents would become more active in the kids' lives."

What about us? He kept from shouting out.

If Lindsay moved from Hollydale, another person he cared about would be gone, and it wouldn't be just Lindsay who'd leave, it'd be Evan and Chloe, too.

Yet he couldn't ask her to stay. Not for him.

"Sounds like you have a lot to think about. I'd best get back to work. It's my yard, and I can't slack off." He hurried off and ran into the exact person he was looking for, his grandfather.

Grandpa Joe backed up. "Haven't seen anyone in that much of a rush since your grandmother moved to save those chocolate chip cookies that almost burned."

"Speaking of Grandma Betty..."

Grandpa Joe held up his hand. "I already know. Bree and Tristan are getting a fresh start. A new house, a new lease on life. Can't beat that for my granddaughter. My bride will be back soon enough."

Mason opened his mouth to reply, but no words tumbled out. He should have known Grandma Betty would tell Grandpa Joe. Of all the different reactions, this wasn't one he'd expected.

Same as he hadn't anticipated Lindsay going anywhere. And what did he expect?

For Lindsay to meet him by the fence every night for the rest of her life?

For them to grow old together, her single and alone in her house and him in his?

Nothing stayed the same forever, not even the best things life had to offer.

He scrubbed his chin and stared at his grandfather. "How can you stay so calm? Don't you sort of feel like she's pushing you away by staying there so long?"

"My Betty's as true as the day is long." He patted Mason on the back. "There's so much in this world that changes, but Betty's my constant, no matter where we are."

Goliath ran toward Joe, and his grandfather bent and picked up the small dog. The children and Hyacinth also found their way over.

"My dear, your cheeks are too pink." She waggled her finger at Lindsay. "Gardening should be a delight, a feast for the eyes and a balm for common ailments such as heightened blood pressure. You need an evening free of concerns, no matter how delightful," she glanced toward Evan and Chloe, "those concerns are."

Lindsay eyed him, and Mason shrugged. "I've been saying that for weeks."

Hyacinth let out a little cheer and clapped. "That's the perfect solution for this quandary. Our Lindsay needs time to herself." She adjusted her flowing floral-print scarf. "Sweet Shelby's is having a special pie tasting test this afternoon until early evening. Only a few friends and repeat customers who'll give feedback on what new savory items and desserts will work with our existing menu. Joe and the children can be my guests. That's one advantage of being the owner, or at least, the co-owner."

Lindsay frowned and picked up Chloe. "Thanks for offering, Aunt Hyacinth, but you've done so much for us today."

"Nonsense." Hyacinth bored her gaze into Mason and arched her eyebrow. He received her message loud and clear, without her even speaking a word. He gave a subtle nod of alliance. "I have to leave early to help with the preparations," she continued. "But I insist on having them along. Spoiling them over one dinner by their aunt won't hurt them. And no one can resist my pie, so that's settled. Joe, would you like to tag along tonight with the kiddos? What about you, Mason? Are you coming to Sweet Shelby's later?"

"Pie? Sign me up." Grandpa Joe rubbed his belly and turned toward Lindsay. "I can drive them in my car if you're okay with that."

"Yes. That is unless Mason's going."

Everyone waited for his answer.

"Uh, no. I'm working tomorrow so it'll be an early night for me." With his grandfather occupied, there was no better time to get a first ride on his motorcycle.

"I must go. I'll see the three of you tonight." Hyacinth tweaked Chloe's nose and Evan's before leaving.

Joe reached for Chloe and motioned for Evan. "How about lunch now so we'll be hungry tonight?"

In two seconds, everyone except for him and Lindsay filed out of the garage. Even Goliath opted for the backyard.

Lindsay frowned. "Do you feel like we've been set up?"

"Not at all. Your aunt was clear—this evening's about you, and it'll give you time to reflect on what you want." He stepped back, almost tripping over a rake. "I mean as far as the move."

From there, he left without another word. Tonight would give her time to think about what was best for her life, especially that job in Wilmington. He couldn't stand in her way. He cared too much, and if leaving Hollydale would be the best thing for her, he'd have to say goodbye.

The thought made his stomach hurt. If this was what caring for someone did to a person, made you feel empty and twisted, maybe he was better off alone.

LINDSAY HAD A quick shower and put on fresh clothes, but then wasn't sure what she should do next. The house was almost too eerie since she wasn't used to the silence.

Why hadn't Aunt Hyacinth asked her to come with them? She loved pie almost as much as she loved the thought of a night to herself.

Everyone else, though, had other plans. Becks and Penelope were reviewing paperwork, and Kris was heading to Asheville to see the latest animated movie with her mother and daughter. She went over to Mason's garage and banged on his door, releasing her frustration on the innocent wood. Mason opened the door enough for her to see the helmet in his hand. "Don't worry. I'm being as quiet as a mouse so you can enjoy your night off," Mason said.

"Hello, Lindsay. How are you after a morning of work and an afternoon of making my yard look the best it's ever been, Lindsay? You could start with some pleasantries, you know?" She elbowed her way into the garage.

Mason's motorcycle took front and center with his tools hanging in place on particleboards and surfaces clear of parts. If it weren't for the faint whiff of oil and paint, she wouldn't even guess he'd built it here from the ground up. She walked over, a quiver of apprehension running through her. She'd never ridden a motorcycle before.

"Thanks for the hard work. It's a changed yard. It's terrific." He clicked on a button and the main garage door opened.

She noticed the motorcycle's silver metallic paint. "Silver. Interesting choice. Why not something else?"

"It stands out without standing out. It's also a suitable alternative to other colors that show off the dirt and grime more quickly." He tucked the helmet under his arm. "I'll see you later?"

"Nope. You lost a bet, and I'm collecting on it." She enjoyed asserting herself. It felt good.

"Okay." His voice was wary, almost as if he was backing away from her.

Good thing she was persistent. A gardener had to be patient, and something told her the fruit of her patience this time would be worth waiting for. "Stop assuming you know everything about sweet ol' Lindsay. I'm full of surprises."

"I don't like surprises, remember?" He rested his helmet on the worktable and placed his elbow on it. "What do you need? I only have a little light left, and I want to get rolling."

"Perfect." She pointed to his helmet. "You got an extra one of those?"

"Why?"

"Because I'm going with you." She went over and straddled the bike before she lost her nerve. "This holds two people, doesn't it?"

"I've only driven around the block once. This is the genuine test." He arched an eyebrow and shook his head. "I can't take you. What if we get stranded on the road or something goes wrong?"

"You put it together, right? With the intention of it working?" She waited for his nod. "That settles that. One helmet, please."

He went over to the cabinet and pulled out a spare. "This is the smallest one I own."

"Good to know I don't have a big head."

He stared at her for a long moment. "If you're really going, you need to change first. Pants and a jacket along with gloves, okay? Boots if you have them."

"You won't leave without me?"

"A bet's a bet."

"And you'll throw in dinner? I'm in the mood for fried chicken." She grinned.

"Sounds good."

"Bet aside, would you have taken me, anyway? If I had asked nicely." She smiled and patted the seat, the rich leather hiding a layer of thick foam.

"I don't know, to be honest." He laid both helmets on the workbench. "I'm used to traveling solo."

He'd driven that point home ever since she'd met him. "Then it's a good thing I accepted that bet, isn't it?" She hurried off before he could change his mind.

Or before she could change hers.

CHAPTER SIXTEEN

MASON SWERVED INTO the gravel parking lot for the hiking trail that led toward Pine Falls. This was a new sensation, having someone's arms around him with the spring breeze rustling his jacket, the miles disappearing under his feet. Not just anyone's arms, either. Lindsay's.

He cut the engine and removed his helmet, taking a deep breath of the clear mountain air. The Great Smoky Mountains were in their full, breathtaking beauty this time of year. Many tourists came to Hollydale in the fall for the foliage when the leaves went out in a blaze of glory. They didn't know what they were missing in spring—his favorite season. There was something about the hint of cherry blossoms in the air, the wildflowers springing up alongside the river and the trickle of that river giving rise to a full crescendo.

Holding his hand out, he assisted her as she dismounted, her trembling fingers not lost on him. Catching a ride on a motorcycle wasn't for everyone. Lindsay struggled with the chin clasp, and he unhooked the strap for her. She removed the helmet. Her pale face sent alarm bells ringing.

"Lindsay." Her name was but a breath as a crash of feelings flooded through him. "Lin?"

"Where do I put this?" She held up the helmet and he took it from her. She started removing the knapsack from her back.

Mason opened the pannier and swapped the take-out containers from the Holly Days Diner with the helmets. For a few seconds, he let his disappointment wash over him. What had he expected? For her to be as entranced about motorcycles as he found himself about gardening.

He loaded the knapsack with their reusable water bottles and the containers.

"Ready?" He pushed off, but she stopped him at the base of the trail.

"What's with being gruff? It was your idea to stop for the food and to come to the trail."

"You're right. I'm sorry, I just have a lot on my mind." He didn't want to bring up her and the kids leaving town, not when she was standing there looking so open and hopeful.

She nodded and tugged on his sleeve. "Then let me carry something. C'mon. Don't be stubborn. I let you pay for my dinner, the least I can do is carry it. Smelling my fried chicken will make me walk that much faster, although

I'm not sure I'd be in such a hurry for your vegetable plate."

Reluctantly, he extracted the water bottles from the knapsack and handed them to her.

"Not fried chicken, but it'll do." She smiled.

This late in the day, other hikers weren't starting out, but they passed a good number of people returning to the lot. Too many for any conversation and the rocky path also demanded most of their attention. When he thought about it, he didn't mind the silence. Not with the possibility of her moving to Wilmington still unsettled.

The river rushed alongside them. With each step, the muted sound of the falls became more pronounced, as did the incline. She stuck with him, matching him step for step, stride for stride.

They came upon a rock outcropping with water dripping over the lichen surface, an overhang tall enough to shelter hikers. She pulled him under the rocks and inhaled. He did the same, the dampness and the earthy scent filling his lungs.

"Thank you, Mason."

"For what?"

"I would have missed out on this moment if you hadn't suggested the hike. I'm so busy making the gardens beautiful for others and our yards a sanctuary for ourselves that sometimes I forget the simple majesty of the world around me. Timber River, the red maples, the flowering dogwoods. Nature for the sake of nature. You're right. I needed the reminder."

The crest of the mountains surrounding them stood out on the trail. Sharing this with someone was different, he reflected, than usually hiking on his own. No matter how many women he'd dated, he hadn't opened up to any of them about his grandparents' and parents' long marriages or losing his sister and best friend.

Had he used those losses as excuses, ways to keep on a path familiar and level rather than hiking a treacherous trail with a trusted someone by his side?

"There's a flat rock near the falls where we can sit and eat," Mason said.

They made it the rest of the way, with Pine Falls cascading sixty feet into a pool of water. Some hikers milled about while others watched in wonder. Lindsay moved the water bottles under her arm and, with her free hand, squeezed his. "This is perfect. Aren't you glad I won the bet?"

"You're quite the con artist."

Her cheeks pinkened, and they settled at the last unoccupied spot on the rock. He unstrapped the knapsack and lowered himself to the gray slate.

"I love everything about tonight. Thanks for my first motorcycle ride."

Mason stopped unzipping the main compartment. "I thought you were scared. Your hands trembled and your face was flushed."

She put his water bottle in front of him. "Maybe my trembling hands had nothing to do with the ride itself."

"Then why were you shaking?" Her chin snapped up, and she leveled her gaze at him.

He leaned back and almost fell off the rock. Opting to keep this light, he said, "My driving's not that bad." He gave a weak smile and brought forth the food, fried chicken for Lindsay, grilled vegetables and rice pilaf for himself. Even now, she shivered when she accepted the disposable container. "Are you cold?" he asked.

"Not cold, just wondering why you're shutting me out."

Her lips pulled into a straight line as she opened the container. She bit into a drumstick and chewed while he struggled with his emotions. He dared to look at her. He shouldn't be noticing the best qualities of something that would be gone too soon. The thought of her moving away crushed his heart and kept him on his side of the rock. He had to hold back.

"I'm just trying to enjoy the scenery, like you said." His smooth voice didn't match his shaky interior.

"Just so you know, that won't work." She breathed out and closed her container. "Maybe I enjoyed that ride with my arms around you too much. Maybe the reason I was trembling was *you*. I might regret this, but I haven't thought of anything else on the trail."

She leaned into him, her fingers gripping the sides of his jacket, pulling him close. Their gazes met, and she licked her lips. The roar of the falls had nothing on the roar of his heart. "Well, I am hard to resist."

"I'll never be able to keep your ego in check now." She grinned before he curled his arm around her.

With a slight nod, she closed the gap, and her sweet lips brushed his. Her fingers threading through his thick hair.

The kiss was pure Lindsay: truthful, blossoming, giving. The kiss deepened, and he smelled lavender and poppies and everything beautiful. Some barrier inside him broke open, like floodgates letting in water to a thirsty town.

Just as with the unending waterfall, he

wanted to keep kissing her, to keep this feeling of one constant thing in his life going. This kiss was what he wanted, something he would cherish, a reminder that at the end of a bad day where everything went wrong, there was someone open and joyful, and waiting for him.

So he in turn could be that someone for her. For Lindsay.

Chuckling, Lindsay broke away. "Dinner and scenery and lack of interruptions. I can see why this must be a popular dating spot for you." Her face drained of color, and she shrugged. "Not that this is a date. It's…" She glanced at him as though he'd have the right answer.

"A bet, won fair and square." He waited for her nod and then he opened his food container. He devoured the rice pilaf, and also kept an eye on her. "You're wrong, though. You're the first person who's walked this trail with me."

Her face went from ashen to rosy in less than ten seconds. He liked her different expressions, whether here, by the fence or downtown. He especially loved the shades of pink on her cheeks, at times revealing her innermost self.

"I'm one of a kind. Thanks." She tossed her hair back and offered a grin.

He speared a bite of grilled zucchini. "Have you been out on a date since Tim?"

Why every topic during their nightly conversations had come up except this one, he couldn't say. Maybe, on some level, he hadn't wanted to know.

"A couple. They ended before they began."

His phone echoed somewhere in the deep recesses of his backpack, and he broke away. "Sorry, but I have to check in case it's a work emergency." He looked at the screen. "It's my brother-in-law. I should take this."

Before he could say more than hello, he was hearing the news. "Bree wasn't feeling well this afternoon after she talked to you. It happened suddenly. She's having tests done." Worry consumed Tristan's voice. "Your grandmother and I are in the emergency room."

"I can be there in a few hours. I just have to throw some things together and find someone to cover my shift."

"Hold on." Muted voices came over the line, and Mason strained to make out any of the words.

Mason stared at the waterfall, the constancy of the flowing water no longer a romantic refuge. Lindsay's hand covered his; he thought he should pull it back, but didn't.

"That was Bree's doctor. She has an infection, but they're confident they caught it in time. She'll be on an antibiotic drip and if all goes as expected, she'll be discharged in the morning." Relief came through the line. "Your grandmother wants to talk to you."

"Stay with Joe." His grandmother sounded older than her usual self, but steady. "We'll keep Bree safe, and then we'll plan a long weekend for you and Joe to come get me at the end of the month." Grandma Betty was quite emphatic, too much so for his taste.

"Grandma, I can be there…"

"Mason, trust Tristan and me. I'll be back in Hollydale soon enough, where I won't get to see my granddaughter as often as I'd like. With you there, I know my Joe has someone looking after him." He must get his stubborn streak from his grandmother rather than his grandfather.

"Wait a minute. Lindsay's right here. I'll ask her if she'll watch Goliath. Then I can bring Grandpa with me."

"If you're with Lindsay, let me talk to her."

He handed over the phone to her. Lindsay pressed the phone to her ear. "Hello, Mrs. Ruddick… Oh yes, Betty."

He caught Lindsay's eye and they smiled at each other.

He tried following her conversation with his grandmother, but gave up and ate his dinner, not tasting anything. He stared out at Pine Falls.

Lindsay tapped his arm with the phone. "She said it's your call, but she'd feel better if you stay here. Bree's doctor doesn't think she's in any real danger."

"Grandpa Joe needs Grandma Betty. I'll take him with me."

"She also said to tell you she wants to finish your knitted blanket with Bree, and they'll give it to you at the end of the month together."

"Did the two of you plan everything out?"

"You probably also missed me promising her that I'd make Joe my world-famous meatballs tomorrow night." She smiled and shrugged. "But only if you think you should stay. Betty's concerned, but not controlling. There's a difference."

Mason glanced at his disposable container, which was empty, and then hers, which was still half full. "Are you going to finish that?"

She chuckled and clasped hers to her chest. "Next time order your own fried chicken."

Next time? Could there be a next time? He'd love to kiss her again, sure, but what if things changed between them? What if she and the kids moved to Wilmington? As much as he'd like to take a chance that he could find the type of rare love his parents and grandparents had, this wasn't the right time to try. He might have to leave for Bree's side at a minute's notice, and Lindsay might be permanently leaving.

Three days on the job would give him some perspective.

He'd never been so thankful for a long shift in his life.

IN THE SMALLER of the two greenhouses on the western side of the botanical garden, Lindsay checked the labels on the plants she finished transplanting and jotted some notes. A new employee called in sick today, and so Lindsay had done double duty, arriving at six this morning. Waving goodbye to one of her assistants, she stretched and yawned. How could thirteen hours have passed so quickly? A long shift but a fruitful one as she caught a mistake in the soil levels for the rare North Carolina plant exhibit scheduled to open next week. The extra alkaline wouldn't have helped the *Cardamine* flowering plant and monitoring the sulfur addition was a must so the roots wouldn't scorch.

With the sulfur added, she started her rounds and found one of the timer's screens blank. After she changed the batteries, she texted Aunt Hyacinth and let her know she was running late. She rubbed her eyes, then headed along the employee's path to the main building. To her surprise, Phillip flagged her down. "Something's come up and I'll be out of the office for the next two days."

Her jaw dropped. The dedication was a little over a week away, and she'd been doing twelve-hour days and several weekend mornings, giving her all.

Phillip opened the door for her. "It's not what you think."

"I was just thinking I've been working a lot of hours, and I'd have loved a break." Frustration at everything boiled over. "My kids are only little once, and I've put in overtime on this project, the rare plant exhibit and my other duties."

"And Heather will also be away, but she's arranged for extra help for you." Phillip kept talking and walking until they arrived at her office. "There will be a group of high school students, coming to assist you for the community service hours."

Lindsay groaned and retrieved her purse from the bottom drawer of her desk. Then she exchanged her green blazer for her coat. "The last time that happened I had to explain the difference between the blade and the handle of a trowel to more than a few of the kids."

Phillip shook his head, propping her door

open. "She personally talked to the agricultural teacher. All these kids are looking for careers in the field and have experience with landscaping."

That sounded more promising, but she wouldn't hold her breath. "The supplier said the substitute plants I ordered should arrive by ten tomorrow morning, so the help would be appreciated."

He went over to her desk and examined her pink stapler with her name written in Sharpie on the top and also on a label affixed to the bottom. "Did you give any more consideration to that position in Wilmington?"

"Yes, I've given it more consideration, and no, I'm not applying. I have no desire to become the director of any botanical garden. I'm all about the plants and flowers. I'm glad you're the one in charge of the budgets and keeping the donors happy."

That stapler became that much more interesting to him, as he never raised his gaze. "You wouldn't even be interested in applying for my position then if it became open?"

"Nope." Funny, she expected a boulder on her shoulder, but relief was a small price to pay for speaking her mind to her boss.

"Good to know." He placed the stapler back on her desk. "See you in two days."

"Why are you taking time off so close to the ceremony?"

Phillip zipped up his jacket. "Heather and I have done nothing but talk about Wilmington since we left, so I've applied for the position. My interview's tomorrow."

"Good." *Oops.* That came out a little too fast. "What I mean is…"

"No need to explain. Heather's picking me up here and we're driving tonight."

It'd been a full day, and Phillip was interviewing for another job. Thank goodness tonight was Mason's first night off in three days. She missed their fence discussions and needed one.

A yearning to see him swept over her. She sank into her office chair. This wasn't just a need to talk life over with a friend and a cup of coffee at The Busy Bean. This was about something else. Something more. In the past few months, a casual chat had developed into an intense connection. That kiss proved the attraction wasn't one-sided or a mere crush, and it wasn't a friendly peck on the cheek, either.

When they'd first started these backyard chats, she'd gone along with them because Mason was so safe and so off-limits. What better person to chat with than a perpetual bachelor who liked his freedom? What better person than her husband's best friend who'd keep her at arm's length?

When did something easy and comforting become something that skirted the edge of disaster?

That kiss, tender yet mind-boggling, dynamic and breathtaking, left her reeling and wanting more. She hadn't ever meant to be anyone but a friend to Mason, especially with Tim being their common link. Yet here she was, thinking about him—his character as loyal as the perennials that grew every year, his personality as colorful as the flowers she loved to surround herself with.

And yet there was no one worse for her than Mason. He lived for the moment, whether it was an unplanned trip to surf, or hike, or even his job, dedicating himself to that brief window of time when he had to stabilize a patient and rush them to the hospital. She tended to her garden and her children, where patience and a steady hand guided the day. For the first time in years, she was reconnecting and expanding her circle of friends.

So his kiss caused her heart to crash in her chest, the same way the waterfall collided with the rocks.

She craved solidity and constancy, two attributes that would never describe the man who didn't wear a watch unless he was on duty.

She found her keys and exited the garden, stopping for a minute to chat with the night security guard before driving home.

The drive didn't take long and Chloe greeted her at the door, where Lindsay swept her into her arms, nuzzling noses with her daughter. Chloe giggled.

Aunt Hyacinth came into the living room, removing her apron, the one with the sunflowers. "Dinner's in the oven. A lovely chicken pot pie with my signature flaky crust. Do let me know whether the dish is as delicious as it is fragrant. Belinda and I wish to accommodate our customers who would like to partake of something heartier, and you're my taste testers."

A loud crash came from upstairs, followed by a wail. Lindsay quickly lowered Chloe to the carpet and ran toward the sound.

Lindsay rushed into the guest room at the same time Mason descended from the ladder, paintbrush in hand. She flicked off the speaker, playing rock and roll. Evan was sitting on the floor, his lower lip jutting out. He burst into tears.

"Evan, are you okay? When did you come in here?" Mason shucked his protective goggles and kneeled beside Evan, laying his hand on her son's shoulder.

Evan cried louder and pointed to an overturned can, where paint was pooling on the beige carpet. Mason set the paint can upright. Evan wailed, and she tried to console him.

"What happened, Ev?"

He sniffed and scrunched his eyes shut. "I only wanted to help Mason. But I tripped and the can fell over and—" Then crying began afresh.

She hugged Ev and sighed, seeing the huge glob of white paint on the beige carpet. Her parents were set to arrive in three days. Moving the bed might cover the spot.

Mason disappeared, and she let go of Evan. "You knew Mason was in here painting the ceiling. Sometimes adults need helpers, and sometimes they don't."

Mason returned with dish soap, a black garbage bag and two rolls of paper towels. Chloe toddled in behind him, and he handed Evan the soap. "No use crying over spilled paint. We need to clean this up while it's still wet. Chloe, you can mix the bubbles with your mommy, and Evan, you can scrub with me."

Chloe giggled but took her job of using a paint stirrer to mix the water and dish soap to heart. After another fast hug, the four of them set to working and within minutes, the carpet looked better, although Lindsay would still have to rearrange the furniture so her mother wouldn't notice.

"Sorry." Mason pulled the plastic drawstring of the trash bag closed. "I thought I had closed the door. I didn't hear him enter."

"I'm sorry, Mommy." Evan sniffled once more, and she kept still for a second, monitoring his breathing and reaction to the paint fumes.

Nothing. At least that was one relief. "Accidents happen." Something beeping sounded in the distance, and Lindsay tapped her forehead. "That must be the pot pie. If Joe's not doing anything, you can call him and see if he and Goliath want to join us for dinner."

The rest of the evening progressed smoothly. After helping with the kitchen cleanup, Mason threw the dish towel over his shoulder. "I'll put everything away in the guest room before I take Grandpa Joe home."

She glanced at Joe, reading a book to Evan and Chloe. "I'll come with you and check on the stain."

They went upstairs, and Mason's phone rang. "Is it Bree?" Lindsay held her breath until he shook his head.

"It's work."

He stayed in the hallway, and she examined the spot and the furniture arrangement. There should be enough room to move the bed, but until everything was put away, she'd have to leave it as is. Mason joined her, but his face reflected something was bothering him.

"What's wrong?"

He grimaced. "Tomorrow's crew is out sick. Jordan and I are covering their shift."

"Be careful. Even if you're okay with the extra shifts, watch over him and keep your guard up." She examined his eyes, weary enough after a recent three-day stint.

Without warning, Goliath rushed into the room, barking playfully. He zigzagged in the open space and headed toward the table with the paint supplies. Mason scooped him up before the dog caused another accident. "Nope, not today, Goliath." He stopped at the entryway and glanced over his shoulder. His gaze fell on her and she wondered what he was thinking now.

Maybe she hadn't been the only one dwelling on that kiss and hoping there'd be another. It had been one thing, though, to realize he was wrong for her but to have kissed and just walked away from it was another. Should she bring it up? Why hadn't he? Did that mean he wanted to forget all about it? The accident with the paint might not have been the only one to have happened recently.

Rather than aiming for the dartboard and seeing whether another kiss would score a bull's-eye, he'd swooped out, conceding before anything began.

He was right. Their kiss was an accident, one that could cause irreparable damage to their friendship were it to happen again.

She'd gotten the hint. If only her heart had gotten the hint before the kiss, though.

CHAPTER SEVENTEEN

LINDSAY OPENED THE refrigerator and peeked into the container with the chicken pot pie. There was just enough for three servings. She placed the leftovers on a cookie sheet and opened the preheated oven. *Thank you, Aunt Hyacinth.* After her exhausting day, heating dinner and getting Evan and Chloe ready for bed were on top on her short list of evening activities. Since Mason was working and Joe was elsewhere, she'd paint the guest-room ceiling by herself after Evan and Chloe were asleep. She plugged in her coffeepot, eager for one last caffeine surge even this early in the evening.

Her doorbell rang, and she glanced at her watch. She wasn't expecting company. The doorbell rang again, and she clicked on the coffeepot before checking on Evan and Chloe, watching their favorite animated cartoon in the living room, and then she peered through the peephole.

No, it couldn't be. Not this early. The muscles in her shoulders tightened. Her parents had arrived one week ahead of schedule.

"Lindsay, darling!" Her mother rapped at the door. "Are you there? I see your truck in the driveway. It's your mother."

"Mimi! Pop-Pop!" Evan and Chloe scrambled off the floor and ran toward Lindsay.

After a deep breath, Lindsay opened the door, her mother on the stoop, her father at the trunk of their rental car, unloading the luggage.

Her mother never changed. White bangs protruded from her silk scarf with a jungle pattern of leopards and elephants hiding her cap of short hair. Dahlia was one of a kind, and she sailed inside, her black stilettos sinking into Lindsay's carpet. "Evan and Chloe! Look at you two angels. Are you eating enough? When was the last time you went outside? Your cheeks seem pale." She bent and patted Evan's cheek, then Chloe's, before blowing air kisses on either side of Lindsay's cheeks. "Lindsay, dearest. You have dark circles under your eyes. Don't you fret about anything. Mother is here, and I'll do everything I can to make sure you get plenty of rest."

Her father, the same as ever with his lanky frame, rolled two suitcases along her walkway with two smaller ones stationed next to the car.

Barefoot, Lindsay rushed out and helped him. "Let me get those for you."

"Nonsense. This way I'm balanced." He laughed as though he'd told the funniest joke. Up close, there were a few more crinkle lines around his gray eyes. "I know where your guest room is. I won't be but a minute until I can join you all."

She gasped and bit her lip. The guest room still had paint cans and drop cloths everywhere. "Put the luggage in my room, Dad."

She'd finish the ceiling tonight and then once it dried and everything was back where it belonged, she'd put her parents there and then sleep in her bed again. For now, the living room sectional would suffice for her bed for a couple of nights.

Her mother faced her. "Your room? Is there something wrong with the guest room?"

"Mommy almost fell through the ceiling in the middle of the night and Mason helped get her out and there was a big hole until Mason and Grandpa Joe fixed it and then I spilled paint, but Mason wasn't mad at me." Evan blurted all of that out before Lindsay could stop him.

"A man? And the middle of the night?"

Right. Her mother would zero in on that. "It wasn't a big deal. You remember Mason

Ruddick, don't you? He was Tim's paramedic partner. He moved in next door, and now he's my best friend." Even though her feelings now had changed.

"Hmm." Her mother's expression didn't change.

Dahlia started for the stairs, and Lindsay smelled the fragrant aroma of tonight's dinner. "You're early. I wasn't expecting you. I don't think there'll be enough chicken pot pie for five." She glanced at Chloe. "I might have something in the freezer for Evan and Chloe."

Her mother stopped halfway up the staircase. "Don't be silly, darling. Of course, your father and I don't expect you to cook for us."

"So, you ate on the way here?" Lindsay stepped toward the kitchen, not wanting a burnt crust.

"At six in the evening? Hardly." She waved her hand dismissively. "That's far too early for dinner. No, I'll freshen up and then your father and I will take you and the children out for our repast. Dominic's is one of my favorites even after traveling almost everywhere."

"Dominic's is rather elegant, and I thought they recommended reservations. Mario's Pizza is more Evan and Chloe's speed."

"Then again, your father and I probably have too much detritus from the plane trip for such a fine establishment as Dominic's." A grudging acceptance, but Lindsay would take it. "Before we leave for the next leg of our trip, I insist on taking you and Mason there for dinner. It'll give your father a chance to get better acquainted with him. It won't be that long before our townhome is finished, and we'll be returning to Hollydale for good."

Her mother started walking again.

"Mason and I aren't a couple." And another stop. This time her mother turned and smiled.

"Thank goodness your father and I arrived when we did. You need someone to pamper you. Since Dominic's is off-limits tonight, let's settle for the Holly Days Diner. I've already booked us appointments at the new spa the day after tomorrow. You know, at that wellness center, started by Patsy Appleby's daughter. We're having the works. A facial, mani/pedis, everything."

Lindsay counted to ten while her mother went up the staircase. "I can't go. I have to work."

"They won't miss you if you show up relaxed and beautiful, especially with that ceremony in only a week. Think of all the cameras and news agencies. You need to look your best."

Lindsay rolled her eyes and clutched the

newel post. "The gardens will look their best, and that's what people are coming to see."

"We'll discuss this at dinner."

Something smelled like it was burning, and Lindsay rushed into the kitchen. After reaching for an oven mitt, she pulled the pot pie out of the stove and clanged the baking dish on the stovetop. A burnt mess stared back at her, and she no longer had an excuse to reject her mother's invitation. From here, she could see her patio and the fence, and more than ever, she needed the support of her best friend.

Although a kiss would be even better.

MASON PULLED INTO his driveway, and Jordan parked next to his SUV. Mason clicked the key fob, and his garage door opened, revealing the beauty that was his new motorcycle. In the glow of the setting sun, the silver metal gleamed. He waved at his new partner, who followed him to the bike.

"I haven't driven it over a long distance, but it accelerates well, and the brakes work on a pin drop. Following the proper maintenance and regular precheck procedures, this one ought to last forever." A twinge of something that almost felt like betrayal ran through Mason while he stared at the bike.

"Hey, Mason, are you finally home?" Lindsay's voice called out from the yard.

"We're in here," he called back.

Lindsay stopped in front of his garage. Her gaze went from Mason to Jordan. "Oh, hi, I'm Lindsay Hudson."

She extended her hand to Jordan, who shook it and nodded his head. "Jordan Bonetti."

"Oh, you're Mason's new partner. Nice to meet you. I'm glad to see you're taking an interest in Mason's motorcycle. Being friends away from work builds a better team."

Jordan eyed the bike. "The framework is sweet. Can I examine the exhaust first?"

"Go ahead."

Jordan lay on his back and scooted toward the bike. "The exhaust is solidly built. I'm impressed. How much are you asking for it?"

"What?" The word burst out of Lindsay, and she grabbed Mason's arm. "Mason, can I see you over here for a minute?"

Mason followed Lindsay out to the driveway while trying hard to ignore how much he liked being in her presence. On this spring day, everything in the neighborhood was in full bloom. The pink tulip trees were her favorite, but then again, everything in a garden was Lindsay's favorite. Everything about Lindsay screamed out for love and he didn't think he'd ever be ready. She needed someone pre-dictable, not someone who wanted last-minute motorcycle rides into the sunset,

"Oh, first, my parents arrived yesterday. They're watching a movie with Evan and Chloe tonight. I've already seen it so I'm meeting Becks and Jillian at the bar and grill, but never mind about that. He's under the impression you want to sell your motorcycle."

"That's because I asked him if he wanted to buy it."

"What? You've been working on it for years. You can't just sell it like that." Lindsay snapped her fingers.

Mason folded his arms over his chest. "Why not?"

"You poured hours into that bike. For the past year, you've talked about nothing else but the trips you're going to take on it, driving to the beach, to the mountains," Lindsay sputtered and imitated him, folding her arms across her chest. "You love this bike."

"I love the challenge of this bike. Welding parts, painting it, seeing it come together, but now that it's done, I'm off to the next adventure. Something new, something different."

She winced. "That's it? You're willing to just walk away from something that's so meaningful to you?"

The disappointment welling in her eyes was almost too painful for him to watch.

"Something new will strike my fancy and that'll be that."

She'd done more than strike his fancy. He could see himself with her every day, waking up next to her, loving her, yet he wasn't convinced he was what was best for her. Someone else would give her everything she deserved.

Seeing how hurt she was, however, almost stopped him in his tracks. More than anything, he longed to sweep her into his arms and tell her they should face the future together, but he couldn't.

"I see." Comprehension lurked in that beautiful face, which almost penetrated the armor he'd built around himself, but didn't. "You can sell the motorcycle, but you should know that you can't sell what it represented. You still have to face whatever led you to spend all that time ripping it apart and putting it back better than ever."

She turned on her heel and rushed away. A hand brushed his shoulder. Mason faced Jordan, who let out an enormous yawn. "I'll think about the bike, but I'm too tired to test drive it tonight. Four days in a row? That's some heavy workload."

Jordan kept talking, but his words were lost on Mason.

Lindsay'd pierced his armor.

LINDSAY SWIRLED HER straw around her glass of Cheerwine cola and stared at the bubbles rising to the top. She'd left Mason's driveway only a few hours before. Was he waiting at the fence for their nightly talk while Goliath strutted around the yard? Or was he picking out his next motorcycle to build? A newer, flashier model...

"Earth to Lindsay." Her friend's voice cut through the noise of the crowd at the Timber River Bar and Grill.

Lindsay faked a smile at Becks and Jillian, who sat on either side of her. "Sorry I'm not better company tonight, Becks."

Becks shrugged. "Nope, don't apologize. That's why we're here. To support each other." She picked out a fried pickle from the appetizer plate. "Secretly I'm enjoying a night away from Nat's baby shower preparations."

Jillian nodded and selected a fried mozzarella stick, dunking it in the marinara sauce. She faced Becks. "What's this I hear about your former fiancé moving back to Hollydale?"

"Huh? Carlos has come home? Last I heard, he's fighting forest fires out of state." Lindsay noticed how Becks' pink cheeks had turned as red as her pixie cut. Becks reached for another fried pickle. "Not that I was keeping track of him or anything. See, Lindsay? Everyone needs to share and listening is what friends are for."

Friends. For too long, she'd put aside her friendships thinking that she could manage her grief alone, but that wasn't the case. She needed them as much as they needed her. She wished she could say the same about her next-door neighbor.

"Thanks." This time her smile was genuine.

"So, why aren't you better company?" Becks grinned. She was tenacious to the core.

For the first time tonight, Lindsay was hungry, and she reached for a chicken wing. "My parents arrived early for the dedication. Mom is still upset with me about turning down her offer for a spa day with her. She'd scheduled it for tomorrow. However, I did say I could arrange a night out with the girls if they were willing to babysit. They said yes, which was sweet, so she and Dad are watching a movie with Evan and Chloe."

"Isn't that a good thing that they're here?" Jillian dabbed her napkin at the corners of her mouth. "Oh, maybe it's Evan? Does his asthma give you cause for concern?"

Lindsay brushed some of the ranch dressing onto the chicken. "My dad knows what to do in case Evan has an asthma attack."

"Please keep the rest of this fried food away from me." Becks pushed at the appetizer tray. "Wouldn't your next-door neighbor pitch in during an emergency? Do your parents have Mason's contact information?"

Lindsay bit into her chicken wing with a little too much force and the ranch dressing splattered everywhere. She swallowed and then wiped away the sauce. "Mason is..."

She couldn't finish the sentence.

Becks sipped her drink, her gaze not leaving Lindsay. "Mason is what?" She placed her elbows on the table and leaned forward. "We won't tell anyone."

"He's loyal and infuriating. He's charming and obstinate." She placed the rest of the wing on the small plate. "He's selling his motorcycle when he's worked so hard on it, and he's not coming to the ceremony."

"And you're upset about all of this, why?" Becks asked.

"Same reason I'm upset he hasn't kissed me again." The words had slipped out faster than she could stop them.

Becks glanced at Jillian, who placed her hand over her mouth to hide a laugh before looking at Lindsay. "We kind of suspected you guys were close. Did you tell him that? About the kissing?"

Lindsay picked up her appetizer again. "No."

"You should." Becks passed a napkin to Lindsay and squeezed her hand. "I'm no Mason Ruddick, but if you need a friend at the ceremony, count me in. I'm sure my mom will watch Pippa."

Jillian checked her phone for the time and then gave her regrets as she was scheduled to work. But that she'd come out at all and joined them touched Lindsay.

Her friends had rallied around her tonight. Becks was also texting Kris and Penelope about their attendance at the dedication. Becks held up her thumb, her indication more people would be backing Lindsay's efforts at the botanical garden.

With the support of her friends, she'd somehow make it through the next few weeks and she'd be there for her friends, too.

She wasn't alone, and that felt good. She reached for another wing in celebration.

CHAPTER EIGHTEEN

LINDSAY TURNED ONTO Holly Cove Lane and soon was parked in her driveway. Dread knotted her stomach at what her parents might have done on this, the fifth day of their visit. Yesterday, Saturday, she'd arrived home to find her living room rearranged and a new, larger television hanging over her fireplace mantle. Her mother mistook her stunned silence for joy. But this wasn't like the bell wind chime Lindsay didn't care for but had kept in her front yard ever since Aunt Hyacinth had staked it there. The television was a massive and expensive purchase made without consulting her, a complete disregard for the sanctity of her home.

Somehow, she'd have to screw up the courage and tell her mother thank you, but no thank you. She never had a problem telling Mason what she thought, so why was she hesitant to tell her mother the truth?

Mason.

Then again, she wasn't being honest with

herself. She hadn't told him about how her romantic feelings for him were strengthening. Losing that friendship connection would be devastating, and yet? This strain was equally draining. She couldn't decide what was better, though, the thought of never having their fence talks again or the thought of never kissing him again.

She sighed and took the keys out of the truck's ignition. *The kisses. Definitely the kisses.* Time to find out if her mother made any changes or purchases today. Maybe she'd been so occupied taking care of Evan and Chloe, she hadn't had the chance to even rearrange a coaster.

With that hopeful thought in mind, she bounded into her home and stopped at the suitcases lined up in the foyer. Her breath stuck in her lungs. She hadn't expected them to leave Hollydale so soon. No, that wasn't right. Maybe the owner of the bed-and-breakfast had a cancellation and called her parents about the early vacancy.

No one greeting her, not even Evan or Chloe, brought a frown. "Mom? Dad?"

Her mother emerged from the kitchen, a disposable cup from The Busy Bean in hand. "Your father is playing in the basement with Evan and Chloe." She set the cup on the closest end table and grasped Lindsay's hands. "I have the most wonderful news, darling."

Lindsay braced herself. "Are you leaving before the dedication?"

"No, dearest. I talked to Lucie Appleby. Oh, what does she call herself these days?"

"Lucie Spindler."

"That's right." Her mother squeezed her hands and smiled. "Well as you know, I was at her fabulous retreat at the edge of town, and her salon isn't half bad. It's a shame you weren't able to make our appointment on Friday. When I was there, we spoke about the cabin her husband lived in while they were dating and now it's available for rental."

"So, you and Dad will stay there for the next week?" Lindsay glanced at the number of suitcases in the foyer. Somehow the luggage seemed to multiply in the short time her parents had stayed here.

"With you and Evan and Chloe." She clapped her hands, a look of delight gracing her expression. "Even though it's the weekend, I've arranged for a construction company to come and take care of the ceiling in the guest room starting tomorrow. They'll also rip out all the carpet and put in hardwood floors, which are ever so much better for someone with asthma. Carpets can trap allergens, you know. Your father is very sensitive to that sort of thing, and he had to use his rescue inhaler this morning."

Lindsay broke free of her mother's grasp. "Why didn't you tell me about Dad's asthma attack before I left?"

"You had already gone to the botanical garden. You seem to be there all hours, by the way." Her mother tapped her own cheek. "I'll call and talk to Lucie about a facial that will do wonders for the bags under your eyes."

"Thank you, but no thank you." She was now grateful Evan and Chloe weren't here. They didn't need to see this confrontation.

"I'll pay for it, of course." Dahlia tightened the animal-print silk scarf around her shoulders. "If you're concerned about money, which must be an issue for you as you didn't hire someone to fix the ceiling, don't be. Your father and I are only too happy to help our only child. And, of course, while we're here, we need to go to Asheville to buy some quality clothes for Evan and Chloe."

"Mother, please stop." Lindsay waved her hands in surrender. She glanced at the suitcases, three of which looked familiar, since she saw them in her closet every day. "Wait. Did you pack for me?"

"Of course, darling. You were working, and the construction crew will be here bright and early tomorrow morning. You need your beauty sleep and those hammers?" She visibly shivered.

"You had no right to go through my things and pack for me. Mason and Joe helped me with the guest room out of the kindness of their hearts. It was the neighborly thing to do." There was that word, *neighborly*, when her feelings for Mason were beginning to be anything but neighborly. "Thank you for offering to have the repairs done, but I'll get to them when I can afford them. I can also afford to make sure *my* children have clothes."

Dahlia huffed and raised one curved eyebrow. "I was in labor for forty-eight hours with you. I think that entitles me to show a little concern."

"A little concern, yes. Doing everything for me, no."

"Well, I don't have to stay where I'm not wanted." Dahlia made her way to the door that led to the basement.

"Mom, that's not true. I want you and Dad here but as guests."

Her mother swung the door wide open. "Jonah, it's time to go to that delightful guest cabin." The patter of footsteps up the stairs preceded laughter and excited shouts. "Sorry, darlings, only Mimi and Pop-Pop are going. You two are staying here."

Evan and Chloe reached her. "But Mommy, Mimi said it's going to be a party and we get to stay up late." Evan gazed at her with those enormous eyes.

"And I get a new teddy." Chloe also looked at Lindsay as if four against one would work.

"You have a perfectly good teddy bear, and I'll be dropping you off at day care in the morning so it's bedtime as usual tonight." Groans met her words, but Lindsay remained firm.

Her father reached the top of the stairs. "What's this I hear? Your mother has a perfectly reasonable plan."

"That she didn't run by me first." Lindsay folded her arms across her chest. "But she had no problem informing my children without asking me if I approved."

"Because I knew you'd be unappreciative and wouldn't think about our comfort, including your own." Dahlia raised her chin. "Fifty hours in labor and for what?"

By tomorrow, the number would probably reach sixty. "I appreciate what you're trying to do, but I have to raise Evan and Chloe my way, and that means being strong enough to stand up for myself. I hope you both understand that. And you're both more than welcome to stay here."

"We'll be staying at Lucie's. I made reservations at Dominic's for tomorrow night in a private room to accommodate Evan and Chloe if that's not too presumptuous on my part." Her mother's icy tone didn't slip by unnoticed, but at least she was still talking to Lindsay. "Since we'll be returning to India as soon as the ceremony is over."

Jonah frowned at Lindsay. "I understand, honey, but you could have agreed to this."

Yes, she could have, but not at the expense of her self-respect. "We'll be there tomorrow night."

Her parents spoke little as they departed, and soon Lindsay was left with two crestfallen children. "But Mimi said she wanted to look out for you." Evan bit his lip, and Lindsay's heart went out to her son and how considerate he could be.

"You know how the tulips are blooming now?" She waited until each child nodded. "They require a lot of work and attention from the moment the bulbs are planted until they grow, and it's like that with parents and their children. Parents help little ones until they can be themselves and blossom."

Their faces were still scrunched up. They

might be too young to understand what transpired, but not too young to help her outside. After they changed into older clothes, she hustled them into the sunshine flooding the yard with springtime warmth.

Ever since Lindsay could remember, she'd sought refuge from her overprotective mother at her aunt and uncle's house, the wind chimes and bright colors a place of nurturing and happiness. There'd be darts with Uncle Craig while her Aunt Hyacinth would show her how to care for plants and flowers. Then they'd share a meal and laugh over one of Aunt Hyacinth's pies before her mother would arrive to take her home.

The truth was she'd always felt a connection with Aunt Hyacinth.

The splash of color Lindsay had added to Mason's yard boosted the basic design. Not that it mattered to him that much since Mason only rented the house, not wanting to settle down and own a property.

He'd made it all too clear he didn't want to settle down at all, selling the bike he'd invested so much in for such a long time.

If she didn't know better, she'd think he was pushing her away on purpose. Same as any prospect of a future relationship with him. Even their yards didn't mesh together, their approaches to life too different, too substantial. And yet, there was something about Mason that made her yearn for a second glance. Maybe their friendship was the base layer and romance could be the topper, which would lead to something real and lasting, not a simple flash in the pan.

Lindsay looked at his house with longing, but the scene with her mother held her back. She put herself out there once today, and that led to a disaster with her kids' disappointment still lingering in the air.

No, it was better to hold back.

GRANDPA JOE GLANCED out the window, and Goliath jumped on his lap, trying to peek out, too. Mason cleared away the rest of the lunch plates, aware his grandfather had picked up on the tension between him and Lindsay. He and Grandpa should get away from the house and do something together for the rest of the afternoon.

"Grandpa, how about a visit to the Night Owl Bakery?" That had distracted him once before. "Or we could see if the fish are biting at Sully Creek?"

His grandfather turned away from the window. "Lindsay, Evan and Chloe are outside. I think Goliath and I will see if they need any help." He snapped on Goliath's leash. "Are you coming?"

"In a minute. Let me finish cleaning up first."

Nothing had gone right with Lindsay since his grandfather came to visit. Not that he could blame Grandpa Joe for his mistakes. Here his best friend was a vibrant, caring woman, who raved about and loved the thirty-one different types of peonies and could also cast a mean dart. He kept her at arm's length, and he wouldn't blame her if she finally listened to him and stayed away.

She and Tim had truly loved each other. He couldn't be a replacement for his best friend. He kicked himself for that very idea. But had he actually been depriving himself of happiness out of some sort of guilt? And what about Lindsay's happiness? He looped the dish towel over the oven handle. If he truly cared for her, he couldn't get in her way.

Distance between them didn't seem the answer, though, so he started for the back door. Mason's phone pinged, and he checked the screen. A reply from Jordan. Mason scanned the text. Jordan understood why Mason had changed his mind about selling the bike. His throat clenched at how close he'd been to giving up his motorcycle. Not having it around would only represent something else he'd missed out on.

With that settled, he joined his grandfather and Goliath in Lindsay's garden. There she was, showing Chloe and Evan how to harvest zucchini.

"You've been patient for forty-five days, and now it's time to reap the rewards," she told the kids.

Was a relationship like that? Could her patience with him lead to new adventures and something beautiful down the line?

"That's a good way to think about life in general, kiddos," Grandpa Joe's voice broke through Mason's reverie, and Lindsay looked their way.

She sent them a smile. "How's Bree doing?" Lindsay plucked another zucchini from the ground.

"She's much better, left the hospital last week, and she's now packing boxes with Betty," Grandpa Joe replied.

Lindsay rose and patted Grandpa Joe's arm. "You and Betty are my role models. I'm glad you're so supportive of each other."

"She's the best." Grandpa glanced at Mason, then at Lindsay again. Why was Mason reminded of the Cheshire cat?

Chloe tugged at Grandpa Joe's sleeve. "Chloe wants a hug."

He complied with her wishes. "Evan and Chloe, I'm at your service. It's time to collect zucchini."

The children led him to the first row, and Mason cleared his throat. "Lindsay, do you have a minute?"

Lindsay lingered but looked his way. "Is there something you wanted to say to me?"

So much, too much. "I'm not selling the motorcycle."

"That's good. You'd have regretted it before the ink was dry on the title transfer. If you'll excuse me, I have vegetables to harvest."

She moved away, and it occurred to him that he really didn't like the space growing between them. "Want to meet at the fence later?"

"I don't think so." Lindsay stooped to examine some flowers. "I've had one of those weeks. My mother is being domineering, I'm under pressure from my boss regarding the Wilmington position and I feel like I've lost my best friend."

Mason glanced at her driveway, but he didn't see another car. "Where are your parents? I don't see their rental."

She scuffed the ground with her gardening boot and then covered the mark. "They told me in no uncertain words how ungrateful I am about not allowing them to hire renovators and not giving them permission to fix me."

"You're not broken."

"Try telling them that." Her smile was forced, a far cry from the usual happy feature he craved seeing.

"I will. Anytime," he told her and meant it.

Her muscles loosened, and the smile became more genuine, more an extension of her true self. "Thanks, but I'm the one who needs to do that. Not you. Seems we both need to learn to talk to our relatives."

"Mom! Come look at my zucchini. I grew it all by myself." Evan held up his green gourd.

Lindsay hurried over, and Mason followed. Chloe's face was the miniature version of Lindsay's as she concentrated on pulling hers off the vine. She plucked off a huge zucchini and fell on her bottom for her efforts. Mason rushed over and knelt beside her. "Are you okay?"

"Mine's bigger than Evan's." She laughed until her giggles became hiccups.

Evan scowled and jutted out his bottom lip. "Mine's gonna taste better."

Lindsay stood between them and placed both zucchinis in a basket. "Gardening's not a competition at this house. You both did a magnificent job."

They seemed to accept that, and she helped them harvest the rest. She'd taken what could have escalated into a fight and made each child feel special.

It wasn't long before the kids grew tired, and Lindsay asked Grandpa Joe to take them inside. Mason could have kissed her for that alone, as his grandfather was also looking wilted, although he'd have been the last to admit it.

Lindsay kept harvesting the zucchini, and Mason worked beside her. She glanced his way. "I thought you disliked gardening."

"I seem to like it if there's a certain someone around." She had no reply so he knew cute, charming lines weren't what she wanted to hear. She wanted more from him, and he liked how she wouldn't settle for anything less than his entire self. "Okay, here's the truth. Without you, I might not be outside gardening. I'd be on that motorcycle heading to who knows where. That doesn't mean, though, this is something I don't enjoy. It's not the first thing on my list, but it's now on my list."

"Because of me?" She sounded a little flattered and a lot skeptical.

"Partly." He cut the last of the zucchini and

tossed it in the basket. "There's a peace that goes along with doing this, the same type I find with the wind all around me and the road flying under my feet. I wouldn't have found that without you."

He scrambled from his position and offered her his hands. She accepted his offer, and he helped her stand.

"So, what you're saying is gardening could become something you look forward to, something like a hobby?"

Her light tone expressed much more. He swept that errant strand of hair behind her ear. "You, Lindsay, could never be a hobby. You're the real deal. Twenty-four seven and worth every second."

She raised her chin, her lips full of sweet promise. Without another word, he leaned down and kissed her. More than coming home, the kiss held the promise of light and hope, and everything he never dared to dream could come his way.

Her lavender scent entranced him, and he deepened the kiss, the taste and feel of her as heady as the first ride on a motorcycle after a long winter. He wound his hands through her honey hair. He couldn't get enough of her, and he wasn't sure he ever would.

Lindsay broke away and, out of the corner

of his eye, he swore he glimpsed Grandpa Joe peeking out from the window, smiling before he replaced the curtain.

"Are you sure, Mason?" She sounded torn. "Many people love the idea of gardening when they're at a nursery and everything is alive and vibrant around them, but then they bristle at the work and dedication that goes into cultivating something sustaining and real."

The subtext wasn't lost on him, and he used his willpower to stop from kissing her again. That wouldn't solve the issues between them, although the appeal of her soft lips pulled him toward her once more. With Lindsay, though, it wasn't just mere attraction. He wanted to be around her and share the simple pleasures of life with her; it was a new feeling that he'd never experienced. "I won't deny that gardening is appealing."

Would this last? The plants and flowers Lindsay loved so much provided a glimmer of beauty for a short time, and then poof, they went out in a blaze of glory. He saw that same question in her expressive eyes.

"There's more to gardening, you know, than meets the eye." She led him to the basket of vegetables. "You'd think these zucchini would be uniform, since they came from the same batch of seeds and were planted in that patch of soil receiving equal sunlight and water."

"So?"

She smiled and held up two of the zucchini. "This one, though, was in Chloe's patch." She raised the larger one. "Where she randomly scattered fertilizer. She's more spontaneous while Evan is more methodical, but both vegetables will end up tasting delicious in your zucchini muffins."

"I can handle methodical. You follow a set of instructions for a motorcycle, and you get a finished product that purrs along the highway."

"And, in your line of work, you know the procedures that are best for each patient." She tapped her hand against the zucchini and threw it back in the basket. "You're calm in crisis situations, but you're a rebel at heart. There can be rebels in gardening. Chloe's zucchini's proof of that. It's not staid or boring."

This part of Lindsay fascinated him, the side of her that was calm and knowledgeable on the outside but could still be open to new experiences, like her first motorcycle ride. Somehow, she turned his idea of relationships upside down. "You make gardening sound like a team effort."

"You say that like it's an awful thing. Teamwork's not a terrible concept. There are advantages of leaning on someone."

She walked away, leaving him behind. She was right, but the prospect of leaning on someone and then having them disappear from his life wrenched his heart in two. Even now, there was a chance she'd be moving to Wilmington. It was hard to want to join a team when the star player's transfer was imminent. For Mason, it was time to step back and let her bloom.

CHAPTER NINETEEN

WITH ONLY FOUR days to go until the dedication of the memorial plaque, Lindsay wasn't sure she had enough time on this Tuesday evening at Sweet Shelby's Tea Room for Natalie Murphy's baby shower, but here she was nursing a cup of raspberry herbal while her parents spoiled Evan and Chloe, promising to get them to day care tomorrow morning.

Aunt Hyacinth and her frenemy-co-owner, Belinda Chastain, had transformed the elegant private room into a celebration of fun for the impending arrival of Miss Murphy, Natalie and Aidan's second child after they'd adopted his nephew Danny, who seemed quite happy to be gaining a sister. Pink-and-silver balloons formed an arch at the doorway, and more balloons surrounded the table with a pink tablecloth and a three-tiered strawberry cake.

All around her, thirty-five women, give or take a few, wearing pink string necklaces with safety pins on them, milled about in groups talking to each other, laughing and exchanging the pins if anyone was caught saying *baby*. Lindsay fingered her necklace and wondered whether anyone would miss her if she ducked out and finished planting the impatiens at the botanical garden.

"Whatever you're thinking, the answer is always yes." Becks, the co-host of the shower, was at her side. Although they were identical, Becks's cropped red hair always made it easy to tell them apart, along with their different fashion styles. Natalie preferring sundresses while Becks always sported shorts or jeans. "Except if you're thinking of leaving early, then the answer is no."

Becks's dry sense of humor was one reason they'd been friends in high school, although they'd lost touch when Becks moved across the country. Now their friendship was going full steam again, but one thing bothered her. "Tell me again why we didn't stay in touch." Lindsay raised her voice so Becks could hear her over the din.

"That's on me. Sometimes when you lose yourself in a person and it doesn't end well, it takes a while to find yourself again." Becks sipped her cup of tea. "I don't think I ever extended my condolences about Tim. Sorry I didn't make it home for his funeral or reach out after he died."

"This isn't exactly the type of conversation I expected to have at a baby shower."

"I get your pin. You said the b-word."

Lindsay unhooked her safety pin and handed it over to Becks, whose necklace sported a fair amount of silver.

"Natalie's a much better partygoer than me. I'm too competitive." Becks shrugged as another woman approached.

"You two look like you're not discussing the forty-nine different ways to change a diaper. Count me in." Georgie, the other cohost, tapped her foot. "I knew we should have held this at the gazebo. Only the best events take place there."

She grinned, and Lindsay remembered the day Tim escorted her to Georgie and Mike's wedding at the gazebo in the heart of downtown Hollydale. It was the last formal event they attended together.

This is a celebration of new life. Not that she'd ever forget Tim and the life they'd shared, but she had to keep living.

"Except for the ones at the botanical garden. I've heard those are pretty decent." Lindsay raised her teacup and smiled.

"My stepdaughter Rachel is enamored of the wishing fountain there. Mike and I didn't know she wished for a new member of the family, and that same night Natalie announced she was pregnant. We haven't taken her back to the garden since." Georgie laughed and then turned to Lindsay. "Isn't the dedication coming soon?"

"This Saturday." Lindsay nodded and tried to deflect the attention away from herself. "By the way, when is Natalie due?"

"In two weeks." Becks clutched her lower back and squirmed. "I shouldn't have run those extra three miles this morning. I've had a backache all day."

"Before I return to my hostess duties, the same as someone else should be doing," Georgie cleared her throat and glared at Becks, "what's your guess about time, date of birth and weight of the baby, Lindsay?"

"I'll take your pins, thank you very much." Becks pounced with glee and added Georgie's four to her growing collection. "This is fun."

Lindsay glanced at Natalie, who was speaking to her son, Danny, and her mother, Diane. If she didn't know better, she'd guess Natalie was due much sooner from the way she was carrying the baby quite low. "Um, tomorrow, and six pounds even?"

"I hope not, but you're not the first person at the party to guess she won't go another two weeks before the baby comes." Georgie waved goodbye and returned to the crowd, giving a five-minute warning for the pin game.

"That long until cake?" Danny's question brought a round of laughter, and Becks clutched her back again.

Lindsay moved toward her. "Are you okay? Did you put up the decorations for Aunt Hyacinth? Maybe you wrenched your lower back muscles."

"I'm fine, but I haven't felt like this since Pippa was born." Becks mentioned her daughter and then waved away Lindsay's concern. "Listen, we have to plan on those Girls' Nights Out becoming a regular event. The first couple were such stress relievers for me. Jillian's under all sorts of pressure with her mother, and Penelope's trying to make more friends in Hollydale."

Lindsay saw straight through her transparent friend. "I'm guessing you won't take no for an answer, huh?"

"Darn right. I'm persistent. It's one of my best traits." Becks laughed. "Time to hostess. The things I do for my twin sister." She strode away, waving enthusiastically at a couple of late arrivals.

Aunt Hyacinth floated by with a tray of mini tartlets. "Would you like one, my darling niece? I especially recommend the strawberry rhubarb." She selected one and placed it on Lindsay's plate and then added a couple more. "I'm sweetening you up on purpose. Could you be a dear and help with the cleanup?"

Since her parents had Evan and Chloe tonight, she was able to say yes. She'd help here, check on that one problem with the thermostat in the smaller greenhouse and get an extra early start tomorrow. "Sure thing."

"Lovely, my dear. Isn't this so beautiful? A celebration of future life coming into the world. My one regret is Craig and I weren't blessed with children, but I'm so fortunate to have you and Evan and Chloe."

Aunt Hyacinth sailed away, offering her selection of desserts to the next taker. Regrets and life? Would she regret not telling Mason of her growing feelings for him? She filed that away for later reflection and joined Kris as Becks announced the next party game.

MASON BOUNDED UP the front steps of Sweet Shelby's Tea Room. He'd promised Hyacinth he'd break down the tables after Natalie's baby shower in exchange for leftover pie for the paramedics' staff kitchen. Not a bad deal if he did say so himself.

The main area of the tearoom was empty, reflective that serving hours were over. He peeked into the gift shop, and there was no one there either.

"Hello," he called out, but only silence answered.

He then grabbed his phone from his back pocket, confirming this was the time Hyacinth had asked him to be here. It was, so he repeated his greeting.

Lindsay, a sight for sore eyes in a beautiful floral dress that brushed her knees, came around the corner from the kitchen. "I thought I heard you." She wiped her hands on a towel. "Everyone's busy at the moment and Aunt Hyacinth had to run home to let out her dogs, but she'll be back in a little while."

Their gazes met, and they burst out laughing. "Hmm. Likely story, huh? What excuse did she use to get you here? Gosh, gee, where I happen to be..."

He slipped his phone back into his pocket and flexed his muscles. "Hey, I'll do anything for pie."

Lindsay arched her eyebrow. "Ever get the feeling you're being set up with your next-door neighbor?"

He stepped closer and gave her a warm smile. "Don't you think we're past that stage?"

"Hello?" Natalie came from the kitchen,

making a beeline for Mason. "You're a paramedic, right?"

Uneasiness skittered down his spine. Those
words rarely led to anything good. "Yes," he
drawled and took in Natalie's appearance. "Are
you in labor?"

"No, I'm… Oh my, this baby packs a punch.
Ow!" Natalie cried out and reached for a chair.

Mason tossed his keys to Lindsay. "My SUV
is parked in the back lot. There's a medical
bag in the trunk with supplies. How fast can
you get it?"

"In a minute. Two if you want me to call
9-1-1."

"Take two then." Mason laid his hand over
Natalie's before reaching to her neck and taking her pulse rate.

"Take three minutes and call my husband
too." Natalie breathed in and out. "E-e-e, o-o-
o." And she kept repeating the mantra, along
with panting breaths.

"I don't have Aidan's number." Lindsay
reached the door. "I'll call him on your cell
when I get back."

Mason searched for the best place for Natalie to lie down. "Natalie, the truth is the baby
might be here before we can get to the hospital."

She practiced her deep breathing techniques

and began to move. "The private dining room." Her knuckles turned white. "I don't want my baby being born in a gift shop no matter how pretty it is."

She wailed again and dug her fingernails into his shoulder. If the contractions were coming this close together, his instincts were telling him the baby would be delivered here. He helped her to the room decorated with pink-and-silver balloons.

Lindsay rushed in with his bag, and she brought Natalie's twin sister with her. "Well, this explains the backache I've had all day." Becks knelt beside Natalie and held her hand. "Did you have sympathetic labor pains when Pippa was born?"

"Hello?" A male voice called out from the other room. "Natalie? Becks? Anyone here?"

Becks rose. "I'll explain to Aidan what's going on while you find out if my niece is going to be born in a tea room or the hospital."

Natalie cried out again. "Hurry!" Her teeth ground together. "Something's happening."

Mason turned to Lindsay. "Do you know where your aunt keeps the clean linens?" She nodded. "Bring whatever you can and a pot of hot water."

He focused on the mom-to-be and slipped

on a pair of gloves he took from his bag. "Your water broke during the shower, didn't it?"

She nodded and gulped. "I've heard first babies take forever."

"This one is in a hurry to meet you." *Forget the ambulance.* He'd likely be delivering this baby. A man with short black hair wearing jeans and a blue Oxford shirt with the sleeves rolled up rushed into the room, and Mason recognized Natalie's husband. He ran over and clutched Natalie's hand.

"The baby's not due for another two weeks. I don't understand." Aidan glanced at Mason, his eyes full of concern. "Is Natalie okay? I can't lose her or the baby."

Natalie cleared her throat. "I'm right here, Aidan, and I'm fine, just rather busy." She stopped and let out another cry. "The baby, though, didn't get the memo about the due date."

"But we have a birth plan all written out to a *T* mapped everything to the smallest detail, and it's at home." His deep voice sounded more fraught with every word. "Your suitcase… phone list…the baby's going-home outfit!"

"Aidan, listen to me." Natalie performed more breathing exercises and pulled him close to her face. "I know you love your plans, but babies sort of throw plans out the window and sometimes they decide when they want to be born."

Lindsay returned with table linens and hot water. Mason took a hard look at everyone. "Well, this baby is saying she wants to be born in the next minute. You two are the father and sister, right?" He waited for affirmation. "You're supporting the mom-to-be." Then he faced Lindsay. "And you're helping me deliver the baby."

Lindsay met his gaze, released a deep breath and nodded. "It's good that we're on the same team then. Natalie, you're doing great."

Mason met Natalie's gaze. "You are doing great. The baby's about to crown."

In less time than it took for his motorcycle to accelerate, the baby made her entrance into the world. "Congratulations, Mom, Dad. You have a beautiful daughter."

Although the new father seemed shell-shocked, he kissed his wife and whooped as if he'd scored the winning touchdown. Gina and Darius, two of Mason's fellow paramedics, arrived. He updated them and then stood back for them to do their jobs.

They loaded Natalie onto the stretcher and swaddled her daughter, who gave a lusty wail, breaking the tension. Gina and Darius were about to roll mom and daughter away when Natalie held up her hand. "Wait." They halted the stretcher; Aidan hovered next to her. "Mason and Lindsay, thank you. I'd like to introduce you to Shelby Diane, named for Aidan's late sister, who was my best friend, and for my mother, who is still very much alive. You two are Shelby Diane's godparents whether or not you want to be." They all chuckled.

Aidan murmured his thanks as well, and he and Becks accompanied Natalie out of the tea room. Lindsay collapsed into a chair and Mason settled beside her, not taking his eyes off the beautiful brunette. She was everything he needed and wanted.

"We're a good team, you and I." He might have just stated the obvious, but today proved what she'd already told him.

Before Lindsay could respond, Hyacinth sprinted into the private room. "There's an ambulance in front of the tea room, and I couldn't get in here any sooner. Is someone hurt?"

Her eyes clouded over with concern, but Mason reassured her. "Natalie and Aidan's daughter decided to come a little on the early side. She and mom are fine. They're on their way to the hospital."

Hyacinth clapped and wiped a tear from the corner of her eye. "How beautiful. What a momentous event for their little family." She glanced around the reception area. "You two have had a full and special day that you'll remember forever. Why don't you go celebrate? I'll clean up and then drop the pies for the first responders at the fire station on my way home."

She ushered the two of them out of the restaurant before either could protest.

"You don't have to walk me to my truck. The lot was full, so I parked on Timber Road a couple of blocks away." Those were the first words she'd uttered to him since Shelby made her grand entrance.

"I want to walk with you." Not just tonight, either. There was something about Lindsay that he'd never expected to find, least of all next door. Her soothing spirit restored his battered soul, which he hadn't even realized had been so wounded from Colette's and Tim's deaths.

He reached for her hand, and she allowed him to take it. The bright red buds of the maples would soon give rise to green leaves, and the air was fragrant with lush blooms. A crowd of teenagers entered Miss Louise's Ice Cream Parlor while a family packed up a picnic basket from the spot on the grassy knoll in front of the gazebo.

He and Lindsay reached her truck and stood on the sidewalk. He didn't want to break the spell yet, but even after magical moments, life continued. Speaking of which, her usual shadows were nowhere in sight. "Where are Evan and Chloe?"

"They're with my parents at the cabin they rented until Saturday." She looked at him with expectation. "Are you coming to the dedication?"

There it was. The wedge keeping them apart. He loosened his grip and leaned against the bumper. "I don't think so. It doesn't bring Tim back."

She reached into her purse and pulled out her keys. "I never said it would."

This might always stand between them. "Lindsay."

She held a finger to his lips. "Before you say anything else, I have to check on the smaller greenhouse. Why don't you come with me and I'll give you a peek at the site? A preview might help you change your mind."

Mason wasn't too sure of that. However, he didn't want this evening to end on a sour note. "How about dinner first?"

Lindsay patted her stomach. "I ate too much at the shower, and I'm pretty proud I kept it down while delivering a baby."

"You're my first choice for a delivery partner any day of the week." His skin grew flushed.

"I'm going home to shower and change, then I'll grab a quick bite and meet you at the botanical garden. Say an hour from now?"

"Sounds good. See you then, godfather."

CHAPTER TWENTY

MASON DROVE INTO the garden's parking lot. Lindsay's truck was nowhere in sight. His cell phone confirmed he was ten minutes late. He leaned back and wondered where Lindsay was. Then again, it wasn't every day someone delivered a baby. He was impressed at how she'd kept her cool and coped throughout, not to mention locating those supplies so quickly. No doubt that adrenaline had finally caught up with her, and she needed a minute.

Now he and Lindsay had yet another special moment in their lives that no one could ever take from them. Life with Lin next door was turning out to be one adventure after another. Could he hold back from kissing her and return everything to the way it was a few months ago? What if she moved? Did he even want to imagine life without her in Hollydale?

He reached for one piece of the spicy tuna roll he'd grabbed at the new Asian fusion café after he'd showered and changed. The stop had taken longer than expected, as the gossip chain had already spread the word about Shelby Diane Murphy's sudden arrival into the world. Everyone wanted the scoop, and he stopped counting the number of times he retold the story.

The first two pieces of sushi disappeared in no time, and he dipped the third into the wasabi sauce. Then he scanned the lot once more. Cars and trucks had left, but none had parked the lot. Where was Lindsay? It couldn't be traffic, not in Hollydale.

After he finished the last bite, worry began to skitter through him, and he wasn't the anxious type. Lindsay loved this place. With that greenhouse issue to deal with, she'd be here unless some other emergency arose. He was gripping his phone when her truck barreled into the lot and stopped next to his SUV.

From his spot, he saw her sitting behind the wheel, staring off into space, her lips mouthing numbers slowly one by one. Concerned, he exited his SUV and rapped on her window. "Lindsay?"

She blinked and hopped out of the truck, her normal smile nowhere to be found.

"Did something happen to Evan or Chloe?"

"They're fine." Her voice sounded faraway, and she clicked her key fob. "Nothing will happen to them on my mom's watch."

He trailed after her as they went past security, and even though he had a good six inches on her, he struggled to keep up with her pace. His side started cramping. He must have eaten too fast. "I need to sit down for a minute."

She glanced over her shoulder. "We're almost to the wishing fountain. We can sit there."

Even with dusk surrounding them, the rose garden shimmered with the velvet petals awash in vibrant color, the aromatic sweet perfume surrounding him like a cloak. At the center of the square loomed a sculpted fountain with water spouting out of a mermaid in a soft whisper. No wonder Lindsay spoke of this facility with such pride. There was genuine artistry in the floral arrangements and the stonework.

He followed her to the edge of the water and sat close to her. "Want to talk about what's bothering you?"

"Why would you think that?"

Everything about her screamed just that. Her shoulders were stiffer than his starched uniform pants. "We just delivered a baby together not even a couple of hours ago. That can be an incredible high, or it can be scary. I have to admit working in tandem with you was the highlight of my year." He paused. He had to say something even though she added distance between them by swinging her legs, bent at the knees, onto the ledge and encircling her arms around them. "And the way we kiss each other. As hard as I've been fighting this, that's special. Extraordinary, really."

She frowned. Whatever happened in the past hour or so was a genuine worry. He and Lindsay hadn't even started, and they might already be over. He'd never felt this type of agony about a relationship before.

"I've never seen you in action. I mean, on the job, responding to a call. Although you were there to help Evan that time. And now today." She stared at the water in the fountain. He shimmied out of his jacket and held it out to her, but she shook her head. "I'm not cold. I'm sad. I don't believe I could take it if something happened to another person I loved in the line of duty."

Her words knocked him back. She'd been thinking about this, about them, and she might already have shut him out.

The full implication of her words hit him like a breaking wave. Did she love him? Her face showed no emotion, so he couldn't tell if it was just a thought or what she really felt.

"You know I'm a paramedic. I love what I do."

"Especially since each call brings something

new, something that could be dangerous and risky."

"There's risk in everything, Lindsay. Even caring holds an element of risk." A risk he was finally willing to accept.

"Do the rewards make it worth the pain?" She still wouldn't look at him.

Were there rewards once someone was gone forever? Colette, Tim, both taken way too young. "I don't know, but risk shouldn't hold you back from anything."

She laughed, a wry sound that twisted his gut even more. "You hold back on the front end while I hold out after my heart's already involved."

Her hand flew over her mouth as if she'd realized what she'd said. He scooted right up to where she was sitting. "Hmm, your heart's involved? I take that type of ailment seriously. I have a reputation as a charmer, you know."

"Oh, I can't ruin your image." Her smile shared that she accepted all of him. She had an inner sense of when to go along with him and when to challenge him.

Although the pull to kiss her was strong, chemistry wouldn't solve their problems. Grandma Betty and Grandpa Joe had the type of love that worked through life together, even when they were in different states. A bond like that could make the tough patches easier, but without him and Lindsay ever being on the same page, how could they connect at that level and make it through the good and the bad?

"Maybe we should talk about why you were late tonight?"

"This makes a change. Mason Ruddick wanting to talk and not run to his garage and work on his motorcycle." Their gazes met, and everything stilled.

The sunset soaked their surroundings in a pink glow, and the woman beside him radiated beauty more substantial and deeper than any of the showy roses. It might sound corny that her calmness rounded out the side of him that loved speed and excitement, but that was the unvarnished truth.

She was more than the woman next door, more than his best friend. Somewhere along the way, in the past year, he'd fallen in love with her, and that scared him as much as his profession scared her.

He wasn't sure if this fear helped or hurt the situation.

"Lindsay—"

"Do you know Tim wanted me to give this up?"

"What?" This was an integral part of her,

and he laughed at the very idea. "Tim would never ask you to do that."

"Yes, he did." Her seriousness reflected in the twilight brought an end to his mirth. "The day before his last shift he asked me to stop working after Chloe was born. He wanted me to stay at home with her and Evan until they were both in school. I didn't even have to think about my answer. I told him no. I love my job—I love this."

A tear slid down her cheek, and she brushed it away with the back of her hand before he could do it for her.

"He never told me." Even if he had, Mason hadn't known Lindsay well at that time. He'd seen her at the barbecues and chatted on a casual level, but that was about it.

"And I haven't told anyone until now. Part of me always wondered if he volunteered for a longer shift because of our fight." Her voice was rough as if she'd struggled with this for two long years.

"That could have been part of it, but honestly, Lin, he also knew I was looking forward to my date that night." Deep down, Mason had struggled with whether he should have been on that helicopter rather than Tim. He'd had that in the back of his mind when he rented the house next to Lindsay's so he could watch over her, only to learn she could more than take care of herself.

Lindsay sighed, the whisper melting into the mountain breeze. "We both know Tim." He noticed her use of the present tense, but it wasn't in a bad way or in denial. "He wouldn't have volunteered if he didn't want to be there."

They both suffered with guilt over the past, and for what? It wouldn't change things, any more than a plaque would, and it might hold them back from the future.

"You've been keeping these feelings inside you all this time? You never mentioned any of it before." And Lindsay had always been more open than him.

"I couldn't tell his parents we fought, and who was I going to confide in?"

"Me." He'd thought their friendship had been cemented over those fence-side chats they'd had so often. "You're my best friend."

"And I don't want to lose my best friend. We need to go back to the way it was for us before Pine Falls."

Decision time. He looked hard at the poised woman on the ledge, and he knew his answer. "We don't have to lose each other. We might end up gaining so much more."

She stilled, and the soft sound of the fountain carried the night. "The thought of losing you was why I was late tonight. I don't know if I'm scared of losing my best friend or losing something more. You yourself have thought something might happen to you. That's why you made Chloe and Evan your beneficiaries."

The raw emotion in her face made him want to sweep her into his arms until she was happy once more. Yet the memory of Tim hovered between them.

But if they didn't address Tim, could he ever move forward with Lindsay?

"That was just me being practical. I'm not planning on going anywhere, but I can't promise that won't ever happen. Same as you. Same as anyone." He placed his hand under her chin and tapped it with two fingers. "I can't be someone else, other than who I am. And I'll never be Tim."

Her gray eyes narrowed. She seemed to see through him like no one else ever had or ever wanted to. "I've seen you, the real you. The serious side of you around Evan and Natalie and Bree, but you like being laid back like no one else either."

"I like to leave the world behind."

"It's not a light switch, you know. You care all the time. More than you let on."

Until now, he'd let the blithe side of him make the world think he was only that. That was one reason he felt so much for Lindsay. He didn't have to pretend or put on a façade when he was with her. She knew the real him and still wanted to stick around.

"It's the same with you but in a different way. You love working here, you're tough and determined, but you love gardening at home just as much and there you're open and almost carefree."

"So much seems uncertain right now. I don't even know what's going to happen here in the long run. Take that Wilmington position, for instance."

The one she'd talked about. They'd be lucky to have her, but where would this leave them? Mason rose, antsy and ready to release some of this nervous energy. Changing topics came to mind. "I bet Wilmington has nothing on this botanical garden. I should have visited here properly long ago. What's your favorite spot?"

"Choosing one would be hard. I can't. I love this spot, though. There's something wistful about the fountain. It merges the natural with the whimsical." A lot like Lindsay herself. When she allowed it, her peaceful side merged with her playful self, surprising and complex.

He reached into his pocket and pulled out two coins, then handed her one. "Make a wish."

"What?" She laughed and shrugged. "The wishes don't come true. We use the money for our outreach program."

"What?" He placed his hands over his heart and pretended to faint. "Wishes don't come true?" He waggled his finger at her. "Don't tell Evan or Chloe, and definitely don't tell Grandpa Joe and Goliath."

"Very well." She snatched one of the coins from him, closed her eyes and threw it into the fountain. Then she opened them again. "There."

"What did you wish for?"

She laughed. "You know I can't say, or it won't come true. That's part of Wish Making 101."

He tossed in his quarter and pulled her close. "There's a way to disprove that. I wished I kissed you."

"That's not technically true if I kiss you first."

She leaned in and kissed him, his breath stolen from the sudden move. He wound his arm around her waist, pulling her toward him. Since she instigated the kiss, he wasn't sure whether that technically meant his wish hadn't come true. He was too happy to care. If she moved to Wilmington, whether he'd follow her there remained to be seen.

Until then, he kissed her back and believed this might be the best fifty cents he'd ever spent. A taste of paradise right here in Hollydale.

LINDSAY RUSHED BACK to the fountain, hoping Mason would still be there. After their incredible kiss, she'd received an urgent text from the night horticulturist in the biggest greenhouse regarding that broken thermostat. With the problem finally solved, she rounded the corner, half expecting Mason would be gone.

Her breath caught as she drank in the sight of his strong features in the dusky gloaming. Those broad shoulders, the bright indigo of his tie-dyed shirt, and that ginger hair were familiar but new, leaving her breathless. Though she'd never expected her heart to open to someone else, let alone the paramedic next-door, Mason was hardly typical. A rebel, a charmer, a family guy at heart, all rolled into one.

A great kisser, too. Her toes still tingled from their latest kiss. As she'd swapped out the broken thermostat, she considered whether there'd be more kisses tonight. The notion her relationship with him might end up like his previous ones with women had also weighed on her. But she already felt this was different.

From what she could tell, this relationship was unchartered territory for both of them.

If she only had herself to consider, she wouldn't care, but she was Evan and Chloe's mom, too. As much as Mason made her tremble in the best way, she needed to know he cared, some indication he'd fight for her with that Mason intensity.

She neared the wishing fountain enough to see his jaw clench, and he moved his cell to his other ear.

His knuckles were white around the edges of the phone, and she hurried over before placing her hand on his shoulder. A speck of dirt marred the fabric of his T-shirt. She brushed it off and he ended his call.

Underneath his stubble, his tanned skin had become pale. "What's wrong?"

"That was Bree."

She held his hand, ready for whatever news he shared.

"She, Tristan and Grandma Betty went to Atlanta to close on a house and for her first visit to a new primary care provider. Her bloodwork revealed Bree has anemia from her treatments and probably from the bout with that infection."

That muscle tic in his jaw was back, and she leaned into him, hoping that would relax him and comfort him. "What's anemia, and can they treat it?"

"It's an iron deficiency, making her feel tired and listless. She outlined what the doctor advised her, basically plenty of rest and a new diet, rich in leafy greens, beans and certain types of meat. If her red blood cell count gets any lower, they'll admit her and give her a blood transfusion."

She heard a *but* in there. "What else are you holding back?"

"I'm packing tonight and leaving as soon as I can find someone to cover my shift. I'm driving to Atlanta and doing what I should have done weeks ago. Making sure my sister is taken care of." His blue gaze stared straight ahead.

If he was in Atlanta, he wouldn't be here for the dedication. "I know this is a lot to ask, especially since your sister is fighting cancer, but can you postpone going until after the ceremony? We're talking hours, not days or weeks. You can leave for Atlanta straight from here." Her heart thudded against her chest. She'd put everything into this project.

Tim had wanted her to quit work, and here Mason didn't want to celebrate her work with her.

Then again, was she in the wrong? His sister was undergoing treatment for cancer. Although the initial results were promising, Bree had faced an uphill battle with setbacks ever since.

He shook his head. "I've waited too long as it is, and Grandpa Joe needs Grandma Betty back."

"I'm just asking you for a couple of hours." She blinked and wanted to say more, but her throat choked up, her words inconsequential. Had something wonderful slipped through her fingers? "You'll be rested for the drive if you take off later in the day." Driving right after a two-day shift would be brutal if he couldn't find another paramedic to cover for him.

"Bree needs me."

"You didn't fail Colette and Tim, you know."

He froze. She remained in place, too, letting her words sink in, offering absolution he might have needed to hear for some time now. His throat bobbed, but he kept silent.

"I know Bree and your grandmother need you." She wanted to reach out and assure him, whether with words or a gentle touch, but she also had to stay strong for herself. "I'm only asking for a short delay. This memorial is many things to me—I'd like you to support my work."

All of this was too overwhelming. Her secure little bubble was gone. For a while now, Mason made the world around her bloom again. More than that. She'd seen him look out for his grandfather ever since Joe arrived, and many others too. These past few weeks, she'd seen through the cute charm and uncovered the substantial man underneath. One who loved his family, lived his life with candor and grace. She and Mason shouldn't have meshed, but she'd fallen head over heels in love with him.

"She sounds fragile."

Lindsay hesitated. "She must be if she asked you to drop everything and come to Atlanta to be with her."

Silence greeted her, and she inhaled the sweet scent of the roses all around her, too aware of how often those thorns had pricked her. "She doesn't know you're coming." Lindsay clenched her fists by her sides. "Does she?"

"I do things on the spur of the moment. You know that. I go surfing at a minute's notice and don't bother with a watch when off duty."

"You've repeated your mantra to yourself so often you believe it." She stepped toward him. "Deep down you distance yourself as soon as you think anyone is getting too close. You hide behind your reputation and run from your problems when it's convenient."

She borrowed a page from his playbook and ran.

CHAPTER TWENTY-ONE

SEEKING THE COMFORT of her living room, Lindsay rubbed her forehead and considered what her grandparents must have gone through raising Dahlia and Hyacinth.

"Hyacinth, you must listen to me. Lindsay is my daughter, and these are my grandchildren." Her mother threw her animal-print scarf over her right shoulder. "If I want to employ a housekeeping service to allow Lindsay to enjoy extra time with them, what business is it of anyone's except mine? It will make her life so much easier."

"While the beneficence of doing what you can to make someone's life easier is a sweet notion, dear sister, Lindsay's a grown woman and can make her own decisions." Her aunt threw her sunflower scarf over her left shoulder and winked at Lindsay. "You've raised a beautiful daughter, Dahlia, who intertwines kindness with intelligence. Did you ask her if she wanted you to pay for a housekeeper or did you forge ahead and hire the service?"

This little tête-à-tête had gone on long enough. If Lindsay could hold her own against Phillip, she could stare down her mother and her aunt, the two most formidable women in her life. She was made of sturdy stuff.

"Thank you both for your insights." Lindsay stepped into the middle of the fray. "Mom, my mind says thank you for the offer of a cleaning service, but I must decline. I don't want a housekeeper." The minute those words were out, she winced. She must be clueless to turn down that kind of offer. *The principle, Lindsay, it's the principle.* With that reminder, she stiffened her shoulders. "Aunt Hyacinth, that bell chime, um, thingamabob in my garden is beautiful, but it's not my taste and I'd love to donate it to the botanical garden. I know the perfect spot for it."

Her aunt's face wilted for a second before her usual radiance came through. "I was wondering when your inner courage would allow you the generosity of telling me the truth. And the joy of spreading the wind chime's beautiful colors to a multitude of visitors is a gift in and of itself."

Lindsay interrupted before Aunt Hyacinth could really get going. "I love both of you, but it's been a long day and I'm going to tuck in Evan and Chloe. I've been awake since four.

The memorial is in less than two days. I hope you both can still make it."

She ushered them to the door and threw it open, only to find Joe, his face ashen, phone in his hand. The poor man looked like he was close to collapse. Something must have happened to Bree or Betty.

"Joe?" She glanced around for Goliath, but the chiweenie wasn't anywhere in sight. "Is it Betty?"

He shook his head, and his eyes looked vacant and shocked. He opened his mouth, but no words came out.

Aunt Hyacinth and Dahlia hooked their elbows around Joe's and pulled him inside to the sectional, where he slumped down into the cushions.

"Is it Bree?" Lindsay sat next to him, but he didn't meet her gaze.

If something had happened to Bree before Mason traveled to Georgia, he'd be devastated, and they'd never be able to get past her asking him to delay his trip. Lindsay reached for Joe's hand, only to find an ice-cold block. She rubbed his hand, trying to bring back some warmth and blood flow.

Joe blinked, then focused on them. "It's not Bree. There was an accident at work. Mason's at Dalesford General." He clutched her hand,

and she squeezed back. They'd support each other. "He's unconscious."

A sense of dread overtook her. She'd never even told Mason she loved him. Lindsay's emotions spiraled, her world fading around her at the thought of anything awful happening to Mason.

Aunt Hyacinth came over to her. "There's always hope, sweetheart. I've often found that searching for that hope and acting on it precipitates a better outcome."

Her mother knelt in front of her until Lindsay had to meet her gaze. "Although my twin sister put a flowery spin on it, as with everything, she's right. There's no use sitting around here if Mason needs you. Hyacinth knows Evan and Chloe better, so she'll stay and I'll drive you and Joe to the hospital."

Should Lindsay go to the hospital? Or would she be an unwelcome reminder? When they'd last talked about this exact possibility happening, she ran away. The truth sank into her bones. Loving Mason was worth the risk. Any risk.

He was worth so much more.

The next minutes passed in a blur. Before she knew it, her mother had taken charge, and, for once, Lindsay was thankful. She stared out the rental car's backseat window while her mother drove her and Joe to Dalesford General.

Once there, Dr. Wang delivered an update about Mason's condition, serious with the next four hours being the most crucial for his head injury.

"Can I see him?" Joe asked. It was as if he was aging before Lindsay's very eyes.

"We're running tests. After that." The doctor gave a tense smile and nodded before leaving them.

The shock finally was wearing off. Lindsay asked, "Does Betty know?"

Joe replied, "I called her, but Bree has a doctor's appointment tomorrow morning and they may do more tests, so she can't drive. Tristan's on a flight home from his latest business trip."

"Then I'm going to get Betty." Lindsay jumped up and clutched her purse. "Mom, will you and Dad watch Evan and Chloe while I drive to Atlanta tonight? I'll be back before sunrise."

"No, I can't let you drive alone at night." Her mother stood as well.

"Mom, I'm capable of…"

"I'm going with you. I'll be the passenger and sleep on the way. Then after we pick up Betty, I'll drive back. You can talk to her or sleep then." Her mother came up to her and slipped an arm around Lindsay's shoulder. "It's me or your father, but he'll take an hour to get ready."

Lindsay was grateful. "What are we waiting for? We'll call Bree and Betty on the way."

MASON BLINKED AND realized he was in bed with strange noises happening all around him. Why was he at home? He should be at work. His head grew fuzzy. Hold it. There was a patient waiting inside the ambulance. He just had to close the rig's doors, but then the pain came. He licked his lips and tried to sit up. Instead, he found himself connected to wires. The quiet beeps of the monitors registered, and he jolted awake.

By his bed, Grandpa Joe slept in an uncomfortable-looking chair, and a nurse, whom Mason vaguely recognized, entered the dim cubicle and rolled a cart toward him. "Well, hello, sunshine. Glad to see you're awake so I can take your vitals."

"What happened?" Mason tried to sit up once more, and the nurse gave him a stern look. He worked through the pain in his head until he remembered her name. "You're Sunny, and you call everyone Sunshine."

"That's good." She pressed a digital thermometer to his forehead. "Do you remember your name and why you were brought in today?"

"Mason Ruddick." He reeled off his date of birth and other relevant statistics before the pain blocked out everything else. The dark wall frustrated him. "I don't know why I'm here."

She clicked her tongue and checked the monitor behind him. "Your temp's normal, and your vitals are good. You have a concussion, so take your time. Don't force it. According to Jordan, you hit your head hard on the patient's lawn ornament after a freak accident involving a Great Dane, a skateboard and a gnome. You've rambled a few times, always something about Lindsay, but you're finally coherent and awake. That's a positive sign. Dr. Wang will check on you soon, but the scans were normal. No swelling or bleeding. If you don't fall asleep again, you'll be transferred to a room for overnight observation and hopefully discharged in the morning."

His grandfather stirred. "Mason."

"Grandpa Joe, how long have you been here?"

His hands went to his chest. "Thank goodness you're awake."

"What time is it?"

"A little past nine at night. I've only been

here for about an hour." He pointed to the digital clock above the door. "The sheriff came by the house around eight. He'd heard I was staying with you."

"I want to leave, Grandpa, now. I'll be all right. Can you tell them?"

Grandpa Joe cleared his throat and laid his hand gently on Mason's arm. "Listen to the nurse, okay? You need to take it easy and follow orders rather than pushing your limits."

Mason leaned back against the pillow. "Please tell me you didn't call Grandma Betty or Bree or Lindsay." The image of his neighbor's beautiful face swam before him. In fact, there were three of her. He moaned. This was exactly what Lindsay feared. This accident ended any hope of them ever getting together. "They don't need to be worrying about me."

Sunny popped back into the cubicle. "Dr. Wang said to let you know he's running a little late, but I filled him in on your condition. He'll come by probably in a couple of hours. If you fall asleep again, I'll wake you up per standard concussion protocol. We'll transfer you to a room once Dr. Wang signs off on that."

Mason breathed in and out and tried to focus.

"Jordan and your boss checked in on you, but they were called away. Your boss is covering your shift." Grandpa Joe kept talking about the accident, but Mason turned away, too afraid to ask about a certain woman with honey-brown hair. "And Lindsay's concerned about you."

"Can we talk later?"

What would he even say to Lindsay? He yawned and the next thing he knew, someone pushed on his arm, and he blinked away. Sunny was taking his temperature. "Dr. Wang had a priority case come in, but you're next on his list." The nurse smiled and checked the thermometer and then recorded his vitals. "How you feeling, Sunshine? Everything hurt yet?"

Muscles he didn't know he had screamed their reply, but Mason wanted his home, to see Lindsay's house, to see his motorcycle before going inside and sleeping away this monster of a headache.

His grandfather squeezed Mason's hand, the coldness seeping into Mason's skin. "I'll be fine, but I'm worried about my grandfather." He tried to smile, that charming one that usually convinced a patient that everything would be fine if they did as Mason asked, but it only intensified the pain. He gave up and spoke from his heart. "Is there an extra blanket, preferably one from those warming racks that you could spare for him?"

Sunny glanced at Grandpa Joe and waggled her finger at him. "Mr. Ruddick, I've asked you a couple of times if you needed anything. You should speak up. I'll be right back." She winked at Mason. "I'll pluck one from the middle, that way it'll be nice and warm."

"Thanks." Mason laid back and admitted the doctor wouldn't discharge him tonight. Not by a long shot. He closed his eyes, washing away the disappointment.

"Mason?" The worry in Grandpa Joe's voice made him open his eyes. His grandfather had aged a couple of years since Mason left him in the kitchen drinking his cup of coffee with Goliath begging for a morsel of turkey bacon.

"How's Goliath? If he's home all alone, why don't you go let him outside and get some sleep? I'll call you in the morning before they release me."

Speaking of calls, where were his phone and his watch and his multi-tool? He glanced around before his head started to ache again, telling him to stop moving. His grandfather pointed underneath his chair. "I was wondering when you'd ask about your belongings. They gave me your personal possessions in a plastic bag. It's all here and inventoried." He gave a small laugh. "It's not often a grandfather has his grandson's credit card."

Sunny ducked in with a blanket and hurried out again. It must be a busy night in the ER.

Mason fingered the edge of the white sheet covering him and found he was still in his paramedic uniform. If he stayed the night, he'd probably be presented with a lovely hospital gown to change into. "Could you bring me some regular clothes in the morning? And if you see Lindsay, tell her…"

After she'd ended their conversation and left the garden, he meandered along the path. Lindsay had created an unforgettable repose where visitors could get lost in a world of beauty. Peace and calmness. She'd brought those back into his hectic lifestyle.

Knowing Lindsay the way he did now, he'd never ask her to give up such a crucial part of herself.

Still, he thought, the best way to show he supported her career was not to stand in her way. If she was meant to spread her wings and provide her talents to the Wilmington garden, he had to let her go.

Everything once again looped back to the problem they confronted last night. She wasn't his to begin with. This injury only confirmed what she feared.

"Tell Lindsay what?" Grandpa Joe prodded. "Mason, don't shut me out. It felt like I lost you tonight, and we've shared too much these past few months for us to stop communicating now."

Mason took a deep breath. Hadn't he learned anything? Facing his fears about his family, those he'd lost and those he'd lose if he didn't show them his authentic self, that was what Lindsay gave him the courage to do. "Okay, Grandpa, then I need to start off with something important. I haven't forgotten Colette."

Grandpa Joe's brow furrowed. "I never thought you had. Even though we don't talk about someone every minute of the day, it doesn't mean they're gone from our hearts. Different people have different ways of mourning, and you were such a good brother to her. Same as you are with your sister, Bree."

Mason shook his head and winced at the pain shooting through his temple. He stayed still until it was manageable. "A good brother would have been in Nashville every chance he got." And he hadn't helped in Atlanta, either.

"Bree knows you love her. She knows we both love her. Why else would Betty and I have stayed away from each other for so long? There's the house, the town and I need my job at the center and your life is here. In fact, there's a certain next-door neighbor who's part of that life, you know? What are you going to do about it?"

What could he do? Last night Lindsay accused him of distancing himself from her, and then this incident drove home the fact he wasn't immune to workplace injuries.

"Nothing."

"What? Haven't you learned anything from your grandmother and me? I love Betty, and I've treasured every minute we've had together." The blanket fell off Grandpa Joe's lap as he scooted forward. "You have a wonderful, vibrant woman next door who's in love with you."

"No." The word ricocheted around the room like a boomerang as one glance at his heart rate monitor confirmed it had skyrocketed.

Sunny rushed in with a look of alarm. Mason took a few deep breaths and his levels returned to normal. "What's going on? I thought I heard someone shout *no*," she asked.

Grandpa Joe gave a weak laugh. "My grandson is rather obstinate sometimes. He gets that from my side of the family, I'm afraid."

"If this happens again, I'll have to ask you to go." Sunny narrowed her eyes at his grandfather and then left, muttering under her breath.

"Are you saying Lindsay doesn't love you?

I have eyes, perfect vision. She does. Or you don't love Lindsay, which I know you do." Grandpa Joe picked up right where he left off, and Mason gave serious consideration to buzzing for Sunny.

However, having the nurse do Mason's dirty work didn't sit right. "Lindsay told me last night I don't face up to my problems. I run."

"Smart *and* beautiful." Grandpa Joe leaned in, his face lighter since Mason had regained his bearings. "Why don't you snap Lindsay up before some other lucky fellow does?"

"Because Lindsay *is* my problem."

"Oh." A woman's voice from the doorway caught his attention. Not just any woman's. Lindsay's. "I'm your problem?"

"Joseph Ruddick. Here I've come all the way from Georgia in what's practically the middle of the night, and you're lying there talking about another woman!" Grandma Betty appeared from behind Lindsay, a gleam in her bright eyes. "Is that any way to greet your wife?"

Moving faster than Mason had seen him in years, Grandpa Joe rushed to take his wife in his arms. "Elizabeth Ruddick, if you don't know by now you're the love of my life, I won't ever be able to convince you of that. I'm never letting you go."

This moment. This was what Mason had dreamed of having while being too skittish to commit. Even with announcements over the intercom and the thrumming noises of the ER, his grandparents only had eyes for each other. Fifty-six years hadn't dimmed their love. Some might think his grandfather didn't care as much as he did since Grandma Betty had stayed away for so long, but it was just the opposite, it was that he loved her this strongly and deeply that they could do that.

After a few minutes, his grandparents pulled out of their embrace.

"Mason, how are you?" his grandmother asked, coming to his side to squeeze his hand.

"I'll be okay, Grandma. You're a sight for sore eyes, though."

His grandmother nodded. "Lindsay and I have been really getting to know each other. Oh, I should let you have a few minutes with the woman who was nice enough to drive me here from Atlanta. Thank you, Lindsay, I'll never forget such kindness. We'll be back to check on you, Mason." She nudged Grandpa Joe's ribs and they quietly slipped out the door.

Mason drank in the sight of Lindsay. With every depth of his being, he loved her, but he wanted so much for her and he still wasn't sure that included him. He wished that it did.

He'd believed he had learned how to hide his feelings and thoughts rather well over the years. Being a paramedic, he'd adapted a mask for any given situation.

Lindsay settled into the chair. "I talked to Bree while your grandmother packed. Your sister sends her love. Tristan, too. He arrived just as Betty and I were leaving."

Bree. The accident couldn't have come at a worse time. "How is she?"

"She's okay. She said to tell you to call her when you feel up to it."

"I will."

A long silence followed. He was torn between wanting to wrap his arms around Lindsay and knowing that wouldn't be best for her. For her future.

Lindsay winced and then stood, the harsh screech of the chair leg against the linoleum ramped up the pain in his head. "This isn't exactly the kind of welcome I expected. Although, to be honest, it occurred to me on the drive back to Hollydale that I've never told you how I feel about you."

He had to let Lindsay go so she could soar wherever she chose to land. Wilmington, Hollydale...

"Let me speak first. We had a fun couple of months, Lin." He kept from cringing at his words. Anything to allow her to thrive. Ending it first was the right thing to do before he could hurt Evan or Chloe or Lindsay. "After I'm out of the hospital, it's on to new adventures. You know me, I never dip my foot into the same water for too long."

Lindsay pointed at the IV line. "Is that fear going straight into your veins? Because I don't believe the man I've gotten to know over the past year is the one talking right now."

Mason kept his gaze on the clock over the door. "Maybe this accident has reminded me of the real me."

"Since you can't go anywhere, I'll take this opportunity to tell you what your accident taught me. For one thing, I discovered I can be in the car with my mother for five hours straight if it's important." He gripped the thin mattress so he wouldn't look at her and see the fire he knew would be lighting up her eyes. "And love is important, Mason. It's worth fighting for."

"Love?" *Keep your eyes on that clock, Mason. Do not look at Lindsay.* He was doing this for her and Evan and Chloe. "Who said anything about love? We're friends who kissed a few times. I'm your rebound. Thanks, and you're welcome." *Forty-eight, forty-nine, fifty.*

How many seconds would he have to lie to get her to buy into this phoniness act?

"That's a low blow."

"Well, life is too short to tie yourself to one person."

She sat down again. "Life is too short to throw away the best thing that will ever happen to you because you're scared."

He laughed. "I ride a motorcycle, shoot darts in bars and rush into situations I know nothing about so people have a chance to live. That doesn't sound like someone who fears life."

"You're not scared of life. You're scared of me and you're unwilling to fight for a love that's powerful, that you don't understand, something that might make you happy."

You didn't hear that. He'd crack in a second, and she had so much ahead of her if she played it safe once more. A job she was proud of, two kids who loved her, friends, more family, a town that thought highly of her. All of that couldn't include him. "You misjudged me. I'm not the man you thought I was."

She stood and crossed to exit the cubicle. "You're right. You're not. The Mason I fell in love with showed me how to live again and get out from under the rock where I was hiding. He showed me predictability is no way to move forward." She met his gaze, tears clouding her gray eyes. "Instead, it's a dash of un-predictability here, lots of laughter there and a firm foundation with hot kisses thrown in for good measure."

His muscles tensed as she walked away. He waited for the relief to wash over him, some sort of signal he'd done the right thing by letting her go. Nothing like that came. It was the opposite. He was pretty sure he'd just made his biggest mistake yet. Yesterday she'd accused him of purposely putting distance between them, and today she'd told him he was afraid to live. Everything he'd hit home to her about as they sat and watched the sunset together so many times. During the course of the past few months, she'd won his heart, which would twist every time she closed that sliding glass door behind her, and he'd head to an empty house without acknowledging his true feelings for her.

He might be a rebel, but for too long he pushed everyone away. He'd been his own worst enemy when his greatest adventure had been next-door all the while.

He heard his grandparents' voices in the hallway and screwed his eyes shut, hoping they'd get the hint and leave.

"Come on, kiddo, that's the worst acting I've ever seen, and your father, Peter, is terrible at it." Mason opened his eyes and found Grandma Betty hovering over him. "That's better. We've spoken to your parents. Tara said she and Peter will text us their flight arrival time once they arrange their work schedules, and Bree and Tristan are coming for the dedication this weekend. Tristan went to school with Tim, you know."

"But her appointment and tests. She can't come." He sat upright. "Her treatment, the long car ride."

"Bree's a fighter, and her own person." Grandma Betty puffed out her chest. "Like her grandmother."

Mason knew it was true, but still, it didn't seem right. His head pounded. He craved rest and let them know.

They were quick to leave, and then he was alone. *Alone.*

But that was how he wanted it, wasn't it?

CHAPTER TWENTY-TWO

LINDSAY ATTACKED THE potting soil with a spade, today's early staff meeting still on her mind. It was their last chance to get together as a group before tomorrow's ceremony. Meanwhile, Phillip's last day would be a week from next Friday. Until a new director was hired, everyone would take on extra responsibilities, but thankfully none of hers revolved around administration or fund-raising.

A couple of her coworker friends had approached her afterward about whether she'd be applying for the director's position, but interviewing for her boss's job wasn't on her radar. She loved what she did best: growing plants and trees and getting her hands dirty. That phone call with the plaque company two months ago proved how much she didn't want to be the new Phillip. Schmoozing and worrying about revenues and receipts weren't her calling.

Although, that day resonated since it was the beginning of how her friendship with Mason had bloomed gloriously before wilting away to nothingness.

No, not nothingness. Never that. Thanks to Evan and Chloe and her friends and family, her life was full and rich. She stuck the spade into the dirt with a vengeance. How one man could not see the nose on his face and realize he was running away from love was beyond her...

"Good morning, darling daughter. So, this is your workplace, is it?" Dahlia whipped off her designer sunglasses and peered at Lindsay, who was elbow-deep in soil.

Unsure of the reason for her mother's sudden appearance, Lindsay decided she'd take a wait and see approach.

The mother who'd accompanied her on the Atlanta drive was someone she could see having lunch with and talking to regularly. Somehow, her mom had been more relaxed and less overbearing than the woman in front of her with her manicured nails and stylish dress, a contrast to Lindsay's dirty khakis and blunt, short nails. "Yes, and I love it."

Dahlia swung a basket covered with a red plaid napkin onto the worktable, a warm aromatic smell of cinnamon, nutmeg and sugary goodness overcoming the mint and other herbs in the greenhouse. "According to Betty, who dropped them off at the cabin this morning,

these are zucchini muffins with cranberries."
Lindsay peeked and found six plump muffins.
"And I didn't come here to start a fight."

Lindsay removed her gloves and plucked one
of the muffins out of its nest before removing
the paper wrapper. "Why did you come here?"
She sank her teeth into the crumbly delight.

"To see something you love. You're obviously passionate about this place." Dahlia
slipped off her animal-print scarf, her short silver hair perfect without one strand out of place.

"Yes, I am."

"I helped your father out with the billing
and the like, but I was never enthralled the
way you and Hyacinth are about your voca-
tions." She ran her hand over the untidy worktable, her hazel eyes, so like Aunt Hyacinth's
in shape and color, but shrewd and cool unlike
her aunt's amiable warmness.

"Is that why you travel?" Her mom's admis-
sion conveyed so much to Lindsay, even more,
as it also was her mother's way of offering an
olive branch, one she'd accept.

"Perhaps."

Lindsay prodded her. "And?"

"Why did I hear from Betty instead of you
that you and Mason are finished?"

The sweet, dense muffin lost all flavor, and
she swallowed a bite that might as well have

been the paper wrapping. Lindsay rested the other half of the muffin away from the others. "What can I say? I thought we were planting a redwood, and Mason didn't feel the same way."

Suddenly, Lindsay choked up, and her mother opened her arms. She flew into them, her mother's strong citrusy perfume suiting her and soothing Lindsay. She let the tears fall and then stemmed the tide. Stepping back, she gasped at the wet stain on her mother's caramel-colored silk shirt. "Sorry about that. I'll pay for the dry-cleaning bill."

"I'm not sorry, and you'll do no such thing." Her mother lifted her chin. "After the ceremony, would you and the children like to accompany your father and me on a small vacation?" She held up her hand. "It's a gift—I know you can pay for your own trips. This'll be a getaway from the memories swirling around you. What do you say?"

Lindsay sniffled. "I say you really mean for me to get away from my next-door neighbor for a while, don't you?"

"That and I want to send your father to talk to him. Other similar retributive thoughts have also entered my brain."

Her mother's raised eyebrow left Lindsay in no doubt that Mason wouldn't get off lightly. She almost felt sorry for Mason. "You missed your calling. You should have written crime thrillers."

"There's still time for anything, darling."

Anything except a relationship with the man who'd lifted her off the ground and moved her to new heights. One for whom adventure lurked around every corner. "That's a nice thought, but it's not always true. Once a storm is over and a flower's stem is broken, it's gone forever."

"Except sometimes that flower can brighten a room, or the rosebush can be saved." Her mother examined her bright red manicure as if her life depended on it, and it hit Lindsay.

Her mother was fighting for her.

"Dahlias are perennials." Lindsay searched for some way to bridge what she knew about the flower with what she knew about her mother.

"They're also vivid and hardy. You know where you stand with dahlias." Her mother met her gaze and nodded, then reached for the end of her scarf.

With the dedication tomorrow, Lindsay didn't have any time to spare from her duties, so she picked up the spade, reluctant as she was to stop this conversation with her mother. "Will you please quit hovering and let me do my own thing?"

"Of course. I'm glad, though. You wouldn't have confided in me like this before, if your dad and I hadn't made this trip home for the ceremony." Her mother tied the scarf around her neck and reached for the basket.

"I've learned about me over the past few years." Lindsay started transferring the plants into larger pots, adding a scoop of wood ash to neutralize the soil. "My friends have waited in the wings, and now when I need help, I ask for it."

Her mom smiled. "I'd say you have an excellent support system in Hollydale."

She'd need that support even more, given her heartache over Mason, the last man she'd ever expected to fall in love with.

Lindsay kept her focus on the plants and gripped the handle of the trowel tighter. "Are you and Dad still coming back when your townhome is finished?"

"Your father wants to come home sooner. He mentioned something about a group of his friends who fish at Sully Creek most mornings. Fishing, of all things, makes your father happy."

"Would cutting your trip short make you happy?"

"I hadn't realized how much Evan has grown since we've been gone, and Chloe didn't recognize me." Her mother's voice was low and less stern.

"What makes you happy?" Lindsay stilled her fingers, still halfway in the pot, and looked at Dahlia.

"Well, travel often satiates my curiosity." Her mother's gaze grew distant, as if she was remembering a certain trip or locale, before the keen perceptiveness returned. "However, I think we will be staying closer to Hollydale after this. Connecting with my family is a new challenge, and I never back out of one, especially when someone hurts my little girl."

Lindsay swiped at her eyes with her arm and occupied herself once more. This time she placed the dug up plants on the cart. "I've known Mason for a long time." She gave her mom a rueful smile. "You always think you'll be the one who's different from all the others before you, but sometimes you're not."

Her mother smiled back. "Oh, darling, I'd endure this for you if I could."

"I know." And for the first time, Lindsay believed that. "But you have to let me make my mistakes and recover from them. Just be there with some jelly beans when you've come home for good, okay?"

"I'll make sure there are extra cherry ones, just for you."

Her mother knew her favorite flavor of jelly bean? Dahlia left, and Lindsay stood there, her mouth agape.

ON THIS BRIGHT SATURDAY, Mason reveled in the feel of the sunshine soaking the back of his neck and his face. Finally appreciating the outdoors, he hadn't done anything like this since his accident, which he still didn't remember well.

Given the doctor had told him to lay off his motorcycle until he visited his general practitioner—that wouldn't be for another two weeks—Mason had found other things to do, so he wouldn't be cooped up inside. He had to; until his doctor cleared him to work again he had to find ways to stay busy.

The jays and crows in the backyard were creating quite a ruckus, he noticed, and yet the noise he really missed came from Evan, Chloe and Goliath.

As much as he'd once tried to have his grandfather live next door, he missed Grandpa Joe and Goliath deeply ever since they'd returned home with Grandma Betty. But not as much as he missed Lindsay. He craved another chance to feel her silky hair, to taste her sweet lips and to talk. Thanks to his stubbornness, that would never happen.

He pulled out another weed and added it to the stack he'd accumulated. To his surprise, the exercise was quite calming, almost fun, really. He'd have committed to this a long time ago had he realized how therapeutic it could be.

His grandparents' small SUV pulled into the driveway, and he rose. Grandma Betty soon made a beeline toward him, her dark sweater matched with plaid pants for today's ceremony. He'd made his excuses last night when he'd said good-night to his parents and Bree and Tristan.

"So, you meant it then." She popped her hands on her hips and glared at him.

He brushed the dirt off his gloves. "Good morning, Grandma. Guess this means no hug?"

That glare became more blinding than the afternoon sun. He knew avoiding the botanical garden today might mean no hugs for a long time. He was hoping his grandmother wouldn't be that cruel.

"Have you not come to your senses about Lindsay yet?" She stared at the pile of stems and discards he'd set aside. "Wild mint is not a weed. Didn't you smell it when you plucked it?"

"Concussion, remember? My sense of smell

is haywire." Mason tapped his head. "And I didn't ask you to get involved in my love life."

Grandma Betty stooped and picked up one of the stems. "Do you know all the uses of wild mint?"

"No, but I take it you're going to tell me." The sun hid behind a cloud, a shadow falling over his grandmother's face.

"Well, you should listen to your grandparents. We know you better than you know yourself sometimes." She came over and waved the stem at him. "Wild mint can be used to keep away animals you don't want in your garden. It's also an herb for tea or a salad, and it's quite beautiful in full bloom."

He didn't miss the parallels to Lindsay. She'd kept away the grief and the loneliness, their kisses were full of flavor and she was always beautiful, whether she was halfway through a ceiling or standing next to a waterfall. And he'd run away faster than a motorcycle accelerating on a stretch of deserted highway.

The way he figured it, it mattered less whether his and Lindsay's time together lasted for months or years… While he'd prefer blowing out fifty-six candles on a sheet cake celebrating their anniversary, same as his grandparents, it was the intensity of the love that counted. His next-door neighbor certainly captivated him, made his stomach do wild cartwheels and stopped him in his tracks.

And he'd blown it.

All he could think about was distancing himself so neither of them would get hurt, and the look on her face told him he'd succeeded in doing just that. He'd hurt her by pushing her away.

"I'm afraid, Grandma." He leaned against his house for support. "Here I am, a paramedic who goes anywhere they tell me to try to save a person, but I couldn't save myself from hurting Lindsay. I love her."

"Love makes everything sweeter. We're all afraid sometimes." She stepped over his new hostas and joined him by the house. "Joe says you're old enough to know your own darned mind and to trust you. But I told him last night at bedtime you'll never take that first step toward Lindsay without our help." She checked her watch. "I have somewhere you need to be."

He shook his head. "I can't go." He scuffed the dirt with his boot. "It should have been me. It could be me in the future."

"But it wasn't. You can't change that, just like we can't change what happened to Colette. Here's the thing, Mason." She laid her hand on his arm and squeezed until he met her gaze. "Your sisters are strong and have made tough choices. Colette may have succumbed to cancer, but she gave her all while she was here. Same as Bree is fighting now, and the rest of the time, she's embracing everything she can."

"It's too late for me and Lindsay."

"Is it?" She whispered into his ear, "I know why you pushed Lindsay away, but you're wrong. Distance in miles can make a heart grow fonder, but distancing yourself?"

She turned and started to walk away.

Mason held out his hands. "You're leaving me like that without answering your own question? It's like you stopped in the middle of the sentence that tells me how to win at life, love and everything."

Grandma Betty stopped, but only smiled a *Mona Lisa* grin before climbing into the car. What secret was she holding back about love? He wanted to know.

He stared long and hard at Lindsay's house and thought about everything it represented. His neighbor had become his best friend while he rambled on about his cases. She'd never said a disparaging word when he left her for a late-night date or another session with his half-finished motorcycle. While he couldn't pinpoint a particular minute, everything had changed between them. One day her hair went from plain ordinary brown to smooth honey strands and her eyes were no longer simply gray but the color of a rippling river before a storm.

And seeing her stuck in the ceiling? That was definitely the moment he knew there was no going back.

Shaken, he entered his house and closed the door quickly, not wanting Goliath to get out. Except the senior chiweenie didn't live here any longer.

He chided himself again. In the past few months, Lindsay and Evan and Chloe had become his home, his heart. Lindsay was so kind, so smart to give him space when he needed it and to tell him off when he needed that too. And just be there for him the rest of the time.

Lindsay was everything he didn't know he needed. Until now. And he'd responded by shutting her out. Now it was too late to sit outside with her and a bottle of beer and a glass of Riesling and set things to right.

Or was it too late? Was there still hope they could be together, whether here or anywhere else? He chuckled at how well Grandma Betty did know him. If she'd told him the answer outright, he would have scoffed and done the exact opposite.

He always thought he needed what Grandma Betty and Grandpa Joe had. He was wrong.

What he needed was his best friend to become his partner, his love, his life. Lindsay was not only his best friend, but so much more. A future without her would be boring and empty.

He ran up the stairs, hoping he still had enough time to let her know he'd come to his senses.

CHAPTER TWENTY-THREE

TWO YEARS AGO, she'd said goodbye to Tim, not knowing it would be for the last time. She'd been inwardly fuming because he wanted her to put a pause on her career. Two days ago, she'd said goodbye to Mason. However, she'd known it at the time and had been outwardly fuming because he wanted to distance himself rather than take a chance on love.

So here she was, at a ceremony she'd been anticipating for months, wanting to be anywhere else than wedged between her aunt Hyacinth and her friend Becks. Most of all, what she wanted, despite Mason's stubbornness, was a future with him. She wanted him to wake up to the hard truth that sometimes people didn't come home. That didn't mean love ended; it just meant the people left behind had to find a way to go on.

That was what this memorial rock signified to her. A way of showing Evan and Chloe that Tim's sacrifice hadn't been forgotten and that they would go on.

For this new relationship to end like it did? Her heart broke yet again. She questioned giving Mason space for him to explore the idea of the two of them, when that space had provided distance for him to run away rather than embrace the risk of loving someone.

Their time wasn't a waste, though, and she wouldn't trade it for anything. He'd awakened in her the need to become part of Hollydale again. Reconnecting with friends and finding a new relationship with her mother might not have happened without him and their nightly talks, when she'd laughed at his anecdotes and stories, and embraced the colorful world around her.

During that time, Mason had transitioned from her charming playboy neighbor to her loyal, brave friend who'd taken up a spot close to her heart. Someone whose spirit for adventure and the open road unlocked something profound in her, something she'd never connected with. That time at the waterfall sparked a special moment and she'd always remember it.

When they delivered Natalie's baby together, her feelings for Mason only deepened. That slow burn grew. Mason caring for those in need showed her a side of him he didn't brag about or show off for attention. That was another layer to him, one he hid behind a smile and that ginger charm.

Making house calls in the middle of the night wasn't a bad way to capture her heart, either. Those kisses curled her toes.

The mayor handed her a pair of scissors and she stopped dwelling on what might have been. With Phillip leaving for Wilmington and a new director on the horizon, announced today, one with innovative ideas about attracting visitors and community programs, the botanical garden's future look stronger than ever.

Lindsay smiled at the crowd as the relatives of other fallen first responders took their places next to her. On cue, she cut the ribbon and then she walked to the front row of the reserved seats, searching the crowd for the person she knew wouldn't be there. Her gaze met Betty's. Mason's grandmother sent her a regretful smile, one that told the complete story. Mason wouldn't come for Tim, for Betty or for Lindsay.

With a sigh, she settled into the folding chair and checked on Evan and Chloe. This was one of the few times when both sets of grandparents were in their midst. Lindsay faced the front again, knowing her kids were well cared for and loved.

The commemoration continued with words

from Mayor Wes, his somber stories washing over her. Polite applause brought her back, and she began clapping after taking another quick glance around. This time she made eye contact with Penelope and Kris, both of whom waved and smiled in support. Still no Mason, and so she faced the truth.

Mason really wasn't coming. There'd be no more patio talks, no more motorcycle rides, no more waterfall kisses. Mason didn't want her in his life, and she'd have to accept his decision, no matter how much her heart ached.

Phillip placed his program on his folding chair and approached the dais. "Thank you for being here today. This memorial rock is a loving tribute and the culmination of hard work, and a team that came together for a worthy cause. I'm sad to announce this team will no longer—"

"Don't go!" a voice called out from the back of the crowd. Mason's voice. It rose over Phillip's speech, over Sully Creek, over the pounding of her heart.

She looked and there was Mason, running down the aisle, his formal dark suit, pressed shirt and tie standing out in the mostly casual attire of the attendees. He rushed up to the podium, leaving a stunned Phillip with no choice but to yield the microphone to Mason.

Mason's gaze searched the crowd and landed on her, and his entire face lit up. Then his eyes widened as he caught sight of Tim's parents. He gulped and loosened his tie. "This might not be the best setting to tell someone you love her, but I couldn't risk waiting another moment. Please understand. Today, this ceremony, that plaque are all fine testaments to the first responders who died as they performed their duties. Just as their sacrifices aren't forgotten, neither should it be forgotten that they were people, people like you and me, with dreams and hopes, and most importantly love.

"My friend, Tim Hudson, whose name is inscribed on that rock understood risk. And he understood love. I'd trade anything, including my life, for him to be here, giving this speech, instead of me." Mason stopped and gulped for air, emotion twisting his face. A tear fell and she could see him exhale a deep breath. "I hope Tim's children will always know his love for them was endless. And they do have their mother, Lindsay. A beautiful, kind, compassionate person who deserves to be loved and cherished. Until this year, I never had the chance to know her, but now, I'm up here to thank her, in front of our family and our friends, for being the radiant woman that she is and to ask her not to move to Wilmington." He took another deep breath and exhaled. "Lindsay, if do you accept that job, look for a house with a vacancy next door because I'm moving there, too, supporting you every step of the way."

Lindsay glanced around, half expecting people to be angry or upset at the interruption. Instead, all eyes were on her, many faces with tears falling, others grinning from ear to ear. From the seat next to hers, Lindsay felt Aunt Hyacinth nudge her. "You better go put that man out of his misery and tell him the truth."

She turned to Becks, who nodded her agreement. "That's the type of speech that makes you believe in love again."

Lindsay hurried to the dais. She ignored the emotion caught in her throat, no ready smile coming to her rescue. She wasn't sure whether she should address the crowd or Mason, but decided she'd better take care of the guests first.

Lindsay stepped up to the microphone. "Thank you, Mason, for coming and…for what you said. Mason's also a first responder. And yes, every one of the inscribed names represents someone who lived and breathed, laughed and cried, and was someone we loved and cherished. It takes courage and guts to remind us of that." She turned to Mason, who nodded as the crowd applauded heartily.

Phillip came forward again and she left the dais, tugging Mason along with her. She noted the curious eyes of the onlookers and didn't stop moving until they reached the privacy of the fountain. Then she remembered she was angry at him. "Why did…"

He'd taken out a handful of coins and now dumped them into the fountain. "I need all the help I can get."

A flash of gold on his wrist caught her attention. "What's that?"

He laughed and pushed up his sleeve. "My watch?"

She unclasped it from his wrist, stopping short of throwing it in the fountain too. She handed the watch back to him. "Why did you come after all?"

There was a time to give him space and a time to confront what they both needed. Now the latter approach prevailed. Any chance they had at a lasting relationship demanded nothing less.

"For the right reasons and the wrong ones." He glanced to where sounds from the ceremony could still be heard. "I'm here because my next-door neighbor is the best horticulturist in the world."

"Am I only your neighbor?"

The tension between them zoomed to a fever pitch, the look in his eyes gave her his answer.

With her breath coming fast, he caressed her cheek and kissed her. The whisper of the fountain couldn't match the beating of her heart as the kiss filled her with hope.

She broke away and licked her lips, the taste of him still there. "Do you go around kissing all of your neighbors like that?"

"Only the attractive ones who get stuck in their ceilings." The corners of his mouth rose and then assumed a serious, straight line. "I won't run away again, except to follow you."

"I'm not moving. Phillip and Heather are the ones moving to Wilmington."

"What?" He sat on the edge of the fountain and placed his hands over his face. "Come to think of it, I guess that explains why there are no moving boxes or anything like that at your house. I just ruined a ceremony and for nothing."

"Maybe, maybe not." She sat next to him. "You spoke from your heart about love and sacrifice. I think it was much better than a predictable, prepared speech."

"Can you spare a little change and some more love for your next-door neighbor?"

She shook her head. "No."

His face fell, and he closed his eyes for a long while. Pain marked their depths when he opened them. "I see."

"No, you don't. I meant, no, not like this." She tugged off his suit jacket. "This isn't the Mason I know and love."

He grinned and widened the gap between the first two buttons of his dress shirt to reveal a tie-dyed t-shirt underneath. "He's still here." His expression grew serious again. "I love you, Lindsay, and the thought of losing you forever was more than I could bear."

"Does this mean another trip to Pine Falls?"

"First, I should probably tell you why I ran all those times." His somber expression remained. "I was scared of losing someone again."

"I was scared of finding someone again."

Mason looked at her then and his expression was so genuine, so heartfelt that she knew she'd never forget it. He quickly kissed her, until footsteps sounded behind them. With great reluctance, Lindsay broke away.

There stood Mason's grandparents, giving each other a fist bump. Then Joe brought Betty into his arms, and they stole away.

"Grandma and Grandpa will never let us live this down, you know." Mason laughed. "Part of the reason I didn't want to commit to anyone was thinking I'd have to live up to what they have. Fifty-six years is a long time, and yet with you, it would seem like fifty-six seconds."

"Is that a promise?"

"You better believe it."

Never had the roses in this garden come so alive with their fragrant spring blooms. Such splendor, she thought, and she was grateful. A life with Mason would be unpredictable and spontaneous, and that was the sweetest perfume of all.

EPILOGUE

MASON PUSHED THE last suitcase into the SUV. "I think we're finally ready." Lindsay nodded and turned to Grandma Betty and Grandpa Joe. Goliath was off in the distance, cuddled next to the kids' new puppy, Coco. Evan and Chloe were playing nearby.

Lindsay said, "Now, if Evan has an asthma attack…"

"His nebulizer is right here, and his emergency inhaler is always with the adult in charge. Your written instructions are quite complete." Grandma Betty winked and pointed at Mason. "I raised his father, so I'll keep these two alive for a few days."

Mason smiled and said to Lindsay, "We need to leave before your new boss forgets something else and you can't get away for a couple more hours."

The good news was her boss was a genius at drawing visitors to the garden, with the bad news being that he'd realized how otherwise invaluable Lindsay was. The two of them had come to an understanding after Jules had offered Lindsay a job, with Lindsay seriously considering taking her talent elsewhere. Now her boss only got in touch during regular business hours, not any time it suited him.

"Wait a minute. I almost forgot something." Lindsay ran inside the house and emerged with a big, decorated box. "Your wedding present."

"You didn't have to get me anything," Mason said. Just having her beside him when they woke up in the morning was enough, her honey-brown hair splayed across the pillow.

She held the box away. "Does that mean you don't want it? I know it won't compare with Bree's news she's cancer-free and in remission..."

"Thanks for that visit with them, and only a week before our wedding." He unloaded the box from her hands and ripped off the paper much to the obvious dismay of his new wife.

Lindsay had taken the time to collect each ribbon and cut off a bit of wrapping from every gift for their album.

He broke into a wide grin once he had the box open. "His and hers motorcycle helmets?"

"Even better." She waited for him to take one from the box and then clapped. "A tie-dyed helmet for you, and a white helmet with a rose on the side for me."

Grandpa Joe pointed to the bike. "What are you two waiting for? It's time to ride off into the sunset."

Mason went over to Lindsay, sealing his thanks with a kiss. She beamed and slipped her arms around his waist.

"So, now the fun begins?" she asked.

"I thought it had already started." He leaned in. "I reserved a patio room for our honeymoon, overlooking the beach, and a bottle of your favorite Riesling."

"And next month it'll be a family vacation in Georgia, with a weekend stop at Bree and Tristan's home. We've found the best of both worlds."

To think the adventure of a lifetime had been waiting for him next door. With their family looking on, Mason followed Lindsay onto the bike, knowing they'd have to head to Pine Falls.

The future was in front of them and a gift neither of them would ever take for granted.

* * * * *

For more Hollydale romances from award-winning author Tanya Agler and Harlequin Heartwarming, visit www.Harlequin.com today!

Get 4 FREE REWARDS!

We'll send you 2 FREE Books plus 2 FREE Mystery Gifts.

FREE
Value Over
$20

Both the **Love Inspired®** and **Love Inspired® Suspense** series feature compelling novels filled with inspirational romance, faith, forgiveness, and hope.

YES! Please send me 2 FREE novels from the Love Inspired or Love Inspired Suspense series and my 2 FREE gifts (gifts are worth about $10 retail). After receiving them, if I don't wish to receive any more books, I can return the shipping statement marked "cancel." If I don't cancel, I will receive 6 brand-new Love Inspired Larger-Print books or Love Inspired Suspense Larger-Print books every month and be billed just $5.99 each in the U.S. or $6.24 each in Canada. That is a savings of at least 17% off the cover price. It's quite a bargain! Shipping and handling is just 50¢ per book in the U.S. and $1.25 per book in Canada.* I understand that accepting the 2 free books and gifts places me under no obligation to buy anything. I can always return a shipment and cancel at any time. The free books and gifts are mine to keep no matter what I decide.

Choose one: ☐ **Love Inspired**   ☐ **Love Inspired Suspense**
               Larger-Print   **Larger-Print**
               (122/322 IDN GNWC)   **(107/307 IDN GNWN)**

Name (please print)

Address   Apt. #

City   State/Province   Zip/Postal Code

Email: Please check this box ☐ if you would like to receive newsletters and promotional emails from Harlequin Enterprises ULC and its affiliates. You can unsubscribe anytime.

Mail to the Harlequin Reader Service:
IN U.S.A.: P.O. Box 1341, Buffalo, NY 14240-8531
IN CANADA: P.O. Box 603, Fort Erie, Ontario L2A 5X3

Want to try 2 free books from another series! Call **1-800-873-8635** or visit www.ReaderService.com.

LIRLIS22

COUNTRY LEGACY COLLECTION

19 FREE BOOKS IN ALL!

Cowboys, adventure and romance await you in this new collection! Enjoy superb reading all year long with books by bestselling authors like **Diana Palmer, Sasha Summers and Marie Ferrarella!**

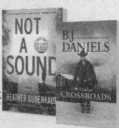

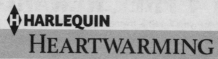
#419 RECLAIMING THE RANCHER'S SON
Jade Valley, Wyoming • by Trish Milburn

Rancher Evan Olsen lost everything, including his son, in his divorce. Now he wants to be left alone. But when a snowstorm traps him with cheerful Maya Pine, he might discover she's just what he needs.

#420 HILL COUNTRY PROMISE
Truly Texas • by Kit Hawthorne

Eliana Ramirez is optimistic but unlucky in love. So is her best friend, Luke Mahan. Single and turning twenty-seven, they follow through on a marriage pact. Could their friendship be the perfect foundation for true love?

#421 THE MAYOR'S BABY SURPRISE
Butterfly Harbor Stories • by Anna J. Stewart

Mayor Gil Hamilton gets the surprise of his life...twice. When a baby is left at his door and when his political opponent, Leah Ellis, jumps in to help! Can a man driven by duty learn to value family above all?

#422 HER VETERINARIAN HERO
Little Lake Roseley • by Elizabeth Mowers

Veterinarian Tyler Elderman has all the companionship he needs in his German shepherd, Ranger. But when he meets widow Olivia Howard and her son, Micah, this closed-off vet might discover room in his heart for family.